THE RED BOOK OF
EMERGENCY
Life Saving Tips

Disclaimer

This Red Book is intended solely for public awareness and educational purposes. It is not a substitute for professional medical advice, diagnosis, or treatment. Always seek the guidance of a qualified healthcare provider with any questions you may have regarding a medical condition. The publisher, editors, and authors disclaim any legal responsibility for outcomes arising from the use of information contained in this book.

THE RED BOOK OF EMERGENCY Life Saving Tips

(Your Life Saving Companion for Medical and Surgical Crises)

Editor-in-Chief

Lokendra Gupta

MBBS MD DNB (CCM) MRCEM (UK)

Director (Emergency Medicine and Trauma Care)
Medanta Super Specialty Hospital
Lucknow, Uttar Pradesh, India
Founder and President
Society of Acute Care, Trauma, and
Emergency Medicine (SACTEM)

Co-Editor

Utsav Anand Mani

MD FISCM FISH FISMN

Emergency Medicine Physician and Assistant Professor
Department of Emergency Medicine
Sanjay Gandhi Postgraduate Institute of Medical Sciences
Lucknow, Uttar Pradesh, India

Foreword

Himanshu Rai

JAYPEE

JAYPEE BROTHERS MEDICAL PUBLISHERS

The Health Sciences Publisher

New Delhi | London

JAYPEE **Jaypee Brothers Medical Publishers (P) Ltd**

Headquarters
EMCA House, 23/23-B
Ansari Road, Daryaganj
New Delhi 110 002, India
Landline: +91-11-23272143, +91-11-23272703
+91-11-23282021, +91-11-23245672
e-mail: jaypee@jaypeebrothers.com

Corporate Office
4838/24, Ansari Road, Daryaganj
New Delhi 110 002, India
Phone: +91-11-43574357
Fax: +91-11-43574314
e-mail: jaypee@jaypeebrothers.com

Overseas Office
JP Medical Ltd.
83, Victoria Street, London
SW1H 0HW (UK)
Phone: +44-20 3170 8910
e-mail: info@jpmedpub.com

EU GPSR Authorised Representative
Logos Europe, 9 rue Nicolas Poussin
17000, La Rochelle, France
Phone: +33 (0) 6 67 93 73 78
e-mail: contact@logoseurope.eu

Website: www.jaypeebrothers.com
Website: www.jaypeedigital.com

Inquiries for bulk sales may be solicited at: jaypee@jaypeebrothers.com

The Red Book of Emergency: Life Saving Tips

First Edition: **2026**

ISBN: 978-93-7202-264-3

Printed in India

Dedicated to

Every patient whose life depended on seconds,
every bystander who chose to help,
and every emergency professional who stood strong in chaos.
Your courage inspired every page of this book.
The passionate team of SACTEM,
who turned a shared vision into a national movement—
your dedication continues to shape the future of emergency care in India.

– Lokendra Gupta

Yogi Adityanath

CHIEF MINISTER
UTTAR PRADESH

पत्र संख्या-364/सीएसओ-सीएम/2025
Lok Bhawan,
Lucknow - 226001

Date : 0 6 OCT 2025

Message

Emergencies strike without warning, and in such moments, every second matters. Timely action can mean the difference between life and death.

The Red Book of Emergency is a commendable effort to bring life-saving knowledge to every citizen. I commend Dr. Lokendra Gupta and his team for this vital work.

Written in simple language, it guides people of all ages and backgrounds on crucial steps during medical emergencies, whether heart attacks, strokes, accidents, burns, poisoning, childbirth complications, or mental health crises.

The Uttar Pradesh government is committed to strengthening healthcare while equally prioritising public awareness and preparedness. If this book becomes a part of every household, like a first-aid box, it will prove invaluable during the Golden Hour.

I urge everyone to read, share, and practice its message. Saving lives is not just the responsibility of doctors; it is a shared duty of society as a whole.

(Yogi Adityanath)

Tel : 0522-2289017 / 2289010 / 2289167 Fax - 0522-2239234 E-mail - cmup@nic.in

Contributors

Abhay Raj Yadav MD (Anesthesia)
Assistant Professor
Department of Emergency Medicine
All India Institute of Medical Sciences
Raebareli, Uttar Pradesh, India

Abhinav Sinha MBBS DNB
Chief Consultant
Department of Ophthalmology
Nalanda Netralaya
Nalanda, Bihar, India

Abhinav Verma MBBS Masters (Sports Medicine)
Resident
Department of Sports Medicine
University College London (UCL)
London, UK

Abhishek Tandon MD DM FAGE
Consultant
Department of Respiratory and Sleep Medicine
Medanta Super Specialty Hospital
Lucknow, Uttar Pradesh, India

Ajay Kumar Verma MD
Professor
Department of Respiratory Medicine
King George's Medical University
Lucknow, Uttar Pradesh, India

Akanksha Kumari MS (Traumatology and Surgery)
Senior Resident
Department of Trauma Surgery
King George's Medical University
Lucknow, Uttar Pradesh, India

Alka Verma MD
Additional Professor
Department of Emergency Medicine
Sanjay Gandhi Postgraduate Institute of Medical Sciences
Lucknow, Uttar Pradesh, India

Alok Ashok Gangurde
MBBS MD (Emergency Medicine) FACEE DMLS
Associate Professor
Department of Emergency Medicine
DY Patil Medical College
Navi Mumbai, Maharashtra, India

Amit Anand MD DM
Assistant Professor
Department of Internal Medicine
King George's Medical University
Lucknow, Uttar Pradesh, India

Amit M Mani MDS (Periodontology)
Professor and Head
Department of Periodontology
RDS, PIMS, Loni, Maharashtra, India

Anshul Jain
MBBS MD (Emergency Medicine) MRCEM CCEBDM
Consultant and Assistant Professor
Department of Emergency Medicine
Amrita Institute of Medical Sciences
Faridabad, Haryana, India

Ashish Kumar Gupta MD (Emergency Medicine)
Medical Officer (Specialist Grade)
Chief Medical Officer
Pratapgarh, Uttar Pradesh, India

Chetan Choudhary MBBS DNB (EM) MRCEM
Associate Professor
Department of Emergency Medicine
Mahatma Gandhi Medical College
Jaipur, Rajasthan, India

D Peeyuusha Abhay MBBS MEM PGDHA
Consultant
Department of Emergency Medicine
Max Super Specialty Hospital
Noida, Uttar Pradesh, India

Debomita Dey MBBS MD PGT
Junior Resident
Department of Pulmonology
Prasad Institute of Medical Sciences
Lucknow, Uttar Pradesh, India

Deepak Singh MD (Anesthesia) PDCC
Senior EMD
Senior Resident
Department of Emergency Medicine
Sanjay Gandhi Postgraduate Institute of Medical Sciences
Lucknow, Uttar Pradesh, India

Devanshi Virani MBBS MD (Emergency Medicine)
Consultant
Department of Emergency Medicine
Unique Hospital and ICU
Jamnagar, Gujarat, India

Devyani Misra MD DNB (Obs & Gyne) MRCOG (UK)
Professor Junior Grade (Obs & Gyne)
Dr Ram Manohar Lohia Institute of Medical Sciences
Lucknow, Uttar Pradesh, India

Digvijay Dhananjay Adake
MBBS MD (Emergency Medicine)
Assistant Professor
Department of Emergency Medicine
Bharatratna Atal Bihari Vajpayee Medical College
Pune, Maharashtra, India

Divya Srivastava MD PDCC FACEE
Additional Professor
Department of Anesthesiology
Sanjay Gandhi Postgraduate Institute of Medical Sciences
Lucknow, Uttar Pradesh, India

Elizabeth Sada MD DA IDCCM
Professor
Department of Emergency Medicine
Bharati Vidyapeeth Deemed University Medical College
Pune, Maharashtra, India

Husain Abbas
MBBS MD (Internal Medicine) DM (Cardiology)
Senior Resident
Department of Cardiology
King George's Medical University
Lucknow, Uttar Pradesh, India

Karthik AR MD DNB DM (Onco-Anes)
Assistant Professor
Department of Anesthesiology
Cancer Institute (Women's Indian Association)
Chennai, Tamil Nadu, India

Kartika Gautam MD
Clinical Observer
Department of Medicine
Dr Yashwant Singh Parmar Government Medical College
Sirmaur, Himachal Pradesh, India

Kushal Pandya DA DNB (EM) MRCEM
Consultant
Department of Emergency Medicine
Aster Whitefield Hospital
Bengaluru, Karnataka, India

Likhitha Dubagunta MD (Anes) IDCCM
Registrar (Intensive Care)
AIG Hospitals
Hyderabad, Telangana, India

Lokendra Gupta MBBS MD DNB (CCM) MRCEM (UK)
Director (Emergency Medicine and Trauma Care)
Medanta Super Specialty Hospital
Lucknow, Uttar Pradesh, India
Founder and President, Society of Acute Care Trauma, and Emergency Medicine (SACTEM)

Melissa Lourdes Carlos MBBS MD (Anesthesia)
Fellow (Pediatric Anesthesia)
Wadia Children Hospital
Mumbai, Maharashtra, India

Mukesh Kumar MD (Anesthesiology)
Assistant Professor
Department of Emergency Medicine
King George's Medical University
Lucknow, Uttar Pradesh, India

Mustahsin Malik MD DM EDIC AFAMS FICCM
Associate Professor and Head
Department of Critical Care Medicine
Era's Lucknow Medical College and Hospital
Lucknow, Uttar Pradesh, India

Narsingh Verma MD FRCP FACP
Principal
Hind Institute of Medical Sciences
Sitapur, Uttar Pradesh, India

Navin Jain MBBS MD FNB (CCM)
Senior Consultant and Intensivist
Max Super Specialty Hospital
Lucknow, Uttar Pradesh, India

Nayan Sriramula
MD DNB (EM) PGDMLE (NLSIU) PGCMDM (Disaster Medicine)
Assistant Professor
Department of Emergency Medicine
Apollo Hospitals Education and Research Foundation
Hyderabad, Telangana, India

Nishant Kanodia MBBS MD (Medicine)
Professor and Head
Department of Medicine
Hind Institute of Medical Sciences
Lucknow, Uttar Pradesh, India

Om Prakash Sanjeev MBBS MD
Associate Professor
Department of Emergency Medicine
Sanjay Gandhi Postgraduate Institute of
Medical Sciences
Lucknow, Uttar Pradesh, India

Pallav Singh MBBS MD PDAF (Cardiac Anesthesia)
Assistant Professor
Department of Anesthesiology
Sanjay Gandhi Postgraduate Institute of
Medical Sciences
Lucknow, Uttar Pradesh, India

Pankaj Parmar MBBS DNB (Emergency Medicine)
Resident
Department of Emergency Medicine
Medanta Super Specialty Hospital
Lucknow, Uttar Pradesh, India

Pooja Gautam MD
Senior Resident
Department of Emergency Medicine
Sanjay Gandhi Postgraduate Institute of
Medical Sciences
Lucknow, Uttar Pradesh, India

Pooja Kanodia MBBS MS
Professor
Department of Ophthalmology
Prasad Institute of Medical Sciences
Lucknow, Uttar Pradesh, India

Prakash Chandra Pandey DM (Neurology)
Assistant Professor
Department of Neurology
Sanjay Gandhi Postgraduate Institute of
Medical Sciences
Lucknow, Uttar Pradesh, India

Pranabh Kushwaha
MS MCh Trauma Surgery & Critical Care (AIIMS)
Associate Professor
Department of General Surgery
All India Institute of Medical Sciences
Raebareli, Uttar Pradesh, India

Pranjal Tripathi MBBS MD (Psychiatry)
Junior Resident
Department of Psychiatry
Andhra Medical College
Visakhapatnam, Andhra Pradesh, India

Prem Raj Singh MD (Anesthesiology)
Additional Professor
Department of Anesthesiology
King George's Medical University
Lucknow, Uttar Pradesh, India

Pushpraj Singh
MD PDCC (Critical Care Medicine)
Assistant Professor
Department of Anesthesiology
Career Institute of Medical Sciences
College of Innovative Management and Science
Lucknow, Uttar Pradesh, India

Rachita Chatterjee MD (Pediatrics)
Assistant Professor
Department of Pediatrics
Baba Raghav Das Medical College
Gorakhpur, Uttar Pradesh, India

Rachna Agarwal MBBS DNB (Ophthalmology)
Additional Professor
Department of Ophthalmology
Sanjay Gandhi Postgraduate Institute of Medical Sciences
Lucknow, Uttar Pradesh, India

Rajeev Kumar Gupta MBBS MD PDCC FACEE CCEPC
Head
Department Critical Care Medicine
Vivekananda Polyclinic and Institute of Medical Sciences
Lucknow, Uttar Pradesh, India

Rajesh Ursekar MD (Anesthesiology)
Associate Professor
Department of Emergency Medicine
Bharati Vidyapeeth Deemed University Medical College
Pune, Maharashtra, India

Ranjitsinh Rathod MD (Emergency Medicine)
Junior Resident
Department of Emergency Medicine
Subharti Medical College
Meerut, Uttar Pradesh, India

Ravi Ranjan Rakesh
MBBS MEM (GWU-USA) Dip Family Medicine (NBE) PGDMT
Senior Clinical Associate
Department of Emergency Medicine
Medanta Super Specialty Hospital
Lucknow, Uttar Pradesh, India

Rohith Gupta Kanisetty
MBBS MD (Emergency Medicine) IDCCM
Assistant Professor
Department of Emergency Medicine
Sri Venkateswara Institute of Medical Sciences
Tirupati, Andhra Pradesh, India

S Prakash Babu MD (Emergency Medicine)
Associate Professor
Department of Emergency Medicine
Sri Venkateshwara Institute of Medical Sciences
Tirupati, Andhra Pradesh, India

Sachin Shakya MBBS MD
Junior Resident
Department of Emergency Medicine
Sanjay Gandhi Postgraduate Institute of Medical Sciences
Lucknow, Uttar Pradesh, India

Saifa Latheef
MBBS DNB-EM MRCEM (UK) FACEE FGID MNAMS
Associate Professor
Department of Emergency Medicine
Sharda University and Sharda Care—Healthcity
Greater Noida, Uttar Pradesh, India

Sajid Ansari MD FRCP
Assistant Professor
Department of Medicine
Hind Institute of Medical Sciences
Sitapur, Uttar Pradesh, India

Samir Misra
MS FACS FIAGES FMAS FICS MAMS FLCS LLB
Professor
Department of Trauma Surgery
King George's Medical University
Lucknow, Uttar Pradesh, India

Santosh Pandey MBBS DNB MRECM (UK) FCCM
Consultant and Head
Department of Emergency Medicine
Maharaja Agrasen Hospital
New Delhi, India
ATLS and ACLS Instructor, New Delhi

Saurabh Jha MBBS DNB (Emergency Medicine)
Junior Resident
Department of Emergency Medicine
Dr Ram Manohar Lohia Institute of Medical Sciences
Lucknow, Uttar Pradesh, India

Shailja Bhamri MD DNB
Assistant Professor
Department of Obstetrics and Gynecology
Hind Institute of Medical Sciences
Lucknow, Uttar Pradesh, India

Shivam Verma MD DNB MD PhD
Assistant Professor
Department of Physiology
Dr Ram Manohar Lohia Institute of Medical Sciences
Lucknow, Uttar Pradesh, India

Shivendra Sinha
MBBS DNB (Medicine) MD (Internal Medicine)
Consultant
Department of Diabetology
Bajaj Diabetic Center, Civil Lines
Ayodhya, Uttar Pradesh, India

Shubhangi Ameet MDS (Periodontology) PhD
Professor
Department of Orthodontics and Dentofacial Orthopedic
RDS, PIMS, Loni, Maharashtra, India

Shyam Sundar MD DNB (EM) Fellowship in Cardiology
Senior Resident
Department of Emergency Medicine
Sanjay Gandhi Postgraduate Institute of Medical Sciences
Lucknow, Uttar Pradesh, India

Somnath Longani MBBS MD
Professor
Department of Anesthesia and Critical Care
Hind Institute of Medical Sciences
Barabanki, Uttar Pradesh, India

SS Tripathi MD PDCC
Professor
Department of Emergency Medicine
Dr Ram Manohar Lohia Institute of Medical Sciences
Lucknow, Uttar Pradesh, India

Subhankar Paul MD DrNB MRCEM
Consultant
Department of Critical Care
Medanta Super Specialty Hospital
Lucknow, Uttar Pradesh, India

Suyash Singh MCh PDF IFSBS
Associate Professor
Department of Neurosurgery
All India Institute of Medical Sciences
Raebareli, Uttar Pradesh, India

Sweta Khuraijam MD DNB (Emergency Medicine)
Assistant Professor and Consultant
Department of Emergency Medicine
Shija Hospitals and Research Institute
Imphal, Manipur, India

Syed Numan Hussaini MD (Forensic Medicine)
Professor and Head
Department of Forensic Medicine
Government Medical College
Seoni, Madhya Pradesh, India

Tanmoy Ghatak MD PDCC FACEE
Associate Professor
Department of Emergency Medicine
Sanjay Gandhi Postgraduate Institute of Medical Sciences
Lucknow, Uttar Pradesh, India

Tushar Parmar MD (Medicine) IDCC FCCS PGDID
Head (Emergency and Trauma) and Chief Intensivist
Sir HN Reliance Foundation Hospital and Research Centre
Mumbai, Maharashtra, India

Utsav Anand Mani MD FISCM FISH FISMN
Emergency Medicine Physician and Assistant Professor
Department of Emergency Medicine
Sanjay Gandhi Postgraduate Institute of Medical Sciences
Lucknow, Uttar Pradesh, India

Vandana Gautam MBBS MD
Assistant Professor
Department of Obstetrics and Gynecology
King George's Medical University
Lucknow, Uttar Pradesh, India

Varnika Agrawal DNB (Emergency Medicine)
Junior Resident (3rd year)
Dr Ram Manohar Lohia Institute of Medical Sciences
Lucknow, Uttar Pradesh, India

Vikram Sarangan MBBS MD (Emergency Medicine)
Senior Registrar
Manipal Hospital
Bengaluru, Karnataka, India

Virendra Verma MBBS MD (Internal Medicine)
Associate Professor
Department of General Medicine
Rajarshi Dashrath ASMC
Ayodhya, Uttar Pradesh, India

Vishwadeep Mishra MD (Radiation Oncology)
Assistant Professor
Department of Radiation Oncology
All India Institute of Medical Sciences
Gorakhpur, Uttar Pradesh, India

Yadvendra Dheer MS MCh (Pediatric Surgery)
Professor (Junior Grade)
Department of Trauma Surgery
King George's Medical University
Lucknow, Uttar Pradesh, India

Foreword

Emergencies do not knock—they crash in, uninvited and unexpected. In those critical moments, what we know—and how calmly we act—can mean the difference between life and death.

The Red Book of Emergency is not just a book. It is a quiet, confident companion in moments of chaos. Dr Lokendra Gupta and Dr Utsav Anand Mani have distilled years of frontline experience into a guide that is clear, compassionate, and—above all—actionable. From heart attacks and strokes to drowning, burns, childbirth, and mental health crises, the book speaks not in medical jargon, but in a language every one of us can understand.

In my own journey, I have often seen how fear takes over when knowledge is absent. And I have also seen how even the smallest right action, taken early, can save a life. This book is about those early actions. It is about recognizing red flags, rejecting harmful myths, and responding with clarity.

We all keep a first-aid box at home. This book deserves a place right beside it.

May it give you not just information, but confidence—and through it, the power to help when it matters the most.

Himanshu Rai
Director
Indian Institute of Management (IIM)
Indore, Madhya Pradesh, India

Preface

Imagine having just six minutes to save a life. In those precious minutes, you must assess the patient, guide your team, extract vital history from panicked family members, and offer them comfort—all while racing against time and fate.

This is the daily reality for emergency physicians like me. Sometimes, we succeed. And when we do, it feels nothing short of miraculous. But other times—despite every effort—we lose the battle. What follows is not just the visible grief of the family, but an invisible storm that rages silently within the heart of the physician.

After two decades in emergency medicine, I often find myself haunted by a single thought: What if someone—anyone—around the patient had recognized the warning signs earlier? What if they had acted faster? What if they had known the importance of the *Golden Hour*?

Time and again, I have witnessed lives slip away—not because medical help was unavailable, but because it arrived too late. Tragically, even among the most educated and well-off, there remains a dangerous gap in understanding how to respond in those critical first moments.

It is that helplessness—those preventable losses—that inspired me to write this book.

"Red Book" is not a medical textbook. It is a simple, clear, and practical guide designed for everyone—parents, children, teachers, workers, elders, and students. It speaks in a language anyone can understand, because emergencies do not ask for your qualifications, background, or age.

If reading this book helps even one person stay calm in a crisis, make the right decision, and save someone's mother, father, child, or friend—then this mission will have been worth every word.

Let's not wait for miracles. Let's become the miracle.

Lokendra Gupta
Utsav Anand Mani

Acknowledgments

This book is a reflection of not just clinical experience, but unwavering support, sacrifices, and a shared vision to empower every citizen in moments that matter most.

First and foremost, I bow my head in gratitude to my parents, who devoted their lives to raising their three sons, providing us with everything we needed, and sacrificing their own happiness so we could build ours. This book, in many ways, is a tribute to their values and strength.

A special mention to my Medanta, Lucknow emergency team—your tireless work, day and night, to save lives is the spirit behind every message this book carries. Your commitment made this journey possible.

To my wife, Dr Devyani, my most honest critic and greatest support system—thank you for holding our world together. While I was immersed in writing this book and leading SACTEM's mission, you cared for Nitya and Navya with unmatched strength, all while working as a gynecologist and educator. Your patience and sacrifice are behind every word.

I am especially grateful to Dr Utsav Anand Mani, my co-author, who stood by me at every step—academically, creatively, and ideologically. Your role in shaping this book and advancing the academic goals of SACTEM is deeply valued.

To M/s Jaypee Brothers Medical Publishers (P) Ltd, New Delhi, India, thank you for believing in this vision and committing to bring this essential knowledge to the hands of the public.

And finally, to my patients, whose love, trust, and stories have shaped my life's purpose—I hope this book helps someone, somewhere, when time is running out.

The Red Book of Emergency is more than a guide—it is an awareness tool for the general public, created to debunk common medical myths, present facts, and offer a stepwise approach during emergencies. It is filled with life-saving tips that everyone should know—because knowledge saves lives, even before a doctor arrives.

Lokendra Gupta

Contents

Section 1: Cardiovascular System

1. **Heart Attack (Myocardial Infarction)** 1
   Husain Abbas, Shyam Sundar
2. **High Blood Pressure Emergency (Hypertension)** 7
   Nayan Sriramula, Abhishek Tandon
3. **Low Blood Pressure (Shock)** 12
   Subhankar Paul, Mustahsin Malik
4. **Breathing Difficulty: Heart Failure** 17
   Pooja Gautam, Ashish Kumar Gupta
5. **Palpitations (Arrhythmia)** 21
   Shivendra Sinha, Virendra Verma

Section 2: Respiratory System

6. **Severe Asthma Attack and COPD** 25
   Debomita Dey, Rajeev Kumar Gupta
7. **Cough** 30
   Kartika Gautam, Ajay Kumar Verma
8. **Choking** 33
   Rajesh Ursekar, Pankaj Parmar

Section 3: Neurological and Mental Health

9. **Stroke (Brain Attack)** 36
   Prakash Chandra Pandey, Deepak Singh
10. **Seizures (Fits)** 41
    Navin Jain, Anshul Jain
11. **Sudden Collapse and Unresponsiveness** 46
    SS Tripathi, Somnath Longani

12. **Head Injury: Danger Signs** 50
Pranabh Kushwaha, Suyash Singh

13. **Fainting and Dizziness** 55
Saifa Latheef, Saurabh Jha

14. **Mental Health Crisis and Suicide Risk** 59
Kushal Pandya, Santosh Pandey

15. **Anxiety and Panic Attacks** 64
Abhinav Verma, Pranjal Tripathi

Section 4: Blood and Metabolic Disorders

16. **Diabetic Emergency (Low and High Sugar)** 68
Shivam Verma, Sajid Ansari

17. **Bleeding Emergencies: Seconds to Survival** 72
Abhay Raj Yadav, Sachin Shakya

Section 5: Trauma and Accidents

18. **Road Traffic Accidents: What to do First?** 76
Samir Misra, Yadvendra Dheer

19. **Fractures and Broken Bones** 81
Prem Raj Singh, Akanksha Kumari

20. **Burns and Scalds** 85
Likhitha Dubagunta, Pushpraj Singh

21. **Electric Shock and Lightning Injury** 89
S Prakash Babu, Rohith Gupta Kanisetty

Section 6: Environmental Emergencies

22. **Heat Stroke and Dehydration** 94
Alka Verma, Divya Srivastava

23. **Cold Exposure and Hypothermia** 98
Devanshi Virani, Ranjitsinh Rathod

24. **Drowning and Near-Drowning** 102
Tushar Parmar, Chetan Choudhary

Section 7: Poisoning and Allergic Reactions

25. **Poisoning: Household Pesticides** 107
Sweta Khuraijam, Alok Ashok Gangurde

26. **Allergic Reactions and Anaphylaxis** 111
Pallav Singh, Ravi Ranjan Rakesh

27. **Snake Bites** 115
Om Prakash Sanjeev, Vishwadeep Mishra

28. **Scorpion Bite** 121
Elizabeth Sada, Digvijay Dhananjay Adake

29. **Animal Bites (Dog, Monkey, etc.)** 125
Tanmoy Ghatak, D Peeyuusha Abhay

30. **Insect Stings** 132
Vikram Sarangan, Amit Anand

Section 8: Pediatric and Obstetric

31. **Child Emergency: Fever with Convulsions** 136
Melissa Lourdes Carlos, Rachita Chatterjee

32. **Pregnancy Emergencies: Bleeding and Labor Pains** 140
Devyani Misra, Vandana Gautam

33. **Childbirth in Emergency Situations** 144
Devyani Misra, Shailja Bhamri

Section 9: Eye, ENT, Dental, and Urological

34. **Sudden Vision Loss or Blurred Vision** 147
Alka Verma, Rachna Agarwal

35. **Foreign Body in Nose and Eye** 151
Pooja Kanodia, Abhinav Sinha

36. **Bleeding from Nose** 156
Mukesh Kumar, Varnika Agrawal

37. **Urological Emergencies in the Elderly** 160
Nishant Kanodia, Narsingh Verma

38. **Dental Emergencies (Tooth Injury, Severe Pain, Bleeding)** 164
Amit M Mani, Shubhangi Ameet

Section 10: Special Situations

39. **Hanging and Near Hanging** 167
Utsav Anand Mani, Syed Numan Hussaini

40. **The Golden Hour in Medical Emergencies: A Quick Overview** 172
Karthik AR, Lokendra Gupta

Index *177*

Video Contents

Chapter 1. **Heart Attack (Myocardial Infarction)** ***(Video)***
Husain Abbas, Shyam Sundar

Chapter 2. **High Blood Pressure Emergency (Hypertension)** ***(Video)***
Nayan Sriramula, Abhishek Tandon

Chapter 3. **Low Blood Pressure (Shock)** ***(Video)***
Subhankar Paul, Mustahsin Malik

Chapter 4. **Breathing Difficulty: Heart Failure** ***(Video)***
Pooja Gautam, Ashish Kumar Gupta

Chapter 5. **Palpitations (Arrhythmia)** ***(Video)***
Shivendra Sinha, Virendra Verma

Chapter 6. **Severe Asthma Attack and COPD** ***(Video)***
Debomita Dey, Rajeev Kumar Gupta

Chapter 7. **Cough** ***(Video)***
Kartika Gautam, Ajay Kumar Verma

Chapter 8. **Choking** ***(Video)***
Rajesh Ursekar, Pankaj Parmar

Chapter 9. **Stroke (Brain Attack)** ***(Video)***
Prakash Chandra Pandey, Deepak Singh

Chapter 10. Seizures (Fits) *(Video)*
Navin Jain, Anshul Jain

Chapter 11. Sudden Collapse and Unresponsiveness *(Video)*
SS Tripathi, Somnath Longani

Chapter 12. Head Injury: Danger Signs *(Video)*
Pranabh Kushwaha, Suyash Singh

Chapter 13. Fainting and Dizziness *(Video)*
Saifa Latheef, Saurabh Jha

Chapter 14. Mental Health Crisis and Suicide Risk *(Video)*
Kushal Pandya, Santosh Pandey

Chapter 15. Anxiety and Panic Attacks *(Video)*
Abhinav Verma, Pranjal Tripathi

Chapter 16. Diabetic Emergency (Low and High Sugar) *(Video)*
Shivam Verma, Sajid Ansari

Chapter 17. Bleeding Emergencies: Seconds to Survival *(Video)*
Abhay Raj Yadav, Sachin Shakya

Chapter 18. Road Traffic Accidents: What to do First? *(Video)*
Samir Misra, Yadvendra Dheer

Chapter 19. Fractures and Broken Bones *(Video)*
Prem Raj Singh, Akanksha Kumari

Chapter 20. Burns and Scalds *(Video)*
Likhitha Dubagunta, Pushpraj Singh

Chapter 21. **Electric Shock and Lightning Injury *(Video)***
S Prakash Babu, Rohith Gupta Kanisetty

Chapter 22. **Heat Stroke and Dehydration *(Video)***
Alka Verma, Divya Srivastava

Chapter 23. **Cold Exposure and Hypothermia *(Video)***
Devanshi Virani, Ranjitsinh Rathod

Chapter 24. **Drowning and Near-Drowning *(Video)***
Tushar Parmar, Chetan Choudhary

Chapter 25. **Poisoning: Household Pesticides *(Video)***
Sweta Khuraijam, Alok Ashok Gangurde

Chapter 26. **Allergic Reactions and Anaphylaxis *(Video)***
Pallav Singh, Ravi Ranjan Rakesh

Chapter 27. **Snake Bites *(Video)***
Om Prakash Sanjeev, Vishwadeep Mishra

Chapter 28. **Scorpion Bite *(Video)***
Elizabeth Sada, Digvijay Dhananjay Adake

Chapter 29. **Animal Bites (Dog, Monkey, etc.) *(Video)***
Tanmoy Ghatak, D Peeyuusha Abhay

Chapter 30. **Insect Stings *(Video)***
Vikram Sarangan, Amit Anand

Chapter 31. **Child Emergency: Fever with Convulsions**
Melissa Lourdes Carlos, Rachita Chatterjee

Chapter 32. **Pregnancy Emergencies: Bleeding and Labor Pains *(Video)***
Devyani Misra, Vandana Gautam

Chapter 33. **Childbirth in Emergency Situations *(Video)***
Devyani Misra, Shailja Bhamri

Chapter 34. **Sudden Vision Loss or Blurred Vision *(Video)***
Alka Verma, Rachna Agarwal

Chapter 35. **Foreign Body in Nose and Eye *(Video)***
Pooja Kanodia, Abhinav Sinha

Chapter 36. **Bleeding from Nose *(Video)***
Mukesh Kumar, Varnika Agrawal

Chapter 37. **Urological Emergencies in the Elderly *(Video)***
Nishant Kanodia, Narsingh Verma

Chapter 38. **Dental Emergencies (Tooth Injury, Severe Pain, Bleeding) *(Video)***
Amit M Mani, Shubhangi Ameet

Chapter 39. **Hanging and Near Hanging *(Video)***
Utsav Anand Mani, Syed Numan Hussaini

Chapter 40. **The Golden Hour in Medical Emergencies: A Quick Overview *(Video)***
Karthik AR, Lokendra Gupta

SECTION 1: CARDIOVASCULAR SYSTEM

Chapter 1

HEART ATTACK (MYOCARDIAL INFARCTION)

HEART ATTACK—A STICH IN TIME SAVES NINE

Story: Crushing Pain, Critical Moments: A Story of Survival

Sudhir, a 40-year-old software engineer, was wrapping up a long day at work when a sudden, crushing pain gripped his chest. It felt like a heavy weight pressing down, making it hard to breathe. Alarmed, his friend Tushar quickly called emergency services—a decision that would ultimately save his life. Tushar knew that Sudhir was a smoker and quickly thought of it as a heart attack. As Tushar was carrying aspirin with him in his wallet, he immediately gave it to Sudhir.

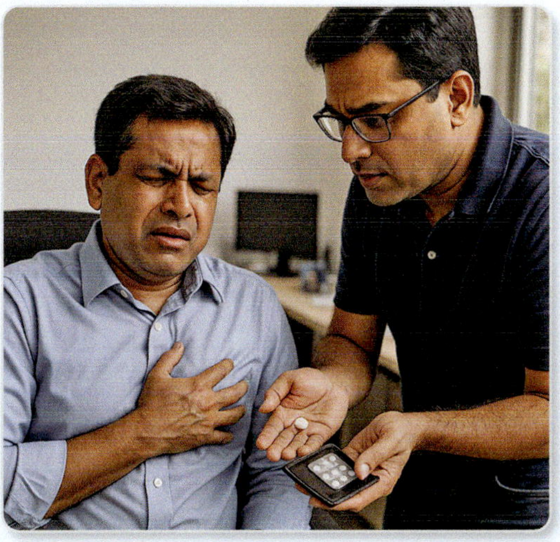

Minutes later, the ambulance arrived. Sudhir, sweating and pale but still conscious, described his symptoms to the paramedics. They immediately recognized the signs of a heart attack. With swift precision, they administered oxygen. Time was critical, and they rushed him to a hospital with a specialized cardiac care unit, alerting the emergency team en route.

As Sudhir arrived, the emergency department sprang into action. An electrocardiogram (ECG) confirmed the worst—an acute myocardial infarction, a heart attack threatening a large portion of his heart. The team acted quickly, deciding on thrombolysis, a procedure to dissolve the blood clot causing the attack. Within minutes of treatment, Sudhir began to feel relief. However, it was clear more was needed to prevent future complications.

He was taken for an emergency coronary angioplasty, a delicate procedure to open the blocked artery. A stent was placed to ensure the artery stayed open, restoring critical blood flow to his heart. The procedure was a success, and Sudhir was stable.

Over the next few days, Sudhir's recovery was closely monitored. The medical team provided him with medication to prevent further clotting and offered detailed counseling on lifestyle changes to reduce future risks. He enrolled in a cardiac rehabilitation program to gradually rebuild his strength and confidence.

After 5 days, Sudhir left the hospital, deeply grateful to his friend Tushar for his second chance at life. With a follow-up plan that included regular cardiology visits, a heart-healthy diet, exercise, and stress management, he was determined to make the changes needed to protect his heart.

Sudhir's story is a testament to the power of quick action, skilled medical care, and the importance of recognizing heart attack symptoms. It is a reminder that timely intervention can make all the difference between life and death.

WHAT HAPPENS IN A HEART ATTACK? WHAT ARE ITS RISK FACTORS?

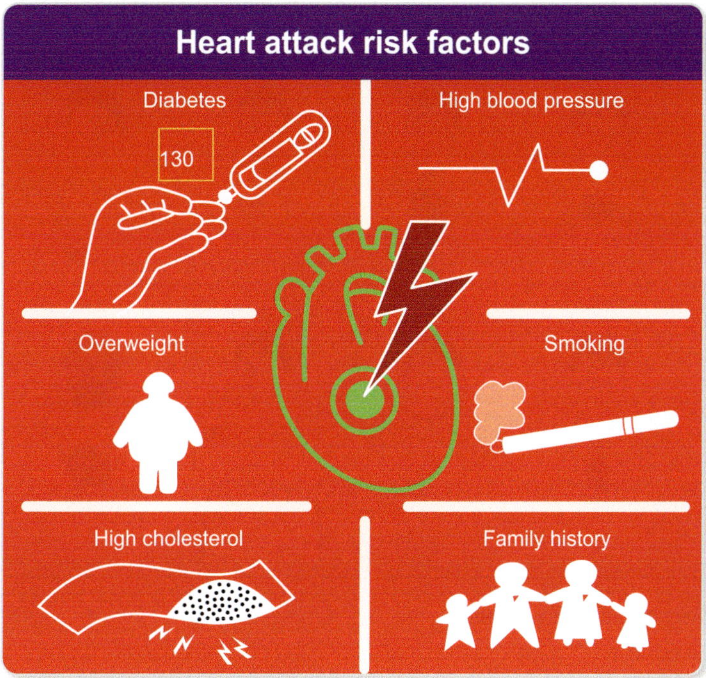

PATIENT PRESENTATION—USUAL

- Pressure-type chest pain originating in retrosternal area (may radiate to arms, neck, or jaw)
- Chest pain occurring at rest or with minimal exertion
- Pain ≥10 minutes
- Chest pain may be triggered by exertion, emotional stress, or temperature extremes
- Chest pain characteristics include: Heaviness/pressure/tightness/squeezing/burning

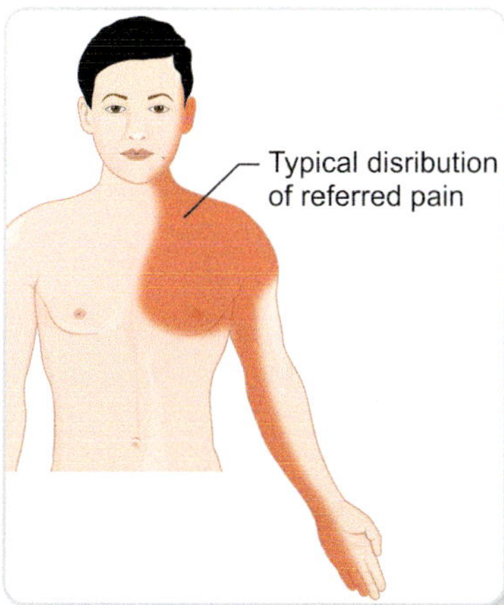

PATIENT PRESENTATION—UNUSUAL

Atypical symptoms are more frequently observed in elderly individuals, females, and those with diabetes, potentially including:

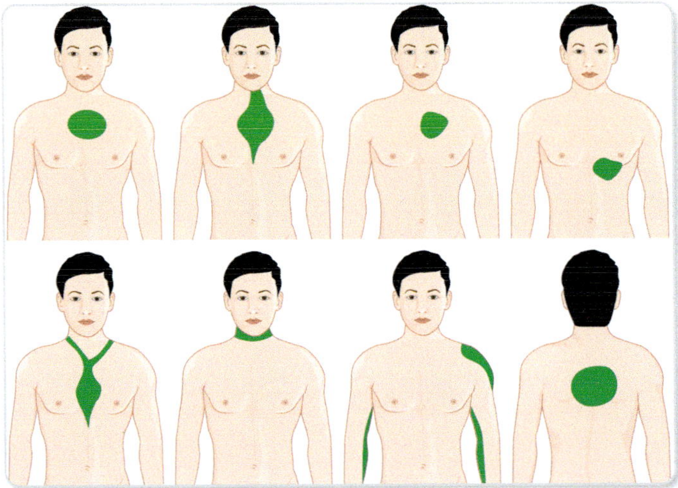

- Discomfort in the jaw, neck, or arm
- Shortness of breath
- Nausea
- Vomiting
- Excessive sweating
- Unusual tiredness
- Pain in atypical regions as shown in the earlier given diagram.

MYTHS AND FACTS

Here are *10 myths and facts* regarding the management of myocardial infarction (MI), commonly known as a heart attack:

Myths	Facts
A heart attack always causes severe chest pain.	Not all heart attacks cause severe chest pain. Symptoms can vary and may include mild pain or discomfort.
Only older adults have heart attacks.	Heart attacks can occur at any age, though risk increases with age. Young adults can also have heart attacks. This is more common in the Indian population.
If you are feeling better, you do not need to call emergency services.	Even if symptoms improve, they may signify a serious condition. Immediate medical evaluation is crucial.

Myths	Facts
Heart attacks can be treated at home with Ecosprin.	While aspirin or disprin can be an initial measure, heart attacks require immediate medical attention and treatment. Ecosprin should not be used in acute management of heart attacks.
Nitroglycerine tablets are beneficial during a heart attack.	Nitroglycerine tablets are detrimental if the patient has a Right sided Myocardial infarction hence should not be used for all patients.
You cannot exercise after having a heart attack.	Physical activity is often part of rehabilitation and recovery, tailored to the patient's condition.
Myocardial infarction symptoms are the same for everyone.	Symptoms can vary greatly among individuals, including differences between men and women.
A heart attack will permanently end your normal life.	Many people return to their normal lives after recovery and rehabilitation, with adjustments for heart health.
Once you have a heart attack, there is nothing you can do to prevent another.	Lifestyle changes and medical treatment can significantly reduce the risk of another heart attack.
All chest pain is a sign of a heart attack.	Chest pain can be caused by many conditions, not just heart attacks. Medical evaluation is necessary. Some common differential diagnosis is Acute Gastritis or Costochondritis.

STEPWISE FIRST AID BEFORE REACHING A HOSPITAL

For pan-India awareness, mention that 108 works in most states, but 112 is the national emergency number

Take the patient to a nearest Hospital having a Cardiologist and an Emergency Physician by 108 Ambulance.

Immediate ECG to be done on arrival in Emergency.

Upon arriving at the hospital describe the details of the chief complaints to an Emergency Physician.

Current recommendation (ACC/AHA, ESC guidelines): Chew 150–325 mg of aspirin as soon as possible (unless allergic).

The time from arrival at the hospital to administration of clot-busting medication should be within 30 minutes.

Angioplasty (a procedure to open blocked heart arteries using a balloon and stent).

CONCLUSION

- The key to tackling a heart attack lies in early recognition.
- Time is muscle – the faster blood flow is restored to the heart, the less damage occurs. Bystanders play a vital role by calling emergency services immediately, and if trained, performing cardiopulmonary resuscitation (CPR).
- Medications can dissolve blood clots, a procedure known as thrombolysis, while minimally invasive cardiac catheterization can open blocked arteries with stents. Not all patients have to undergo thrombolysis followed by angioplasty, leave that decision to the cardiologist.

Scan to watch Dr Lokendra's 1-minute reel on this emergency.

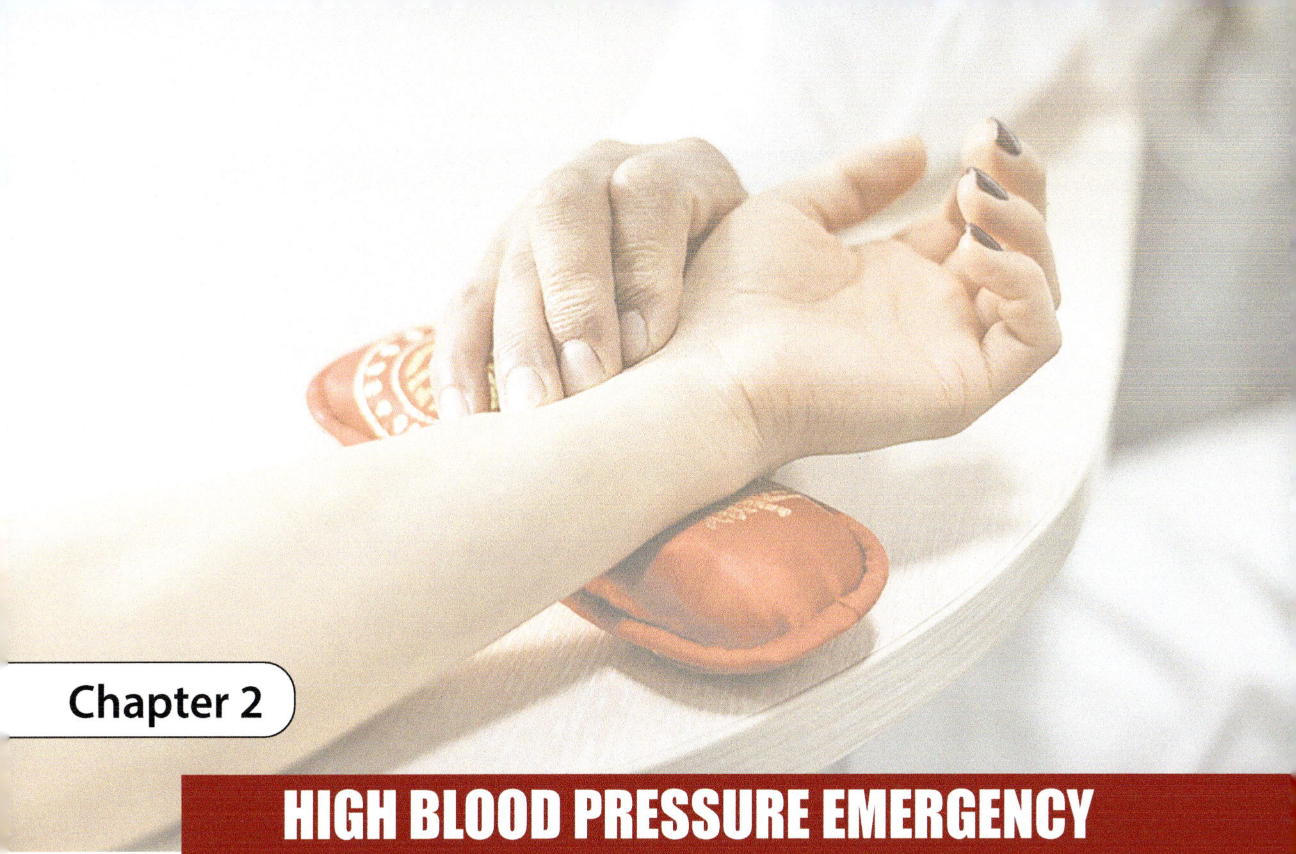

Chapter 2

HIGH BLOOD PRESSURE EMERGENCY (HYPERTENSION)

CLINICAL SCENARIO

A Dangerous Decision: Gopal's Story

Gopal, a 64-year-old retired bank officer, was relishing his post-retirement life in a serene neighborhood. For the past 15 years, he had been managing his blood pressure with prescribed medication. Each morning, he took a leisurely stroll in the park with his neighbor and walking companion, Manish.

One day during their walk, Manish noticed something unusual about Gopal. "Gopal, you do not seem like yourself lately. Is everything all right?" Manish asked with concern. "Everything is fine, Manish. I am feeling great today. I just forgot to take my medicine this morning," Gopal replied casually.

Manish shrugged and said, "Why rely on those allopathy medicines? They come with side effects. You should try the herbal remedy I have been using—it works wonders for blood pressure and has no side effects!"

Gopal listened thoughtfully to Manish's suggestion. Later that day, he began to wonder if he should stop his medications altogether. Trusting Manish's words, he decided to try the herbal remedy and stopped taking his prescribed pills—without consulting his physician.

For 3 days, everything seemed fine. However, one night, Gopal woke up with a pounding headache, severe nausea, and shortness of breath.

Alarmed! His wife, Neelam found him clutching his chest and struggling to breathe.

"Gopal, what is wrong? Are you okay?" she asked, her voice filled with panic.

Hearing the commotion, their son rushed into the room. Grabbing the blood pressure monitor, he checked his father's blood pressure (BP). The reading was a dangerously high 190/110.

"Papa, have you been taking your blood pressure medication?" his son asked anxiously.

After hesitating for a moment, Gopal admitted, "No, I stopped a few days ago. Manish suggested I should try herbal remedies instead."

The family was stunned. Recognizing the urgency of the situation, they rushed Gopal to the nearest emergency center.

At the hospital, the medical team acted swiftly, stabilizing Gopal's blood pressure and addressing his symptoms. Once his condition was under control, the emergency physician spoke firmly.

"Mr Gopal, you are fortunate your family brought you here in time. Stopping blood pressure medication without consulting a doctor can be life-threatening. Uncontrolled high blood pressure can lead to severe complications such as heart attacks, strokes, or kidney damage."

Hearing this, Gopal realized the gravity of his mistake. The doctor emphasized the importance of following prescribed treatments and cautioned against unverified remedies or advice from nonmedical sources.

The incident was a wake-up call for Gopal and his family. He promised to follow his doctor's advice moving forward and encouraged his loved ones to spread awareness about the dangers of ignoring or discontinuing prescribed medications.

Gopal's story serves as a crucial reminder: *"Managing chronic conditions like high blood pressure requires discipline, medical guidance, and trust in science—not unverified shortcuts."*

WHAT IS HYPERTENSION?

Hypertension, commonly known as *high blood pressure*, occurs when the force of blood against the walls of the arteries remains consistently elevated. It is a leading risk factor for heart disease, stroke, kidney damage, and other complications. Blood pressure readings are measured in millimeters of mercury (mm Hg) and consist of two numbers:

1. ***Systolic Pressure:*** The top number, indicating pressure when the heart beats.
2. ***Diastolic Pressure:*** The bottom number, representing pressure when the heart rests between beats. Normal blood pressure is generally defined as below 120/80 mm Hg.

Classification of Hypertension

Stage 1 Hypertension
130–139/80–89 mm Hg
Stage 2 Hypertension
≥140/≥90 mm Hg
Hypertensive Crisis
≥180/120 mm Hg requiring immediate medical attention
Hypertensive Emergency/Severe Hypertension
>180/>120 mm Hg

Causes of Hypertension

Hypertension may develop due to various causes, including:

- ***Primary (Essential) Hypertension:*** No specific cause, influenced by genetics, aging, and lifestyle factors.
- ***Secondary Hypertension:*** Caused by underlying conditions such as:
  - Kidney diseases.
  - Endocrine disorders (e.g., Cushing's syndrome, hyperthyroidism).
  - Obstructive sleep apnea.
  - Medications [e.g., nonsteroidal anti-inflammatory drugs (NSAIDs), decongestants].
  - Excessive alcohol or drug use.

Symptoms of Hypertension

Common Symptoms

- Headaches.
- Fatigue or confusion.
- Dizziness.
- Nosebleeds (in severe cases).

Red Flag Signs of Hypertension

- Severe chest pain.
- Shortness of breath.
- Severe headaches with visual disturbances.
- Neurological symptoms such as confusion, weakness, or speech difficulties.
- Swelling in the legs or sudden weight gain.
- Blood pressure exceeding 180/120 mm Hg (hypertensive crisis).

SIDE EFFECTS OF UNCONTROLLED HYPERTENSIVE EMERGENCY/SEVERE HYPERTENSION

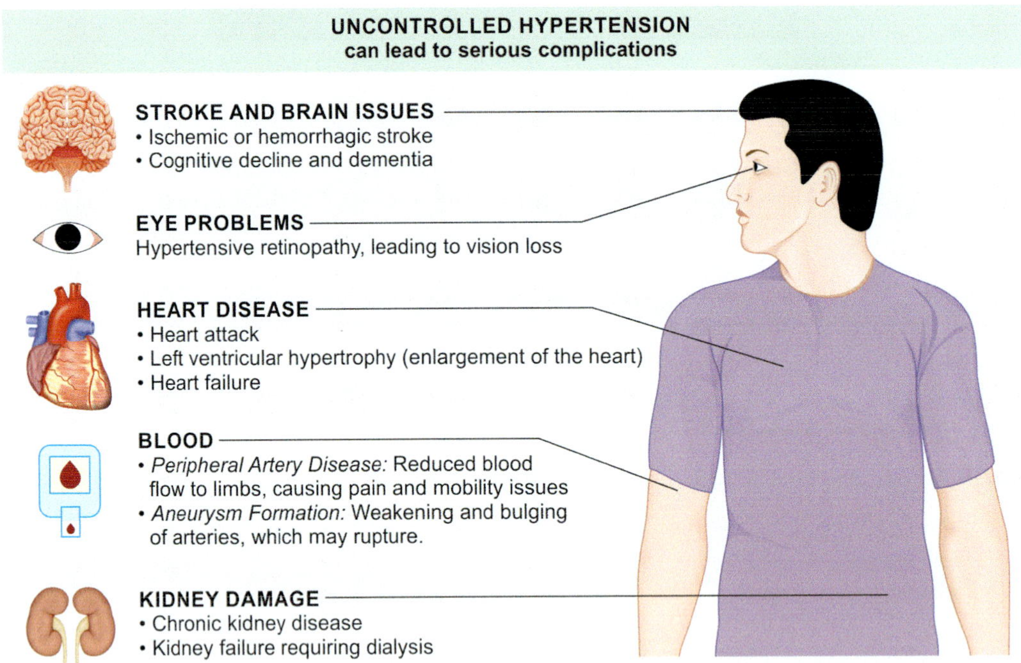

WHEN TO ATTEND EMERGENCIES

Emergency care is essential if:

- Blood pressure exceeds 180/120 mm Hg and is accompanied by symptoms such as severe headache, chest pain, or confusion.
- You experience signs of organ damage, such as heart attack, stroke, kidney failure, eye damage, difficulty in breathing, visual changes, or stroke symptoms.
- Symptoms of hypertensive emergency persist despite home management measures.

STEPWISE MANAGEMENT OF HYPERTENSION: FROM HOME CARE TO EMERGENCY CARE

At Home

- Sit calmly and rest.
- Measure blood pressure using a reliable device.
- Avoid smoking, alcohol, or caffeine, which can elevate blood pressure.
- If prescribed, take short-acting antihypertensive medication as directed by your physician.

Primary Care Visit

- WHO recommends <5 g/day (~1 teaspoon salt).
- Regular check-ups to monitor blood pressure.
- Long-term management includes lifestyle changes (e.g., reducing salt, maintaining a healthy weight, exercising) and medications such as angiotensin-converting enzyme (ACE) inhibitors, medicines that slow your heart and reduce blood pressure or calcium channel blockers.

Emergency Department Care

- Rapid evaluation of symptoms and blood pressure.
- Administer medications to lower blood pressure in a controlled manner.
- Conduct tests to identify organ damage [e.g., electrocardiogram (ECG), blood tests, imaging].

MYTHS AND FACTS ABOUT HYPERTENSION

Myths	Facts
Hypertension only affects older adults.	It can occur at any age, especially people having obesity, sedentary lifestyles, or family history.
Hypertension always causes noticeable symptoms.	Most people with hypertension have no symptoms, earning it the nickname “Silent Killer.”
You can stop taking medication once blood pressure is controlled.	Blood pressure can rise again if medications are discontinued without medical advice.
Low salt diets cure hypertension.	Although reducing salt helps to maintain normal blood pressure levels, still a comprehensive approach including medication and other lifestyle changes is often necessary.

CONCLUSION

Understanding hypertension is vital for prevention and early intervention. By recognizing symptoms, addressing risk factors, and seeking timely medical care, individuals can reduce complications and lead healthier lives.

Scan to watch Dr Lokendra’s 1-minute reel on this emergency.

Chapter 3

LOW BLOOD PRESSURE (SHOCK)

"WHEN THE BLOOD PRESSURE FALLS"—UNDERSTANDING LOW BLOOD PRESSURE (SHOCK)

Story: The Sudden Slump—Life Saved by Awareness

Ravi, a 62-year-old retired bank manager, led a peaceful life. Every morning, he took a brisk walk around his neighborhood, enjoying the fresh air and familiar greetings from fellow walkers.

But one morning, the routine was shattered.

As he stepped into his gate after the walk, Ravi suddenly felt lightheaded. His legs turned weak, sweat drenched his forehead despite the pleasant weather, and his vision darkened. Within seconds, he collapsed on the ground—silently, dangerously.

Just then, his neighbor, Mrs Sharma, noticed something was wrong. *She rushed to him and found him pale, cold to touch, and barely responsive. She didn't panic.*

She called an ambulance immediately.

Then, recalling a community health camp she had once attended, she took quick action:

- *She laid Ravi flat on his back*
- *Elevated his legs using a low stool*
- *Kept speaking to him to prevent unconsciousness*
- *And asked a nearby bystander to bring a* ***BP monitor and glucometer*** *from her house*

Within minutes, they checked his vitals:

- *His blood pressure was dangerously low at* **80/50 mm Hg**
- *His blood sugar was* **normal at 102 mg/dL**

*The low blood pressure confirmed what she suspected—****hypotensive shock.***

Thanks to Mrs Sharma's awareness and the immediate first aid, Ravi's condition slightly stabilized. By the time paramedics arrived, he was semi-conscious but breathing steadily.

At the hospital, doctors confirmed: ***This was a case of hypotensive shock. His vitals could've worsened rapidly without early intervention.***

Remember*: Not every emergency needs a doctor first—sometimes, it needs a* ***neighbor who knows first aid***

Spread the Word. Learn First Aid. Save a Life.

*You don't need a medical degree to be someone's hero—****just a little knowledge, and a lot of heart***

WHAT IS LOW BLOOD PRESSURE (SHOCK)?

Low blood pressure (hypotension) occurs when the force of blood pushing against artery walls becomes too low to supply essential organs with enough blood and oxygen. If severe and sudden, it can lead to shock, a life-threatening emergency.

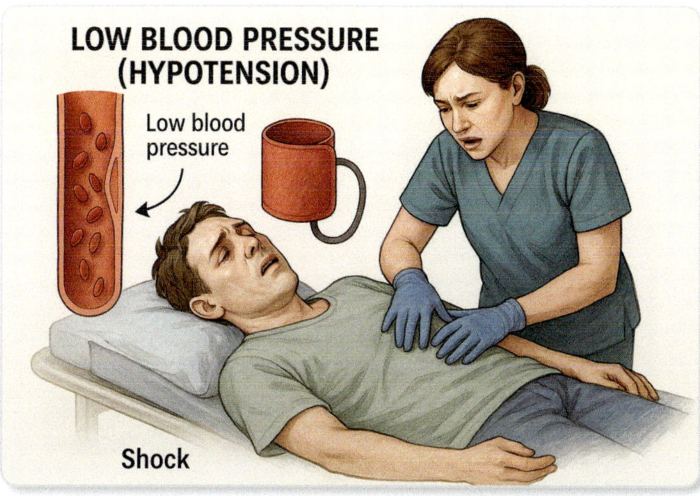

Signs and Symptoms

- Dizziness or lightheadedness
- Fainting or near-fainting
- Cold, clammy, pale skin
- Rapid but weak pulse
- Shallow or rapid breathing
- Confusion or drowsiness
- Nausea
- Weakness or fatigue

Causes/Risk Factors

- Severe dehydration (from vomiting, diarrhea, or heat)
- Heart problems (heart attack, arrhythmia)
- Bleeding (internal or external blood loss)
- Severe infections (sepsis)
- Endocrine issues (adrenal crisis, low blood sugar)
- Medications (such as antihypertensives and diuretics)
- Allergic reactions (anaphylaxis)

Early Red Flags Before Collapse

- Sudden dizziness or blackout
- Excessive sweating without exertion
- Cold hands and feet
- Feeling like "about to faint"

SHOCK POSITION

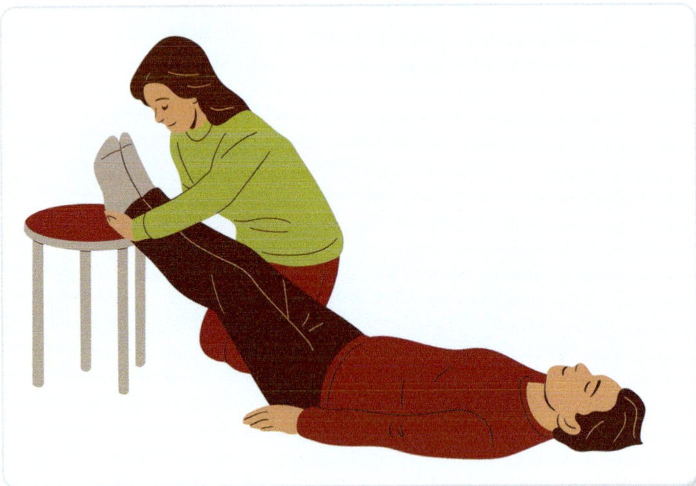

RECOVERY POSITION DIAGRAM

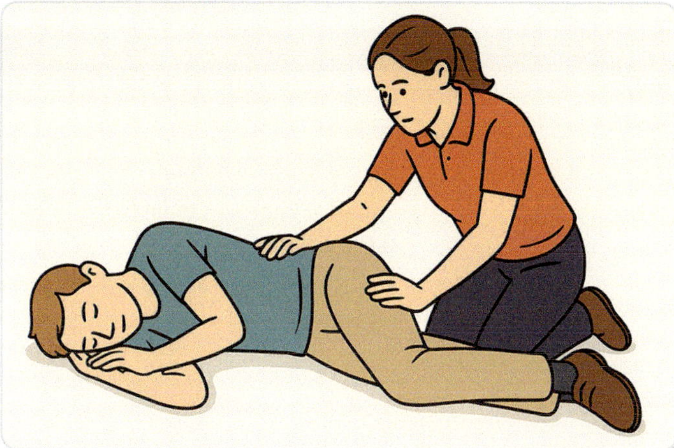

STEPWISE FIRST AID BEFORE REACHING A HOSPITAL

Act quickly—shock is a medical emergency.

- ***Step 1:*** Call for help immediately
  - » Dial 112/108 or the local emergency number.
  - » Mention that the person appears to be in shock or has very low blood pressure.
- ***Step 2****:* Lay the Person Down Flat
  - » Place them on their back on a firm surface.
  - » If no trauma or injury, gently raise their legs about 12 inches to improve blood flow to the brain.
- ***Step 3****:* Keep them Warm and Calm
  - » Loosen tight clothing.
  - » Cover with a blanket or shawl to prevent heat loss.
  - » Reassure them, stay calm.
- ***Step 4****:* Do *NOT* Give Anything by Mouth
  - » No water, food, or medication unless advised by a doctor.
  - » Risk of choking or worsening the condition if unconscious or semiconscious.
- ***Step 5****:* Monitor Breathing and Consciousness
  - » If unresponsive but breathing, place in recovery position (on their side).
  - » If not breathing, start cardiopulmonary resuscitation (CPR) if trained.

WHEN TO SEE A DOCTOR

- Any sudden collapse, fainting, or weakness
- Persistent low blood pressure with symptoms
- Known heart disease, bleeding, or infection along with weakness
- *Signs of shock:* Cold skin, rapid pulse, confusion, or unconsciousness

MYTHS AND FACTS

Myths	Facts
Give water or sugar water to revive fainting people.	Never give anything orally to an unconscious or drowsy person.
Low blood pressure (BP) is not serious.	Severe hypotension can be life-threatening.
You must always sit a person up.	Lying flat improves brain blood flow and is preferred unless there is injury.
Only older people get low BP.	Shock can occur at any age, especially with bleeding or infections.

PREVENTION TIPS

- Stay hydrated, especially in hot weather.
- Eat small, frequent meals to avoid postmeal drops in BP.
- Rise slowly from sitting/lying positions.
- Regularly monitor BP if on medications.
- Follow-up for any heart, diabetes, or adrenal issues.
- Be cautious with diuretics, BP medications, and fasting.

CONCLUSION

- "Low blood pressure may come silently—but its danger is loud. Act fast, lie flat, and never ignore the signs."
- With proper first aid and timely medical help, shock can be reversed, and lives can be saved.

Scan to watch Dr Lokendra's 1-minute reel on this emergency.

Chapter 4

BREATHING DIFFICULTY: HEART FAILURE

SHORTNESS OF BREATH—NOT JUST "BEING TIRED"

"When Breath Becomes a Warning" – Recognizing Hidden Heart Failure

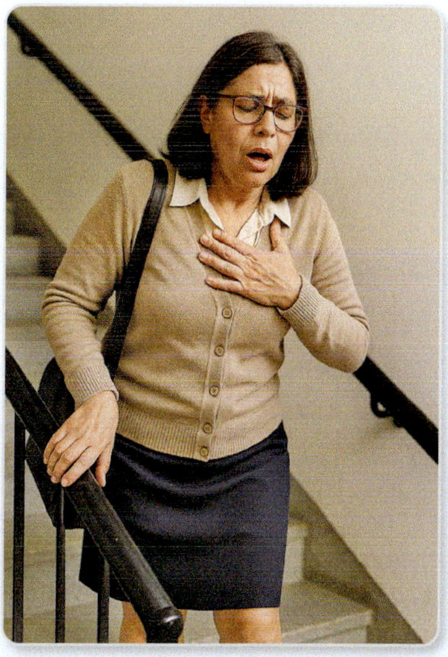

Ritika, a 48-year-old school teacher, had always been the picture of health in her eyes. She juggled work, home, and life's little dramas with ease. A brisk walk every morning, balanced meals, and no major health complaints—what could possibly go wrong?

But over the past few weeks, something had begun to change. Climbing stairs that once felt like nothing now left her breathless, forcing her to pause halfway, pretending to check her phone. Short walks, even conversations with friends, left her gasping, her words interrupted by the need for air.

"It's just stress," she told herself. "May be I've gained a little weight. May be I'm just tired."

So she ignored it.

Her family watched quietly. Her husband noticed how often she sighed heavily after the simplest tasks. Her daughter asked, "Mumma, why do you sound so tired all the time?" Still, Ritika waved it off with a smile. "I'm fine. Just busy."

Until one day, standing in front of her class, explaining a lesson she'd taught a hundred times before, she suddenly couldn't catch her breath.

Her chest tightened like a rope was pulling it from inside. Sweat trickled down her forehead. Her words faltered. Panic flashed across her students' faces. A concerned colleague rushed in, recognizing something wasn't right.

Within minutes, she was on her way to the hospital.

Tests revealed the truth Ritika never expected: Early heart failure.

Her heart, silently struggling for weeks, had finally forced her to listen. The breathlessness wasn't from stress or age—it was her body's alarm bell ringing louder and louder.

With timely care, her condition was managed. But her story is a reminder:

When breath becomes hard to catch, don't catch it late. Listen early. Act early. Your heart might be speaking.

RED FLAG SIGNS OF SHORTNESS OF BREATH YOU SHOULD NEVER IGNORE

Shortness of breath (dyspnea) is your body's signal that something is not right. Seek medical attention if you notice:

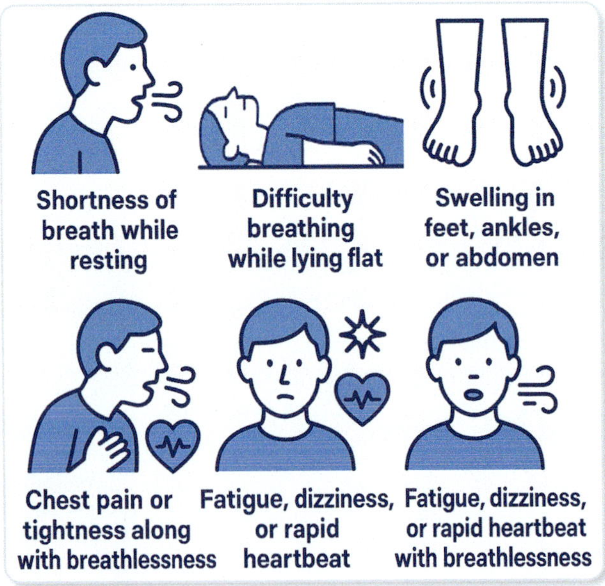

IS IT HEART, LUNG, OR SOMETHING ELSE?

Here is a simple guide to help you *understand the possible cause* of shortness of breath.

Note: This is for awareness, not diagnosis.

Symptom Pattern	Likely Cause	Details
Breathlessness on exertion or lying down	Heart-related	May be due to heart failure. Often with swollen feet, fatigue, or chest heaviness.
Sudden shortness of breath with chest pain	Heart attack or embolism	Needs immediate medical attention. Could be life-threatening.
Wheezing, cough, tight chest	Asthma or COPD	Often worsens at night or with allergens. Relieved by inhalers.
Fast onset with fever, cough, and sputum	Lung infection	Likely pneumonia or bronchitis. May also have chills or chest pain.
Anxiety, panic, with rapid breathing and fear	*Psychological causes*	Often occurs in episodes; breathing exercises may help. Still, rule out physical causes first.
Breathlessness with pale skin, fatigue	*Anemia*	Due to low hemoglobin; heart and lungs work harder to compensate.
Gradual onset with weight gain, fatigue	*Obesity/Deconditioning*	Breathlessness on mild exertion. Improves with fitness and weight control.

(COPD: chronic obstructive pulmonary disease)

SELF-MONITORING TIP

Encourage patients to track:

- Number of pillows needed to sleep without breathlessness (orthopnea).
- Any overnight weight gain (>2 kg in 2 days could suggest fluid retention in heart failure).

MYTHS AND FACTS

Myths	Facts
"I am just out of shape, that is why I feel breathless."	Breathlessness can be a sign of heart or lung disease—even in active people.
"It is anxiety. It will go away on its own."	While anxiety can cause breathlessness, so can serious medical conditions.
"I only feel it while lying down—it is nothing to worry about."	Shortness of breath when lying flat may indicate heart failure.
"I am not old, so I cannot have a serious problem."	Heart and lung issues can affect young people too—especially with lifestyle stress.
"Breathing problems are always asthma."	Many conditions cause breathlessness, not just asthma.

WHAT YOU CAN DO

- Do not ignore or self-diagnose. *See a doctor* if breathlessness is new, persistent, or worsening.
- *Track your symptoms*—note when and how it happens (rest, exertion, lying down, with chest pain, etc.).
- If you have existing conditions like *asthma, heart disease, or anemia,* follow-up regularly.
- *Avoid panic, but do not delay.* Early diagnosis can prevent serious complications.
- *Save emergency contact numbers,* including ambulances and nearby hospitals.

CONCLUSION

- Ritika is now on proper medication and lifestyle management—and doing much better. She learned that *shortness of breath is not a minor inconvenience—it is a message your body is urgently sending you.*
- *Breathe Easy, But Stay Alert.*
- Every breath matters. Do not wait until it becomes difficult to take one.

Scan to watch Dr Lokendra's 1-minute reel on this emergency.

Chapter 5

PALPITATIONS (ARRHYTHMIA)

WHEN YOUR HEART SKIPS A BEAT: UNDERSTANDING PALPITATIONS

Clinical Scenario: A Son's Quick Thinking Saves His Mother

It was an ordinary morning ***for 55-year-old Sudha, a devoted homemaker.*** *She was busy in the kitchen, preparing breakfast like any other day. However, today felt different. A* ***wave of uneasiness swept over her,*** *but she dismissed it and continued working, assuming it was nothing serious. As time passed, the discomfort only grew worse. She felt light-headed, her heart pounding in her chest. Realizing something was wrong, she called out to her son, Ajay.*

Ajay, a software engineer who usually worked in London, was visiting home—a stroke of luck that would soon prove crucial. Hearing the urgency in his mother's voice, Ajay rushed to her side. He noticed she looked ***pale and fatigued.*** *Drawing on his basic health knowledge, he retrieved the medical kit he always kept handy, which included a blood pressure (BP) monitor and a saturation probe.*

As he checked her vitals, ***his heart sank.*** *Her pulse was racing at an alarming* ***174 beats per minute,*** *and her* ***blood pressure had plummeted to 80/54 mm Hg.***

Something was terribly wrong. Despite his shock, Ajay remained calm. He immediately ***called the emergency number*** *he had saved on his phone and spoke clearly to explain his mother's condition. Meanwhile, he reassured Sudha, holding her hand and encouraging her to stay calm.*

The ambulance arrived within minutes. The paramedics quickly assessed Sudha's condition and transported her to the Emergency Medicine Department. Ajay accompanied her, his heart pounding with worry but his mind steady.

At the hospital triage, the medical team moved swiftly. ***An electrocardiogram (ECG) confirmed Ajay's fears: Sudha was experiencing a dangerous arrhythmia,*** *coupled with critically low blood pressure. The emergency physician, recognizing the urgency of the situation, immediately began antiarrhythmic treatment.*

As the minutes ticked by, Sudha's condition stabilized. Within 2 hours, ***her pulse returned to a normal rhythm, and her blood pressure improved****. The crisis had passed. The physician commended Ajay for his quick thinking and timely action, which had undoubtedly saved his mother's life.*

Later, as Sudha rested in the hospital, Ajay sat by her side, holding her hand. He could not help but feel a surge of gratitude—for being home at the right time, for the emergency team's efficiency, and for his own preparedness. This experience had taught him a profound lesson: in emergencies, staying calm and acting quickly can make all the difference.

That day, Sudha and Ajay realized the ***true value of the golden hour and the power of staying prepared. For Ajay, it was not just a rescue—it was a reaffirmation of his love and duty toward his mother.***

INTRODUCTION: WHAT ARE PALPITATIONS AND ARRHYTHMIAS?

Palpitation is the sensation of feeling your own heart beating, which can be described as pounding, fluttering, or irregular skipping beats. It can be felt in the chest, throat, or neck. They can be occasional or persistent and are often benign but may indicate underlying heart rhythm abnormalities known as arrhythmias. While most cases of palpitations are harmless, some can signal severe cardiac issues requiring immediate medical intervention.

Arrhythmias are abnormal heart rhythms that can cause palpitations. They occur when the electrical impulses that coordinate your heartbeats do not work properly, causing your heart to beat too fast, too slow, or irregularly.

Causes of Palpitations

Palpitations can result from a variety of causes, including:

- *Cardiac Causes:* Arrhythmias (e.g., atrial fibrillation, ventricular tachycardia), heart valve disorders, heart failure.
- *Noncardiac Causes:*
    - » Anxiety and panic attacks.
    - » Stimulants such as caffeine, nicotine, or drugs.
    - » Hormonal changes during pregnancy, menopause, or thyroid dysfunction.
    - » Electrolyte imbalances (e.g., low potassium or magnesium).

- » Medications
- » Fever, dehydration, or anemia.

RED FLAG SIGNS OF PALPITATIONS

- Severe Chest pain or discomfort.
- Shortness of breath.
- Dizziness or fainting.
- Severe sweating or pallor.
- Persistent or worsening symptoms.
- A history of heart disease or significant risk factors (e.g., diabetes, hypertension).

WHEN TO ATTEND EMERGENCIES

Seek immediate medical attention if you experience:

- Palpitations accompanied by chest pain, shortness of breath, or confusion, sudden weakness, or loss of consciousness.
- A history of heart disease and new or worsening palpitations.
- Palpitations that last longer than a few minutes or occur frequently.
- Home measures fail to relieve symptoms.

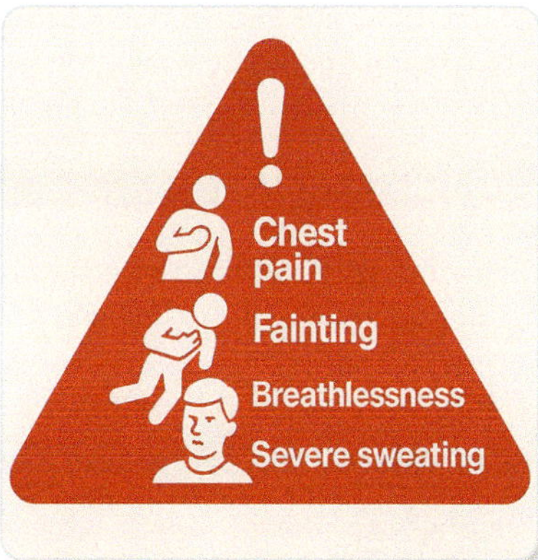

STEPWISE MANAGEMENT OF PALPITATIONS: FROM HOME CARE TO EMERGENCY CARE

At Home

- Stay calm and try to relax.
- Practice deep breathing exercises or vagal maneuvers (e.g., bearing down or gently massaging the neck).
- Avoid stimulants like caffeine or nicotine.

Note the timing, duration, and triggers of palpitations.

Primary Care Visit

- Consult a healthcare provider for a thorough evaluation if palpitations are recurrent or unexplained.
- Tests like an ECG or Holter monitoring may be advised.

Emergency Department Care

- Triage to identify severity.
- ECG and blood tests to rule out life-threatening conditions.
- Advanced treatment such as medications, electrical cardioversion, or catheter ablation for arrhythmias if necessary.

MYTHS AND FACTS ABOUT PALPITATIONS

Myths	Facts
Palpitations are always a sign of a heart attack.	Palpitations can be caused by various factors, not just heart attacks.
Only older adults experience palpitations.	Palpitations can occur at any age, including in young, healthy individuals.
Drinking water can stop palpitations.	While staying hydrated is important, it may not stop palpitations caused by underlying conditions.
Palpitations are always dangerous.	Many palpitations are harmless and temporary, but persistent or severe symptoms should be evaluated by a doctor.

CONCLUSION

Palpitations and *anxiety attacks* are real and common, but with awareness and understanding, we can reduce stigma and offer better support. Recognizing the signs, showing empathy, and encouraging treatment can make a big difference.

Scan to watch Dr Lokendra's 1-minute reel on this emergency.

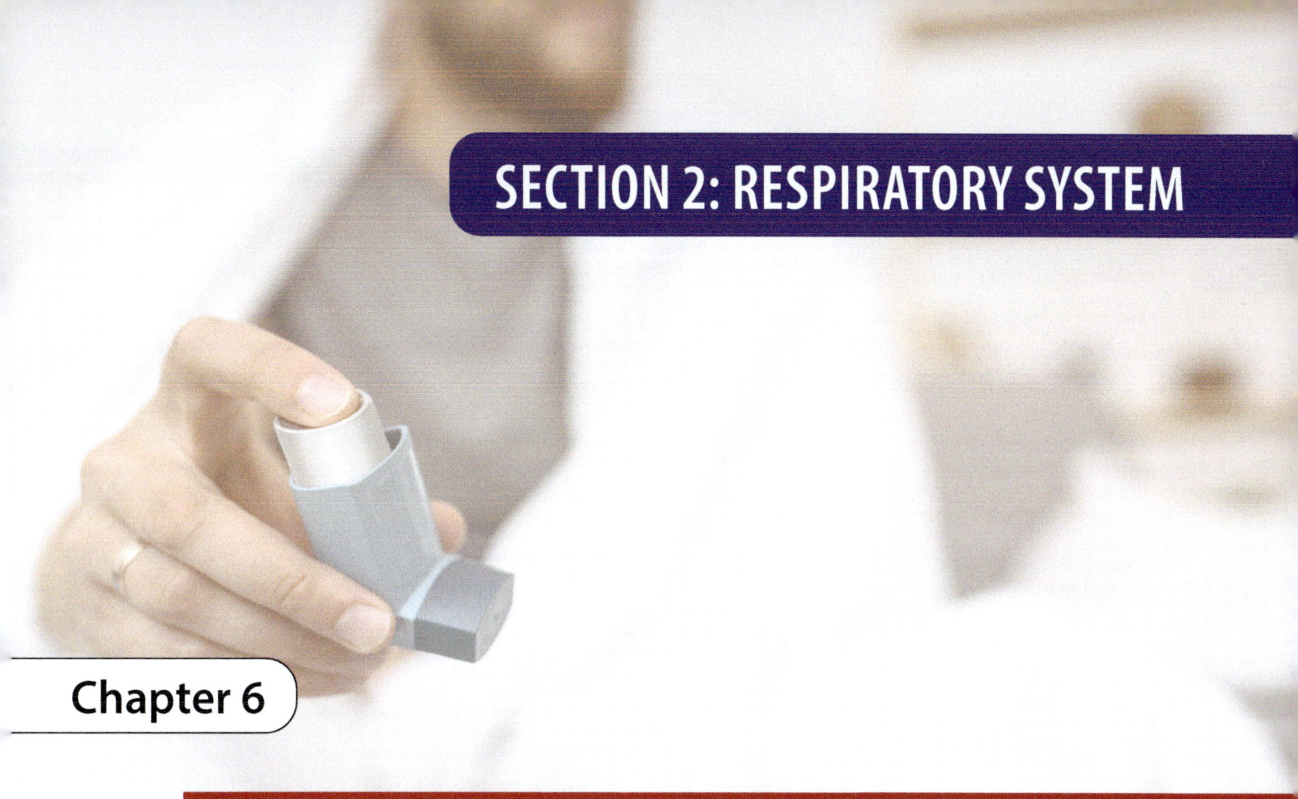

SECTION 2: RESPIRATORY SYSTEM

Chapter 6

SEVERE ASTHMA ATTACK AND COPD

WHEN BREATH BECOMES A STRUGGLE

Story 1: The Whistle Nikhil Ignored

Nikhil was the star forward of his school football team—fast, fierce, and unstoppable. To everyone else, he was the boy who never tired. But behind the cheers and trophies, a silent battle had begun.

It started small. A faint wheeze when he sprinted. A dry cough that refused to leave him, especially at night. "Just the winter air," he told himself. ***"I'm fit. I'm strong."*** *He ignored it. Again and again.*

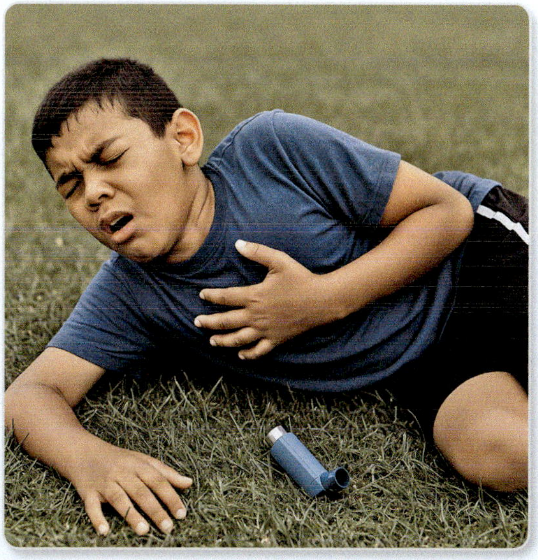

One frosty morning, during the biggest match of the season, Nikhil felt something different. Mid-run, his chest tightened like an invisible hand was crushing his lungs. He slowed, then stumble, then stopped altogether. His teammates shouted. His coach ran towards him.

Nikhil couldn't answer. No words came—just a sharp, high-pitched whistle escaping his throat.

He collapsed, clutching at his chest, his world shrinking to nothing but the desperate need for air.

It wasn't a magic goal, but a simple inhaler—pulled hurriedly from a teammate's bag-that saved him that day. Minutes later, in the ambulance, Nikhil heard a word he'd only half-understood before: Asthma.

He had been living with it, ignoring the signs, risking everything.

Today, Nikhil still plays. Still runs. Still scores. But now, he carries his inhaler with the same pride as his captain's armband.

He shares his story with young athletes everywhere:

Asthma doesn't make you weak. Ignoring it does. Respect your body. Listen to the signs. Breathe safe, play strong.

Story 2: The Smoke in Shankar's Story

Shankar, 60, was proud of his strength. A factory veteran, he often joked, "Smoke, dust, chemicals—I've breathed it all. Nothing can break me now."

His morning routine was as fixed as the sun—tea in one hand, a deep, rattling cough in the other. "It's just my morning cough," he'd laugh, brushing away worried looks from his family.

But behind the laughter, something had been changing.

The stairs he once climbed with ease left him breathless. A short walk felt like scaling Everest. He started avoiding outings, making excuses, masking his fear behind tired smiles.

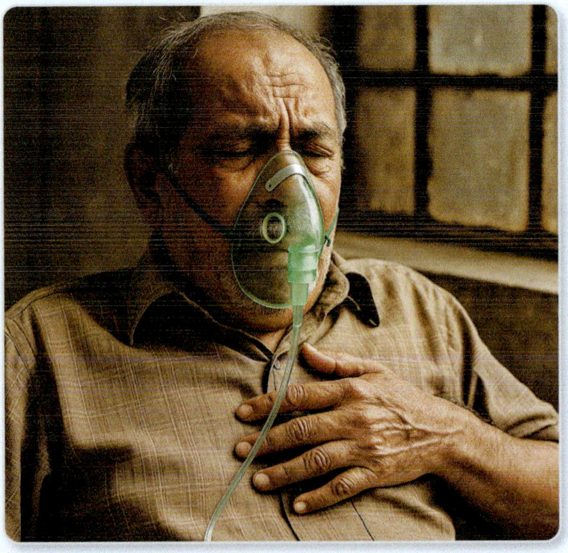

One winter morning, Shankar couldn't even rise from bed. His chest heaved, but no air seemed to reach his lungs. Panic filled the house.

At the hospital, the oxygen mask covered his face before the doctor spoke a word.

***Diagnosis**: Severe **Chronic Obstructive Pulmonary Disease (COPD)**—years of breathing in smoke, dust, and fumes had finally caught up with him. Now, sitting quietly by his window, Shankar reflects with regret: "I thought coughing was just part of life. I thought breathlessness was age. I was wrong. My lungs were screaming for help. I just wasn't listening."*

Shankar, 60-year-old, was a factory veteran. "I have worked through smoke, dust, and everything. I will be fine," he used to laugh, waving off his constant cough.

He called it his "morning cough"—as regular as his tea. But slowly, stairs became his enemy. A 10-minute walk felt like climbing Everest. One morning, he could not get out of bed—his lungs simply refused.

At the hospital, the oxygen mask went on before the doctor could even speak.

The diagnosis?

Severe Chronic Obstructive Pulmonary Disease (COPD)—*a chronic lung disease caused by years of smoking and exposure to fumes.*

"I wish I had taken my cough seriously," Shankar says now. "My lungs were screaming for help—I just was not listening."

WHAT IS ASTHMA?

Asthma is a long-term inflammation of the airways that narrows the breathing tubes, making it harder to breathe—especially during triggers such as cold, exercise, or allergens.

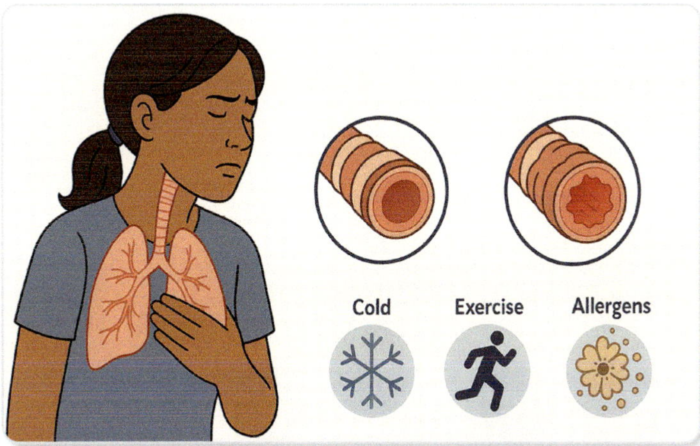

Asthma Symptoms

- Recurring dry cough, worse at night
- Wheezing (a whistling sound)
- Shortness of breath or gasping
- Chest tightness or heaviness
- *Common triggers:* Dust, smoke, pollen, exercise, stress

WHAT IS CHRONIC OBSTRUCTIVE PULMONARY DISEASE?

Chronic Obstructive Pulmonary Disease includes emphysema and chronic bronchitis—progressive lung damage that reduces airflow and oxygen exchange, often due to smoking or exposure to pollution.

Chronic Obstructive Pulmonary Disease Symptoms

- Chronic cough with phlegm
- Breathlessness, even with mild activity
- Frequent lung infections
- Wheezing and fatigue
- Bluish lips or nails in advanced cases

WHAT TO DO IN A BREATHING EMERGENCY—STEP-BY-STEP

During an Asthma Attack

- Stay calm—panic worsens breathing.
- Sit upright; loosen tight clothing.
- Use your rescue inhaler (the blue one).
- Take one puff every 30–60 seconds, up to 10 puffs.
- If no relief after 10 puffs → Call emergency services immediately.
- Avoid known triggers (cold air, dust, smoke, etc.).

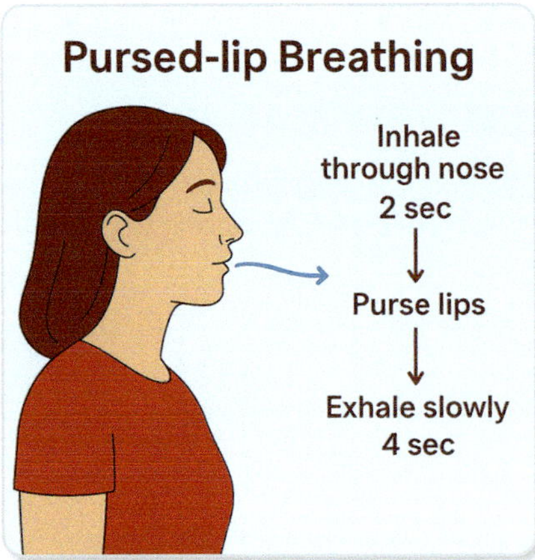

During a Chronic Obstructive Pulmonary Disease Flare-Up

- Sit in a supported position (lean forward on a table if needed).
- Use prescribed bronchodilator inhaler or nebulizer.
- Do pursed-lip breathing to slow your breath rate.
- Take emergency medications if previously advised.
- Seek emergency care if symptoms worsen.

HOW TO USE A METERED-DOSE INHALER

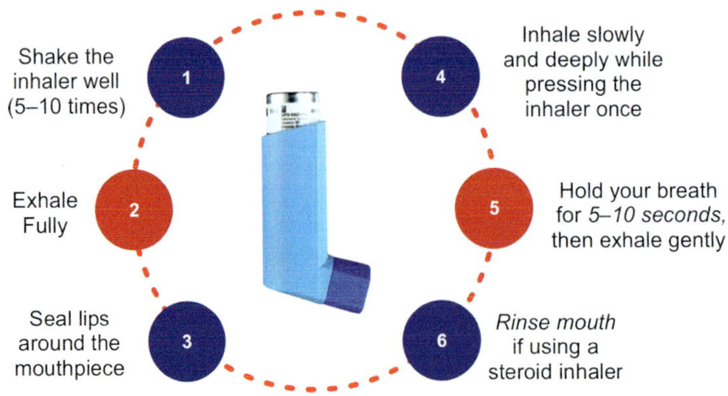

For children or the elderly, a spacer helps deliver the medication more effectively.

CALL EMERGENCY SERVICES IF (RED FLAG SIGNS)

- Inhaler gives no relief after 10 puffs
- Severe breathlessness at rest
- Lips/fingertips turning blue
- Difficulty speaking in full sentences
- Confusion, drowsiness, or collapse

MYTHS AND FACTS

Myths	Facts
"Inhalers are addictive."	Inhalers are *not addictive* and save lives.
"Only smokers get COPD."	*Pollution, Factory fumes and indoor Chulha cooking can cause COPD*
"Asthma is only a childhood disease."	Asthma can occur *at any age* and may persist lifelong.
"I do not need an inhaler if I feel okay."	Even symptom-free days need *maintenance medication* to prevent attacks.
"Exercise is dangerous for asthma."	With good control, *exercise is encouraged* and improves lung strength.

CONCLUSION

Every breath matters. Do not take it for granted.

- If you or a loved one has a *persistent cough, breathlessness, or wheezing—do not ignore it.*
- *Asthma is controllable. COPD is preventable.*
- Proper diagnosis, inhaler use, and lifestyle changes can lead to a full, active life.

Just like Nikhil and Shankar, many people learn the importance of lung health *after* a crisis. Let us help others learn it *before* one.

Scan to watch Dr Lokendra's 1-minute reel on this emergency.

Chapter 7

COUGH

DO NOT IGNORE THE SIGNS: RAVI'S WAKE-UP CALL WITH TUBERCULOSIS

Ravi, a young and ambitious banker, was used to juggling deadlines, meetings, and late nights. So when a mild cough crept into his busy life, he barely noticed. "Just a seasonal thing," he thought. Like many of us, he reached for the usual over-the-counter (OTC) cough syrups and popped a few antibiotics—without any doctor's advice.

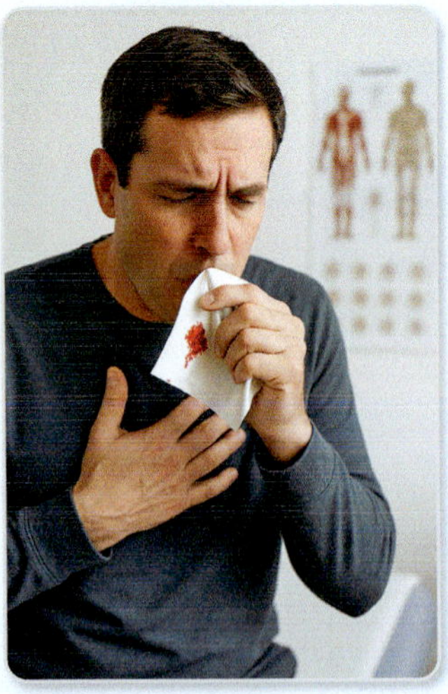

Weeks passed. The cough didn't leave. In fact, it got worse. But Ravi kept brushing it aside. "I don't have time for this. I'm too busy to be sick."

His parents noticed the change. His colleagues commented on his pale look and tired eyes. "Go see a doctor," they said. But Ravi shrugged it off. After all, how serious could a cough be?

Then came that Monday morning—the one he would never forget.

While the rest of the house slept, Ravi woke up gasping, coughing uncontrollably. This time, his sputum was blood stained.

Fear gripped him. His parents panicked—fumbling for emergency numbers they hadn't saved.

Luckily, a doctor living nearby rushed to help and called for an ambulance immediately.

At the hospital, Ravi was stabilized. Oxygen. IV lines. Tests.

The diagnosis? Tuberculosis (TB)—a serious infection that had been silently damaging his lungs. A cavity had already formed.

All those cough syrups and random antibiotics? Useless. Worse, they delayed the right diagnosis.

Today, Ravi shares his story as a warning.

"We take coughs too lightly. We start antibiotics without reason, chase syrups hoping for magic. I learned the hard way—what we ignore today can destroy us tomorrow. See a doctor. Find the reason. Don't gamble with your health."

RED FLAG SIGNS OF COUGH YOU SHOULD NEVER IGNORE

If you have a cough that lasts >2 weeks with any of the following symptoms, consult a doctor immediately:

Cough with fever

Cough with blood in sputum

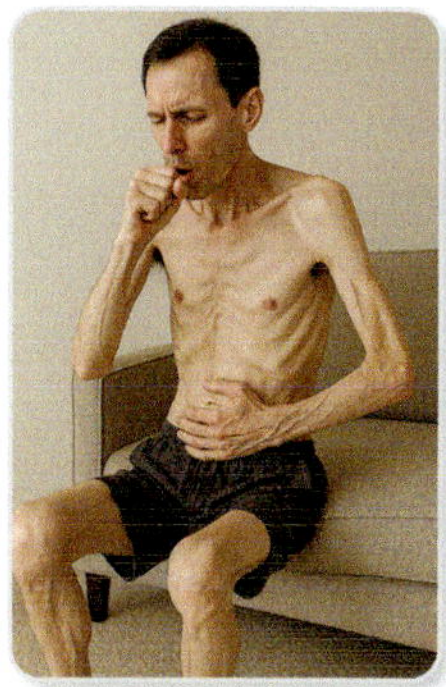

Cough with unexplained weight loss

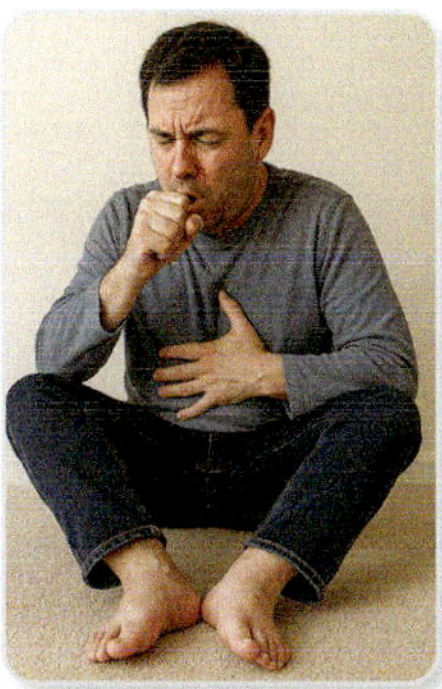

Cough with *chest pain*

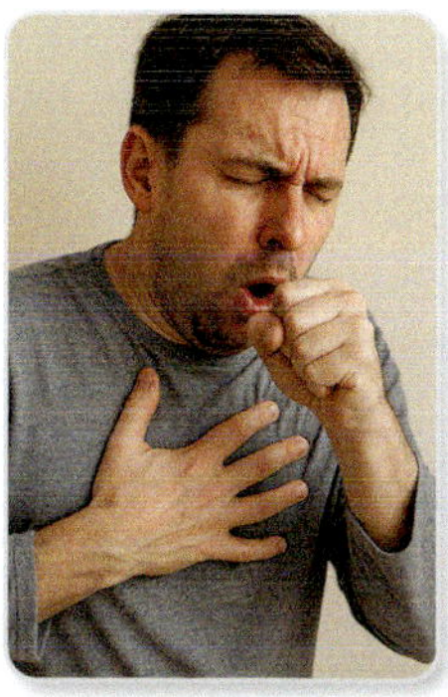

Cough with *shortness of breath*

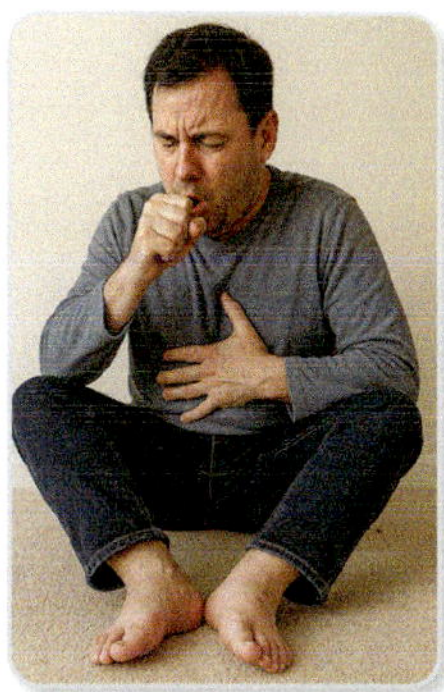

Cough with *swelling in the feet or ankles*

These could be signs of serious lung or heart conditions that need medical attention.

OTHER SERIOUS CAUSES OF CHRONIC COUGH

- Chronic bronchitis/COPD
- Asthma
- Heart failure
- Interstitial lung disease
- Post-COVID lung damage

MYTHS AND FACTS

Myths	Facts
"It is just a seasonal cough. It will go away on its own."	A persistent cough could indicate a serious illness like TB or lung disease.
"Antibiotics will fix any cough."	Not all coughs are due to bacteria. Many are viral or related to other conditions.
"Blood in sputum is just due to strain or dryness."	Blood in sputum is a red flag. It needs immediate medical evaluation.
"If I do not have a fever, it is nothing serious."	Serious conditions like TB or even cancer can present without fever.
"Only smokers get serious lung issues."	Anyone can get lung infections or diseases—smokers and nonsmokers alike.
"Cough syrups are enough to cure most coughs."	Cough syrups only relieve symptoms—they do not treat the root cause.

WHAT YOU CAN DO

- Do not self-medicate. Avoid taking antibiotics or cough syrups without consulting a doctor.
- Seek medical advice early—especially if symptoms persist.
- Save emergency ambulance numbers in your phone and share them with your family.
- Educate others—especially those who might ignore their symptoms due to work or fear.

CONCLUSION

Ravi is now on the road to recovery and has learned a life-saving lesson the hard way. Let us not wait for a health emergency to teach us the same.

Health is not a luxury. Do not ignore the signs.

Scan to watch Dr Lokendra's 1-minute reel on this emergency.

Chapter 8

CHOKING

"WHEN AIR STOPS"—UNDERSTANDING CHOKING EMERGENCIES

Story: The Dinner Table Panic

It was a joyous family dinner. Rohan, a 6-year-old child, was laughing while eating grapes when suddenly he began coughing violently. Within seconds, he was unable to speak, turned blue, and clutched his throat—classic signs of choking.

His elder sister shouted for help. Fortunately, their uncle, who knew basic first aid, sprang into action.

He performed abdominal thrusts (Heimlich maneuver), and after a few tries, the grape popped out.

Rohan burst into tears—relieved but safe.

The family was shaken but grateful. That night, they all promised to learn first aid and cut food into smaller pieces for children. A potentially fatal situation had turned into a lesson in preparedness.

WHAT IS CHOKING?

Choking occurs when an object, usually food or a small item, blocks the airway, preventing normal breathing. It can be partial (some airflow possible) or complete (no airflow) and requires immediate intervention to prevent suffocation and death.

Signs and Symptoms

- Clutching the throat (universal choking sign)
- Inability to speak, cough, or breathe
- Silent or high-pitched sounds when trying to breathe
- Skin, lips, or nails turning blue (cyanosis)
- Panic or loss of consciousness if untreated

Causes/Risk Factors

- Eating too fast or while talking/laughing
- Swallowing large or poorly chewed food
- Small objects (buttons, toys) in children
- Dental problems or dentures in elderly
- Neurological conditions (stroke, Parkinson's disease)
- Alcohol or drug intoxication

STEPWISE FIRST AID BEFORE REACHING A HOSPITAL

Act fast—choking can turn fatal within minutes.

Special Groups

- Infants (<1 year): No abdominal thrusts—use back blows and chest thrusts
- Pregnant or obese patients: Use chest thrusts instead of abdominal thrusts.

If the person can cough or breathe:

- Encourage them to cough forcefully.
- Do not hit on the back while they are upright and coughing.
- Stay close and be ready to help if it worsens.

If the person cannot breathe, speak, or cough (complete choking):

- ***Step 1:*** Ask, "Are you choking?" If they nod or cannot respond, act immediately.
- ***Step 2:*** Perform five back blows—lean them forward and give five firm blows between the shoulder blades with the heel of your hand.
- ***Step 3:*** Perform five abdominal thrusts (Heimlich maneuver)—stand behind, wrap arms around the waist, make a fist just above the navel, and give quick upward thrusts.
- Alternate five back blows and five thrusts until the object is expelled or they become unresponsive.

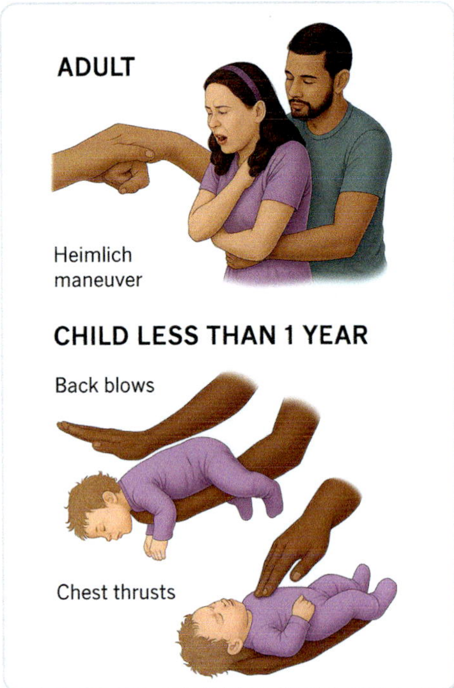

If the person becomes unconscious:

- Call emergency services immediately (112/108).
- Begin cardiopulmonary resuscitation (CPR)—start chest compressions. Check mouth for obstruction before each breath.
- Do not attempt blind finger sweeps—it can push the object further down.

WHEN TO SEE A DOCTOR

- After any choking incident (especially in children or elderly).
- If breathing remains difficult or noisy after the object is removed.
- Coughing up blood or persistent pain in throat/chest.
- If abdominal thrusts or back blows were performed.

MYTHS AND FACTS

Myths	Facts
Give water to someone who is choking	Never give anything by mouth—it can worsen the situation
Slapping on the back always help	Only effective when done correctly with person leaning forward
Choking only happens to kids	It can occur in any age, especially elderly or intoxicated individuals
You can wait a few minutes before helping	Brain damage can occur in 4–6 minutes—act immediately

PREVENTION TIPS

Chew food thoroughly and eat slowly

Cut food into small pieces for children and elderly

Keep small objects away from young

Avoid talking or laughing while having food

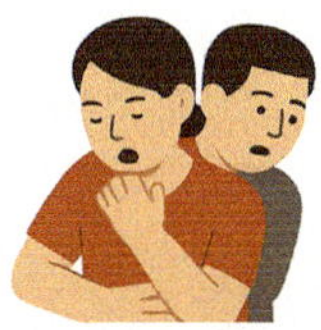

Learn and teach choking first aid

Supervise kids during meals and playtime

CONCLUSION

- "Choking does not come with a warning—your action in the first seconds can save a life."
- Learn the signs, act fast, and empower others with this life-saving knowledge.

Scan to watch Dr Lokendra's 1-minute reel on this emergency.

SECTION 3: NEUROLOGICAL AND MENTAL HEALTH

Chapter 9

STROKE (BRAIN ATTACK)

FROM PARALYSIS TO PROGRESS: STROKE RECOVERY WITH ALTEPLASE (WITHIN 4.5-HOUR WINDOW, DOSE BY WEIGHT)

Story: A Sunday Stroke and a Second Chance: Mr Avatar's Journey

Mr Ram Avatar, a 65-year-old retired school teacher, experienced sudden onset of right-sided weakness and difficulty speaking while gardening at his home on a quiet Sunday morning. Recognizing these alarming signs, his wife immediately called for an ambulance, mentioning the symptoms that strongly suggested a stroke. Upon arrival at the emergency department, the clock indicated that only 45 minutes had passed since the onset of symptoms.

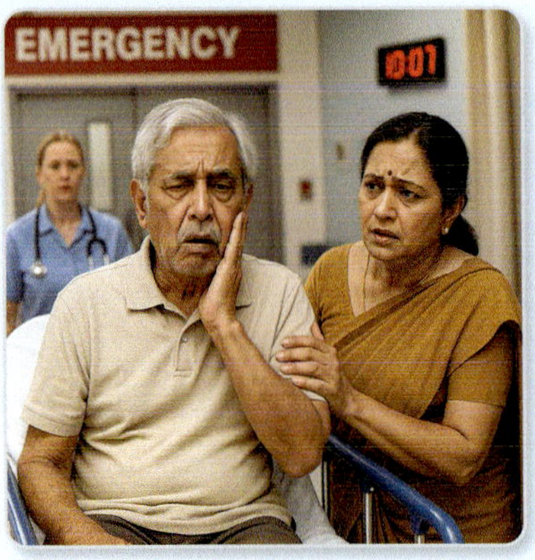

The emergency team swiftly conducted a physical examination and a rapid assessment using the National Institutes of Health Stroke Scale (NIHSS) to evaluate Mr Avatar's neurological function, which revealed a score indicating moderate-to-severe stroke. His medical history was notable for hypertension and type 2 diabetes, both of which are risk factors for stroke. An urgent computed tomography (CT) scan of the brain was performed to differentiate between ischemic and hemorrhagic stroke, revealing an ischemic stroke with no signs of hemorrhage. Blood tests were also conducted to ensure there were no contraindications to thrombolytic therapy (medicine to dissolve the clot).

Given the absence of hemorrhage and the fact that Mr Avatar was within the 4.5-hour window period from symptom onset, the decision was made to administer alteplase, a recombinant tissue plasminogen activator (rtPA), to dissolve the clot obstructing blood flow to his brain. Before administering the treatment, the medical team explained the potential risks and benefits to Mr Avatar and his family, obtaining informed consent.

Alteplase was administered intravenously at the recommended dose, calculated based on Mr Avatar's body weight. The treatment was initiated approximately 2 hours from the onset of his symptoms. During and after the infusion, he was closely monitored for any signs of improvement in his neurological status or adverse effects, particularly bleeding.

Over the next 48 hours, Mr Avatar showed significant improvement in his right-sided weakness and speech difficulties. He was transferred to the stroke unit for continued observation and began early rehabilitation with physiotherapy and speech therapy to aid his recovery. His management also included secondary stroke prevention measures, such as optimizing his blood pressure and diabetes management, starting antiplatelet therapy, and lifestyle modifications including diet, exercise, and smoking cessation.

Mr Avatar's case highlights the critical importance of rapid recognition and treatment of stroke symptoms. His timely arrival at the hospital and the effective use of thrombolytic therapy (medicine to dissolve the clot) within the therapeutic window significantly contributed to his positive outcome. His journey underscores the lifesaving potential of alteplase in acute ischemic stroke management when administered promptly and appropriately. Following is the CT scan angiography of Mr Ram Avatar before and after administration of Alteplase.

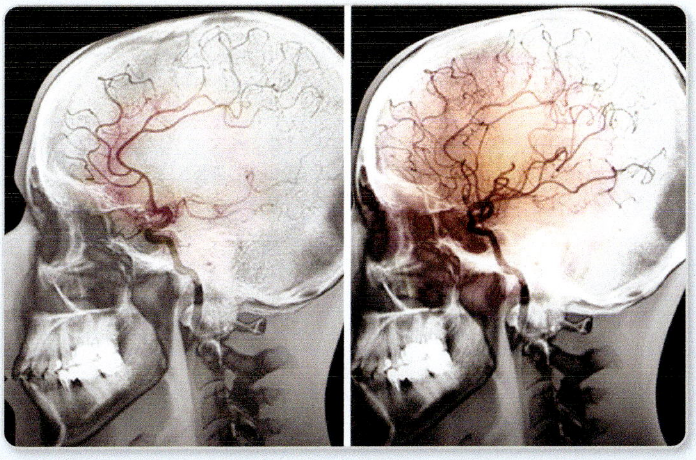

WHAT IS A STROKE?

A stroke is a type of brain damage that occurs when the blood flow to a part of the brain is interrupted.

Types of Stroke

There are primarily two kinds of strokes:

1. ***Ischemic strokes (blood clot blocking a brain artery):*** These happen when a blood vessel that supplies blood to the brain gets blocked.
2. ***Hemorrhagic strokes (burst blood vessel in the brain):*** These happen when a blood vessel in the brain bursts.

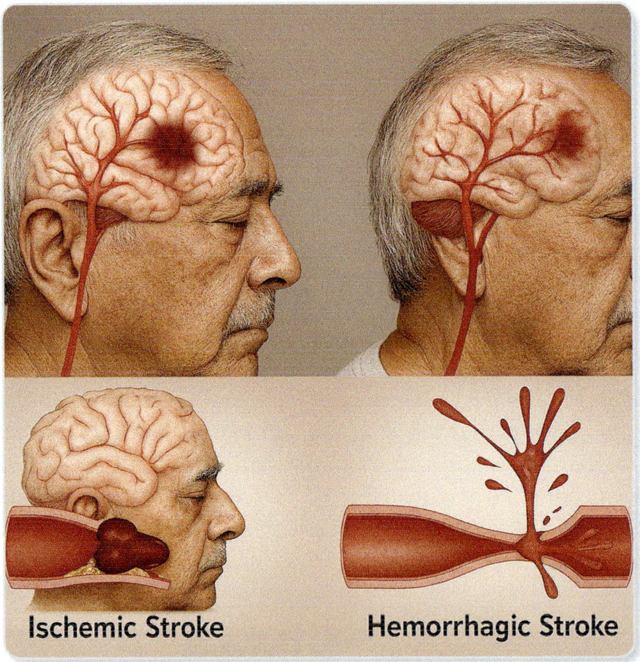

While both types are serious and can be life-threatening, ischemic strokes typically do not cause death within the first hour, unlike hemorrhagic strokes, which can be immediately fatal. For those who survive the initial hours after a stroke, the damage to the brain can rapidly worsen, potentially leading to lasting impairments. It is crucial to distinguish between ischemic and hemorrhagic strokes because their treatments are significantly different.

Signs and Symptoms

BE FAST Reminder of Stroke Signs

B

Balance
Is the person suddenly having trouble **with balance or coordination?**

E

Eyes
Is the person experiencing suddenly blurred or double vision or a sudden loss of vision in one or both eyes without pain? balance or coordination?

F

Face Dropping
Does one side of the face droop or is it numb? Ask the person to smile.

A

Arm Weakness
Is one arm weak or numb? Ask the person to raise both arms. Does one arm drift downward?

S

Speech Difficulty
Is speech slurred, are they unable to speak, or are they hard to understand? Ask the person to repeat a simple sentence like, "The sky is blue." Is the sentence repeated correctly?

T

Time to call 911
If the person shows any of these symptoms, even if the symptoms go away, call 112 and get them to the hospital immediately.

STEPWISE FIRST AID BEFORE REACHING A HOSPITAL

- Immediately call for help.
- Take the patient to a nearest Hospital having a Neurologist and an Emergency Physician by 108 Ambulance.
- If possible check the patients Glucose values with a Glucometer at home.

- Administer simple sugar one teaspoon if sugar is <70 mg/dL.
- The hospital should have a CT scan facility on premises.
- Upon arriving in the hospital describe the details of the chief complaints to an Emergency Physician.

MYTHS AND FACTS

Myths	Facts
Strokes only happen to older people.	Stroke can occur at any age even amongst young adults.
Strokes are not preventable.	Up to 80% of strokes can be prevented by managing risk factors such as high blood pressure and not smoking.
Strokes are rare.	Stroke is a leading cause of death and disability worldwide, affecting millions of people each year.
Stroke symptoms develop slowly over time.	Stroke symptoms usually happen suddenly. Quick action is crucial for effective treatment.
If stroke symptoms go away, you do not need to see a doctor.	Even if symptoms disappear, it might be a transient ischemic attack (TIA), a warning sign of a future stroke.
Strokes are always fatal.	Many people survive strokes. The outcome depends on the stroke's severity and the speed of treatment.
Only people with a history of stroke in their family need to worry about having one.	While family history can increase risk, factors such as lifestyle and medical conditions also play a significant role.
Strokes cannot be treated.	There are treatments for stroke that can reduce the risk of damage or death, especially if administered quickly.
All strokes have the same symptoms.	Stroke symptoms can vary widely from person to person, including speech difficulties, paralysis, and confusion.
Once you have a stroke, you cannot improve or regain lost abilities.	Many people make significant recoveries after a stroke through rehabilitation, although the extent of recovery can vary.

Understanding these facts about stroke can help in recognizing the signs early, seeking immediate treatment, and potentially saving lives or reducing long-term disabilities.

CONCLUSION

- Stroke is a medical emergency.
- Recognizing symptoms early and seeking immediate help can save lives and prevent disability.
- *Remember FAST*—Face, Arms, Speech, Time.
- If you suspect a stroke, do not wait—call emergency services right away.
- Every minute counts. Time lost is brain lost.

Scan to watch Dr Lokendra's 1-minute reel on this emergency.

Chapter 10

SEIZURES (FITS)

"WHEN THE BRAIN MISFIRES"—UNDERSTANDING SEIZURES (FITS)

Story: The Class Shock

Ritika was known in her college for her confidence. Bright, ambitious, and full of life, she was the kind of person who lit up a room when she entered. That morning, she stood before her classmates, delivering a presentation on entrepreneurship—her voice clear, her posture firm.

Then, mid-sentence, something changed.

Her classmates noticed it before she did.

Her words slowed, her eyes seemed to lose focus. For a brief second, she stood frozen—like someone had pressed "pause" on her body. Then, her knees buckled, and she collapsed onto the hard classroom floor with a heavy thud.

Confused murmurs turned to shocked gasps as her body began to twitch violently, her arms jerking uncontrollably, legs stiffening. Some students stood up, panicked. A few rushed to the door shouting for help. Others simply froze, not knowing what to do.

Neha, Ritika's close friend, felt her heart racing—but something clicked in her mind. She had once seen a seizure during a first-aid workshop and remembered the golden rule: Stay calm. Act smart. Don't panic.

"Clear the space around her! Move the bags and chairs away!" Neha commanded her classmates firmly.

She carefully turned Ritika onto her left side, placing her in the recovery position—this simple step could prevent Ritika from choking if she vomited or struggled to breathe. She looked at her watch. "Start timing. It's important."

Neha made sure nothing was placed in Ritika's mouth and gently cushioned her head with a folded jacket. She knew restraint was dangerous, so she let the seizure run its course without interference.

The jerking stopped after two long minutes that felt like hours.

Ritika lay still now, breathing heavily, her eyes fluttering open in confusion. "What happened?" she whispered, frightened, tears mixing with sweat on her pale face "It's over. You're safe," Neha reassured her, holding her hand.

The nurse arrived moments later, followed by the college's medical team. Ritika was rushed to the hospital. There, after tests and a detailed evaluation, doctors confirmed what she had never suspected—Epilepsy. A condition where sudden bursts of abnormal brain activity cause seizures. Not a curse. Not something to fear. Just a medical condition that needed proper care, regular medicine, and understanding.

Today, Ritika continues her studies confidently. She openly shares her story to spread awareness.

"That day was terrifying. But I'm grateful Neha knew what to do. Her calm saved me from serious harm. People fear seizures because they don't understand them. With the right support and treatment, I live a normal life. Don't fear epilepsy. Fear ignorance."

Steps to Place Someone in the Recovery Position:

- ***Protect the Head:*** Gently support and cushion the head throughout the movement.
- ***Position the Arm:*** Move the arm closest to you at a right angle to their body, palm facing upwards.
- ***Cross the Far Leg:*** Bring the far leg across the body so the foot is flat on the ground, forming a bent knee.
- ***Roll Them Towards You:*** Hold their shoulder and knee, and roll them gently towards you onto their side.
- ***Open the Airway:*** Tilt the head slightly back to open the airway. Ensure the mouth is facing downwards to allow fluids to drain.
- ***Monitor Breathing:*** Stay with them. Reassure them as they regain consciousness.

The seizure lasted about 2 minutes, and Ritika was confused and drowsy when it ended. The medical team arrived shortly after and transported her to a hospital. Tests revealed that Ritika had epilepsy a condition that can be managed with the right treatment.

Thanks to Neha's calm response, Ritika avoided any injury during the episode and was able to begin her journey to diagnosis and treatment.

WHAT IS A SEIZURE?

A seizure (also called a fit) is a sudden, uncontrolled electrical disturbance in the brain. It can cause changes in behavior, movements, feelings, and levels of consciousness. Seizures can be a one-time event or part of a condition like epilepsy.

Types of Seizures

- **Generalized tonic-clonic:** Loss of consciousness + shaking (most familiar to public)
- **Absence seizures:** Brief staring episodes
- **Focal seizures:** Jerking or strange sensations in part of the body.

Signs and Symptoms

1 Sudden collapse or loss of consciousness

2 Uncontrolled jerking or shaking of the body (convulsions)

2 Staring spells or unresponsiveness

4 Stiffening of limbs

3 Frothing at the mouth or tongue biting

6 Loss of bladder or bowel control

7 Confusion or sleepiness after the episode (postictal state)

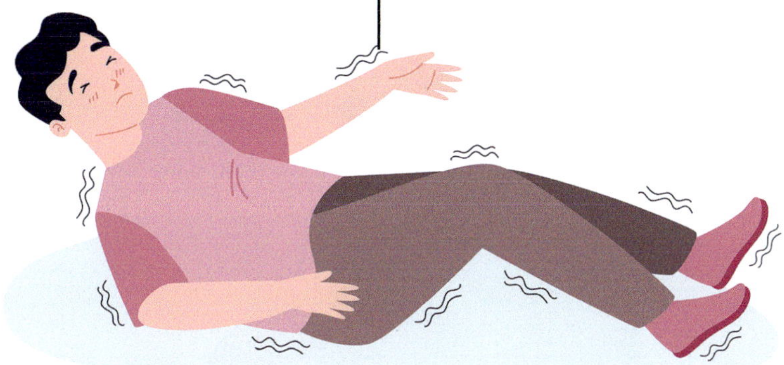

Causes/Risk Factors

- Epilepsy
- High fever (especially in children)
- Brain injury or stroke
- Low blood sugar or electrolyte imbalance
- Drug or alcohol withdrawal
- Infections of the brain (meningitis, encephalitis)
- Sleep deprivation or stress

STEPWISE FIRST AID BEFORE REACHING A HOSPITAL

Stay calm and protect the person from harm.

- ***Step 1:*** Keep the Person Safe
    - » Gently help them to the ground if falling.
    - » Clear nearby objects to prevent injury.

- ***Step 2:*** Turn Them on Their Side
  - » This prevents choking if vomiting or drooling occurs.
  - » Loosen tight clothing around the neck.
- ***Step 3:*** Time the Seizure
  - » Most seizures stop within 1–3 minutes.
  - » Note the duration to inform medical personnel.
- ***Step 4:*** Do NOT Put Anything in the Mouth
  - » Never try to hold their tongue or put objects between their teeth.
  - » This can cause injury or choking.
- ***Step 5:*** Stay Until They Recover
  - » Comfort them once the seizure stops.
  - » Expect drowsiness or confusion afterward.

Recovery Position

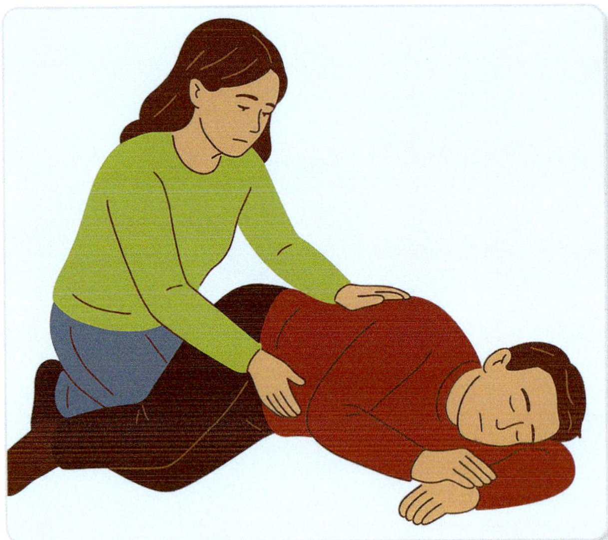

WHEN TO SEE A DOCTOR

- First-time seizure or unknown cause
- Seizure lasting >5 minutes
- Difficulty breathing or waking up afterward
- Multiple seizures in a short time
- Injury during the seizure
- Seizure during pregnancy

MYTHS AND FACTS

Myths	Facts
Put a spoon or cloth in the person's mouth.	This can cause choking or broken teeth—never do this.
Seizures are always dangerous.	Most seizures are brief and stop on their own.
People with seizures are mentally ill.	Epilepsy is a neurological condition, not a psychiatric one.
You should restrain a person having a seizure.	Just protect them from harm—do not try to hold them down.

PREVENTION TIPS

- Take prescribed antiepileptic medications regularly.
- Avoid sleep deprivation.
- Manage stress effectively.
- Limit alcohol intake and avoid recreational drugs.
- Avoid flashing lights or known triggers if photosensitive.

CONCLUSION

- "A seizure can strike without warning—but with the right response, you can protect and support someone until help arrives."
- *Never panic. Protect, time, and turn. Let us break the myths and bring in awareness.*

Scan to watch Dr Lokendra's 1-minute reel on this emergency.

Chapter 11

SUDDEN COLLAPSE AND UNRESPONSIVENESS

"WHEN SILENCE STRIKES"—UNDERSTANDING SUDDEN COLLAPSE AND UNRESPONSIVENESS

Story: The Morning Walk Alarm

Mr Shyamlal, a 68-year-old retired postmaster, was well-known in his neighborhood for his disciplined routine. Every morning, just after sunrise, he would lace up his walking shoes and head to the nearby park for his daily walk.

One such morning, as he was halfway through his usual round, he suddenly felt lightheaded. Before anyone could notice, he ***collapsed silently to the ground****—unresponsive, not breathing normally, and with a pale, lifeless face.*

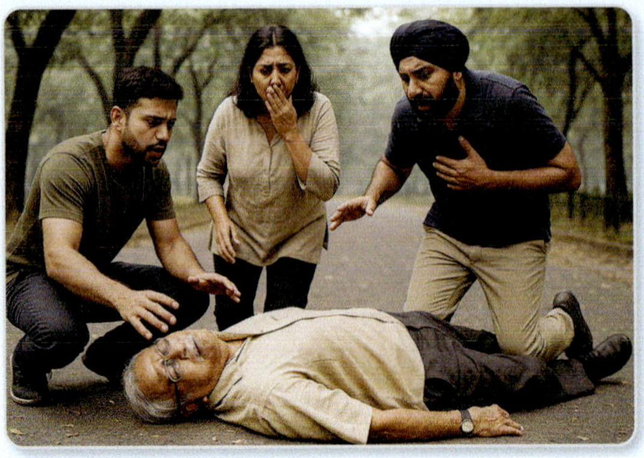

People nearby panicked. Some thought he had fainted, others feared the worst, but no one was sure what to do. Precious minutes passed in confusion.

*Thankfully, a young jogger named **Aakash** had recently attended a **Basic Life Support (BLS)** and **CPR workshop** at his college. He recognized immediately that this was not fainting—this was likely a **cardiac arrest.***

He quickly checked:

- *No pulse in the neck*
- *No breathing*

*Without wasting time, Aakash **called out for help, asked someone to dial an ambulance, and immediately began chest compressions**—hard and fast, in the center of Mr Shyamlal's chest. His calm yet firm actions surprised and inspired the onlookers.*

*For the next few minutes, until the ambulance arrived, Aakash kept going with **continuous CPR.** The paramedics arrived and took over with advanced care. **Miraculously, Mr Shyamlal regained a pulse** and was rushed to the hospital.*

*At the hospital, doctors confirmed it had been a sudden cardiac arrest—something that can happen even without prior heart symptoms, especially in elderly individuals with risk factors like **diabetes, high blood pressure, or underlying heart disease.***

*The doctors praised Aakash's **quick thinking and CPR skills.** They explained to Mr Shyamlal's family and the gathered onlookers:*

"In cardiac arrest, every second counts. Without CPR, brain damage starts within 4–6 minutes. Early chest compressions can double or triple survival chances."

Key Lessons from Mr Shyamlal's Story

- *Sudden collapse with **no response or breathing is a medical emergency—think cardiac arrest.***
- ***Immediate CPR saves lives**. Don't wait for help to arrive.*
- *Learn and practice **Basic Life Support (BLS)**—it can make you a lifesaver.*
- *Be aware: **Age, hypertension, diabetes, heart disease** increase sudden collapse risk.*

WHAT IS SUDDEN COLLAPSE AND UNRESPONSIVENESS?

It refers to a condition where a person suddenly becomes unconscious and fails to respond or breathe normally. This can be due to several critical causes such as cardiac arrest, stroke, low blood sugar, seizures, trauma, and choking. Immediate response is crucial to prevent brain damage or death.

Signs and Symptoms

- Sudden fall to the ground
- No response to tapping or calling
- No breathing or abnormal breathing (gasping)
- Limp body, no purposeful movements
- Pale, bluish, or clammy skin
- Possible frothing, seizures, or tongue bite
- No pulse in the neck

Causes/Risk Factors

- Sudden cardiac arrest
- Stroke or brain injury
- Seizure or epilepsy
- Low blood sugar (especially in diabetics)
- Severe allergic reaction (anaphylaxis)
- Drug overdose or poisoning
- Head trauma or internal bleeding

STEPWISE FIRST AID BEFORE REACHING A HOSPITAL

Remember: Check, Call, Compress (CPR)

- ***Step 1:*** Check Responsiveness
  - » Tap shoulders and shout loudly. Ask: "Are you okay?"
  - » If no response, check for breathing.
- ***Step 2:*** Call for Emergency Help
  - » Dial 112 or 108 immediately.
  - » Ask for an ambulance and inform that the person is unresponsive.
- ***Step 3:*** Check for pulse and breathing, if no pulse no breathing, start CPR
  - » **Place hands in the center of the chest and push hard and fast (100–120 compressions/min).**
  - » Continue CPR until help arrives or the person becomes responsive.

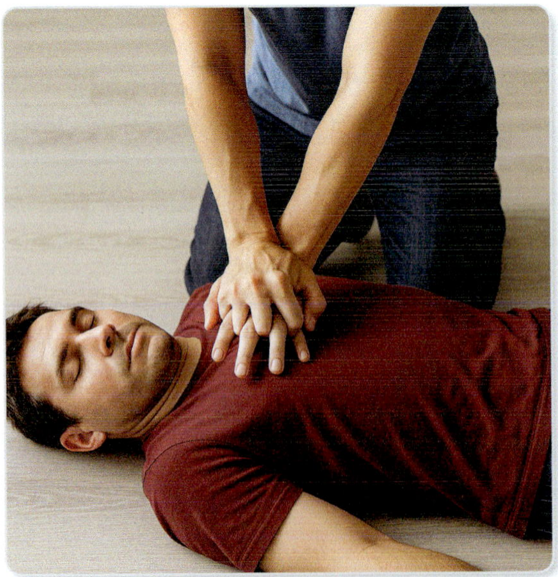

Hands-Only CPR (just chest compressions) is effective for sudden adult collapse and is recommended for untrained rescuers.

- ***Step 4:*** Use an Automated External Defibrillator (AED) if Available
  - » Follow voice instructions from the AED.
  - » Use only if trained or guided by emergency personnel.
- ***Step 5:*** Recovery Position (If Breathing)
  - » If the person starts breathing, turn them onto their side (recovery position).

WHEN TO SEE A DOCTOR

- Any episode of sudden unresponsiveness
- Collapses with chest pain, breathing difficulty, or seizures
- Known heart conditions or stroke history
- Associated trauma, injury, or bleeding
- Recurrent fainting or blackouts

MYTHS AND FACTS

Myths	Facts
Sprinkle water or slap the person to revive them.	Unconsciousness without pulse is a medical emergency—start CPR instead.
Only doctors can do CPR.	Bystander CPR saves lives—anyone can and should learn it.
Wait for the ambulance before doing anything.	Every second counts—CPR keeps blood flowing to vital organs.
Sudden collapse means death.	Many survive if helped early with CPR and medical care.

PREVENTION TIPS

- Regular health checkups for heart, sugar, and blood pressure.
- Learn Basic Life Support (CPR).
- Avoid excessive exertion in high-risk individuals.
- Manage stress and sleep well.
- Carry emergency ID or medical alert bracelets if you have chronic conditions.
- Keep emergency numbers accessible.

CONCLUSION

- "Sudden collapse does not mean the end—what you do in the first few minutes can save a life."
- *Be prepared. Learn CPR. Act fast. Because in emergencies, you might be the first responder.*

Scan to watch Dr Lokendra's 1-minute reel on this emergency.

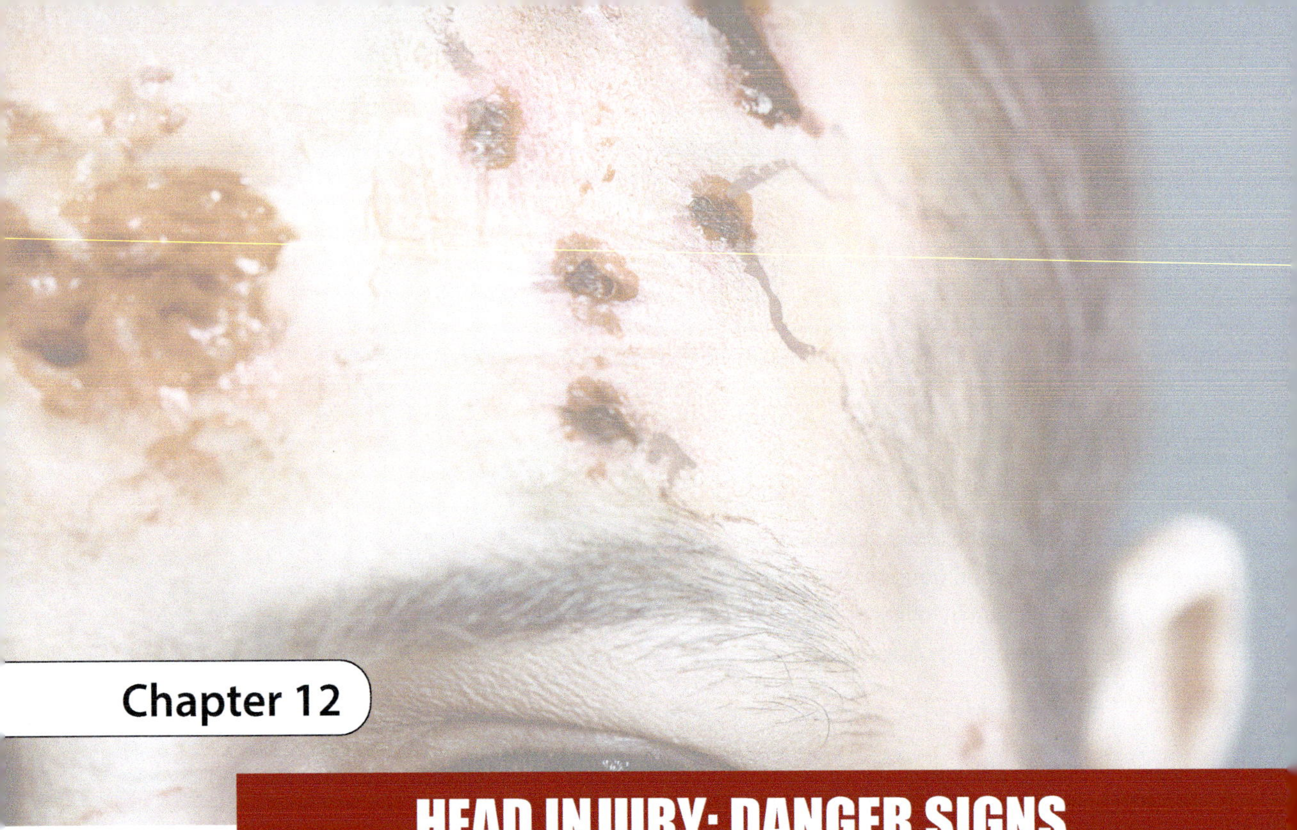

Chapter 12

HEAD INJURY: DANGER SIGNS

"WHEN A BUMP CAN BE SERIOUS"—HEAD INJURY: DANGER SIGNS

Story: The Playground Fall

It was just another cheerful afternoon at school when ***10-year-old Meera*** *and her friends decided to race each other to the top of the jungle gym. In her excitement, Meera climbed too fast, lost her grip, and fell awkwardly from a height of about 5 feet. She landed hard, her head hitting the dusty ground with a loud thud.*

Startled by the fall, Meera cried loudly at first. Her teacher, Ms Anjali, rushed over immediately. She noticed a small scrape on Meera's forehead but no swelling or bleeding from the nose or ears. Meera seemed to calm down quickly, reassured everyone that she was fine, and even managed a weak smile when her friends comforted her.

To be cautious, Ms Anjali cleaned the wound, applied a cold compress, and asked Meera to rest in the infirmary. Initially, everything seemed under control. However, about ***30 minutes later****, things began to change.*

Meera, who was usually chatty and playful, became unusually ***quiet and drowsy. She started to complain of a strong headache. When she vomited twice within the next 15 minutes, Ms Anjali grew concerned. Remembering her school's first aid training on head injuries, she recognized these as danger signs.*** *Without wasting time, she called Meera's parents and explained the situation clearly.*

Her parents arrived promptly and rushed her to the ***nearest hospital emergency department. There, the doctor performed a thorough assessment. Though Meera was awake, the doctor noted signs that suggested a possible concussion with a risk of internal bleeding. A CT scan*** *was advised. Thankfully, it ruled out a large bleed but showed* ***mild swelling consistent with a concussion.***

Meera was admitted for ***observation*** *because symptoms from head injuries can sometimes worsen over hours. Under close monitoring—checking her level of consciousness, pupil reactions, and any further vomiting—she gradually began to improve. By the next day, her headache had reduced, and she was more alert. After 2 days of observation and no worsening signs, she was discharged with strict instructions for* ***home rest*** *and a follow-up visit.*

Why this Story Matters

Many head injuries in children may seem minor at first but can escalate if warning signs are ignored. Observation in the first 24 hours is crucial.

Key Takeaway

A child saying "I feel fine" immediately after a fall does not rule out serious injury. Trust your instincts. If in doubt, seek medical evaluation—early action saves lives.

WHAT IS A HEAD INJURY?

A head injury refers to any trauma to the scalp, skull, or brain. It can be mild (like a bump or concussion) or severe (involving bleeding, skull fracture, or brain swelling). Some head injuries may not show symptoms immediately but can still be dangerous.

Signs and Symptoms

Mild Symptoms

- Scalp swelling or bruising
- Headache
- Nausea or brief confusion
- Drowsiness without loss of consciousness

Danger Signs (Seek Immediate Medical Help)

- Repeated vomiting
- Loss of consciousness (even brief)
- Seizures or convulsions

- Slurred speech or confusion
- Unequal pupil size or blurred vision
- Bleeding or clear fluid from nose/ears
- Weakness or numbness in arms/legs
- Unusual behavior, drowsiness, or difficulty waking up

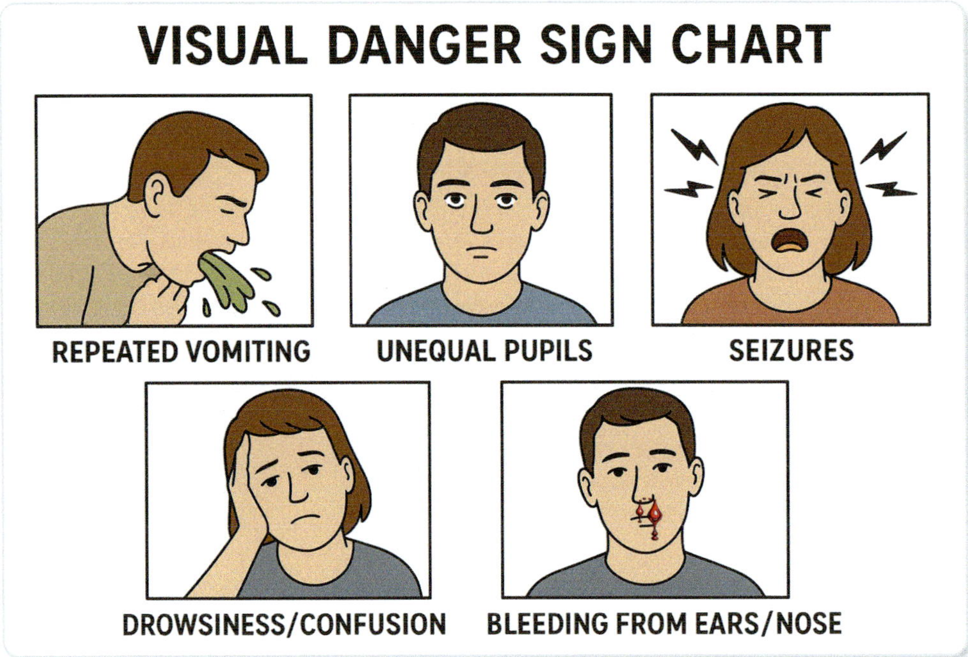

Causes/Risk Factors

- Falls (especially in children and elderly)
- Road traffic accidents
- Sports injuries or fights
- Not using helmets or seatbelts
- Alcohol or drug use
- History of bleeding disorders or blood thinners

STEPWISE FIRST AID BEFORE REACHING A HOSPITAL

Always treat a head injury with caution, even if it seems minor.

- ***Step 1:*** Check Responsiveness
  - » Ask questions to assess alertness. Note any confusion or drowsiness.
- ***Step 2:*** Keep the Person Still
  - » Avoid moving the head or neck.
  - » Lay the person down with the head slightly elevated, if conscious.

- ***Step 3:*** Control Bleeding
- Apply gentle pressure with a clean cloth.
  - » Do not press hard if skull fracture is suspected (e.g., soft spot, deformity).
- ***Step 4:*** Monitor Breathing and Alertness
  - » If unconscious but breathing, place in recovery position.
  - » If not breathing, begin cardiopulmonary resuscitation (CPR) if trained.
- ***Step 5:*** Do Not Give Food, Water, or Painkillers
  - » These can worsen condition or delay care.
- ***Step 6:*** Seek Medical Help Immediately
  - » Especially if any danger signs are present or injury was significant.

WHEN TO SEE A DOCTOR

- Any loss of consciousness
- Vomiting more than once
- Seizures or drowsiness
- Head injury in infants or elderly
- Bleeding from nose or ears after head trauma
- Persistent headache or confusion

PREVENTION TIPS

MYTHS AND FACTS

Myths	Facts
If the person is awake, the injury is not serious.	Some brain injuries show delayed symptoms.
Let the person sleep it off.	Drowsiness after head injury may signal danger—observe closely.
It is okay to give painkillers.	Painkillers can mask symptoms or increase bleeding risk.
Only big hits cause brain injury.	Even a minor bump can lead to a serious internal bleed.

CONCLUSION

- "Not all head injuries bleed—but the danger might be hidden inside."
- *Be alert to danger signs, act promptly, and always prioritize safety with protective gear and preventive habits.*

Scan to watch Dr Lokendra's 1-minute reel on this emergency.

Chapter 13

FAINTING AND DIZZINESS

"WHEN THE WORLD SPINS"—FAINTING AND DIZZINESS

Story: The Morning Commute Scare

*It was a **humid Monday morning**, and the metro was packed with office-goers. Among them was **30-year-old Reema,** standing with one hand holding the overhead rail. She had skipped breakfast after a late night of work, surviving only on a cup of coffee. As the train rattled forward, **she began to feel uneasy**—her vision blurred, her head felt light, and a ringing sound filled her ears.*

*Before she could call out for help, **her knees buckled, and she collapsed onto the floor.** The sudden fall startled the passengers around her. A quick-thinking commuter gently laid her flat on her back, elevating her legs with a bag to help blood flow back to the brain. Another person loosened her scarf and **tight clothing to ease breathing,** while someone checked her pulse and ensured she was breathing normally.*

*A diabetic passenger, **carrying a small portable glucometer,** quickly checked her blood sugar. It was low—likely due to skipping her morning meal. Once Reema regained consciousness, a sugar sachet was mixed with a little water and given to her in small sips, helping her regain strength.*

*Within minutes, her dizziness faded, though she was left shaken. At the nearest clinic, **doctors confirmed that she had experienced simple fainting** (vasovagal syncope) due to dehydration, low blood sugar, and prolonged standing in a hot, crowded environment.*

*This incident was a wake-up call for Reema. She realized the **importance of eating a proper breakfast,** carrying water, and even keeping a glucose sachet in her bag—**small habits that could prevent such scary episodes in the future.***

WHAT IS FAINTING AND DIZZINESS?

Fainting (syncope) is a temporary loss of consciousness caused by a sudden drop in blood flow to the brain. Dizziness is a sensation of lightheadedness, spinning, or imbalance. Both can be caused by benign issues like dehydration or serious conditions like heart problems.

Signs and Symptoms

Dizziness (Pre-Fainting)

- Lightheadedness or unsteadiness
- Blurred vision or dimming of sight
- Nausea or sweating
- Ringing in the ears
- Feeling weak or faint

Fainting

- Sudden loss of consciousness
- Collapse or fall to the ground
- Cold, clammy skin
- Brief confusion after regaining consciousness
- Rapid heartbeat or palpitations

Causes/Risk Factors

- Dehydration or overheating
- Prolonged standing or sudden change in posture
- Skipping meals or low blood sugar
- Anxiety, pain, or emotional stress
- Heart problems (arrhythmias, valve disease)

- Certain medications (blood pressure, sedatives)
- Anemia or low oxygen levels

HEART AND STROKE WARNING

"If fainting is accompanied by facial drooping, arm weakness, speech difficulty, chest pain, or severe shortness of breath, treat it as a possible heart attack or stroke—call emergency services immediately."

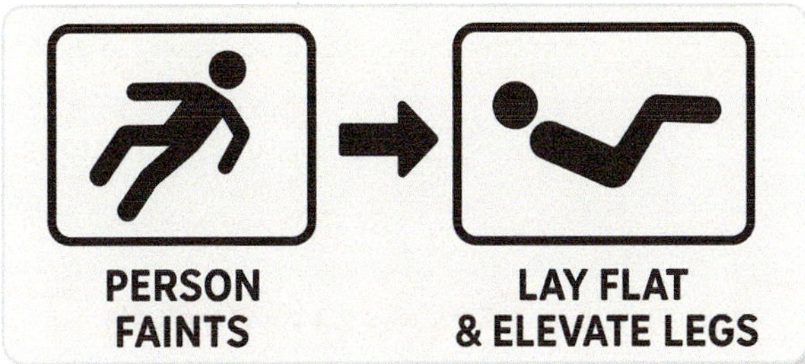

STEPWISE FIRST AID BEFORE REACHING A HOSPITAL

Help the person lie down and improve blood flow to the brain.

- ***Step 1:*** Lay the Person Flat
  - » Gently lower them to the ground to prevent injury.
  - » Elevate their legs about 12 inches to aid blood flow.
- ***Step 2:*** Loosen Tight Clothing
  - » Remove belts, collars, or ties that may restrict breathing.
- ***Step 3:*** Ensure Fresh Air
  - » Open windows or fan them if indoors.
  - » Turn their head to the side if vomiting occurs.
- ***Step 4:*** Offer Fluids or Snack Once Awake
  - » Give water or juice if alert and not nauseous.
- ***Step 5:*** Reassure and Let Them Rest
  - » Avoid sudden standing; help them sit up slowly.
- ***Step 6:*** Seek Medical Help If:
  - » Fainting lasts more than a minute, happens repeatedly, or follows chest pain or seizures.

WHEN TO SEE A DOCTOR

- First-time fainting episode
- Recurring dizziness or blackouts
- Fainting with chest pain, palpitations, or breathing difficulty
- Seizures, tongue biting, or confusion after fainting
- Injury sustained during the fall
- Bood Pressure Check tip: ***Especially for older adults or known hypertensives:*** "If possible, check blood pressure after recovery to rule out a drop (postural hypotension)."

MYTHS AND FACTS

Myths	Facts
Slapping or sprinkling water quickly revives a fainted person.	Lay them flat and elevate legs to restore blood flow.
Fainting is always due to weakness.	It can be a sign of heart or neurological problems.
It is okay to let someone walk immediately after fainting.	Let them rest and sit up slowly to avoid repeat episodes.
Only older people faint.	Fainting can occur at any age due to various triggers.

Prevention Tips

- Stay hydrated, especially in hot weather.
- Do not skip meals; eat regular balanced food.
- Stand up slowly after sitting or lying down.
- Avoid standing for too long in one position.
- Manage stress and anxiety with breathing techniques

CONCLUSION

- "Fainting may be brief—but the danger is real if ignored."
- *Act fast, stay calm, and seek help if it happens repeatedly. Simple steps can prevent serious falls or reveal hidden conditions.*

Scan to watch Dr Lokendra's 1-minute reel on this emergency.

Chapter 14

MENTAL HEALTH CRISES AND SUICIDE RISK

"WHEN THE MIND CRIES QUIETLY"—MENTAL HEALTH CRISIS AND SUICIDE RISK

Story: The Silent Struggle

Nikhil, a 22-year-old college student, was known among his friends for his sense of humor and bright smile. But over the past few weeks, something had changed. He stopped going to classes, stayed in his room for hours, and hardly ate. His friends assumed he was just tired or stressed about exams, but deep down, ***Nikhil was silently battling overwhelming sadness and hopelessness.***

One evening, his roommate, Arjun, returned to find a half-written note on Nikhil's desk and empty strips of medication on the floor. The room was eerily quiet. Arjun's heart sank— ***he realized Nikhil had taken a dangerous step.***

Wiithout wasting a second, Arjun called emergency services and stayed by Nikhil's side, ***shaking him gently, keeping him awake, and talking to him until help arrived.*** *His calmness and quick response ensured that precious time was not lost.*

*At the hospital, doctors confirmed a **drug overdose** but managed to stabilize Nikhil with prompt medical treatment. Over the following days, Nikhil was introduced to a psychiatrist and a counselor who began working on a supervised recovery plan, addressing both his mental health and emotional pain.*

*The incident left a lasting impression on their college campus. Arjun shared his experience, emphasizing that **depression is not just sadness—it is an illness that needs help and understanding.** Nikhil, in time, began talking openly about his struggles, becoming an advocate for mental health awareness.*

*The event highlighted an essential truth: **Listening, noticing the signs, and taking action can save a life.** Asking someone if they are okay, encouraging them to seek help, or calling emergency services when in doubt can make all the difference.*

WHAT IS MENTAL HEALTH CRISIS AND SUICIDE RISK?

A mental health crisis is a situation where a person's behavior puts them at risk of hurting themselves or others, or prevents them from being able to care for themselves. Suicide risk increases when a person feels hopeless, overwhelmed, or sees no way out. Early recognition and compassionate intervention are critical.

Signs and Symptoms

Warning signs of mental health crisis or suicide risk:

- Talking about wanting to die or being a burden
- Withdrawing from friends, family, or usual activities
- Extreme mood swings or sudden calm after depression
- Giving away belongings or writing goodbye notes
- Increased use of alcohol or drugs
- Self-harm (cutting, burning, etc.)
- Expressing hopelessness, guilt, or worthlessness

Causes/Risk Factors

- Depression, anxiety, or other untreated mental illnesses
- Trauma, abuse, or significant loss (relationship, job, loved one)
- Chronic illness, pain, or disability
- History of self-harm or previous suicide attempt
- Social isolation or bullying
- Substance use disorders
- Lack of access to mental health support

STEPWISE FIRST AID BEFORE REACHING A HOSPITAL

Take every sign seriously. Offer presence—not judgment.

- ***Step 1:*** Stay calm and listen
  - » Let them speak without interruption or judgment.
  - » Avoid dismissing their feelings or offering false reassurance.

- ***Step 2:*** Ask directly about suicide
  - » It is okay to ask: "Are you thinking about hurting yourself?"
  - » Asking does not plant the idea—it shows you care.
- ***Step 3:*** Remove harmful objects
  - » Safely remove medications, sharp objects, or weapons nearby.
- ***Step 4:*** Do not leave them alone
  - » Stay with the person until professional help arrives.
- ***Step 5:*** Call emergency services (112/108) or mental health helplines

WHEN TO SEE A DOCTOR

- Any talk or indication of suicide or self-harm
- Sudden behavior changes or emotional withdrawal
- Ongoing depression, anxiety, or insomnia
- After a traumatic event or loss
- Substance abuse with mental health symptoms

PREVENTION TIPS

SUICIDE PREVENTION

Warning Signs

- Withdrawal or isolation
- Recent Loss or Crisis
- Increased Substance Use
- Feeling Hopeless

First Aid

- Stay calm
- Ask directly about suicide
- Remove harmful objects
- Stay with them
- Call for help

Vandrevala Foundation helpline new number +919999666555. iCall counselling service run by School of Human Ecology, Tata Institute of Social Sciences, 9152987821 Available from Monday to Saturday: 10:00 am to 8:00 pm

Help is available. A simple act of caring can save a life.

MYTHS AND FACTS

Myths	Facts
People who talk about suicide would not actually do it.	Most people who die by suicide show warning signs.
Talking about suicide encourages it.	Open conversations reduce stigma and help-seeking increases.
Only people with mental illness die by suicide.	Situational crises can lead anyone to the edge.
Once someone feels better, they are no longer at risk.	Risk can remain even after apparent improvement.

CONCLUSION

Suicide is not just an individual tragedy but a profound public health challenge that deeply affects families, communities, and society at large. While the causes are complex and multifactorial—ranging from mental health conditions and social stresses to sudden crises—the message of hope must always remain central. Suicide is preventable. Early recognition of warning signs, timely psychological support, reduction of stigma around mental illness, and ensuring accessible mental health care can save countless lives.

Equally important is creating an environment of compassion, where individuals feel safe to share their struggles without fear of judgment. Every conversation, every act of empathy, and every effort to reach out may be the step that prevents an irreversible act. By combining awareness, medical care, community support, and policy-level interventions, we can shift from despair to resilience, and from silence to understanding.

Scan to watch Dr Lokendra's 1-minute reel on this emergency.

Chapter 15

ANXIETY AND PANIC ATTACKS

STORY: WHEN A RACING HEART FEELS LIKE A HEART ATTACK

Aarohi, a 26-year-old postgraduate student, had always been cheerful and hardworking. But after a painful breakup, she often felt lonely and anxious. One evening, while preparing for an upcoming exam, she suddenly experienced a frightening rush of symptoms.

Her heart began to race rapidly—her pulse was pounding at nearly ***120 beats per minute***. She felt short of breath, her chest tightened, and her hands turned cold and sweaty. An overwhelming sense of fear gripped her, and she was convinced something terrible was happening, perhaps even a heart attack.

Her roommate, shocked by Aarohi's pale face and trembling body, quickly checked her vitals with a home monitor. The ***heart rate was high, but her blood pressure remained within normal range***. Realizing it might be an anxiety episode, she sat with Aarohi, encouraged her to breathe slowly, and reassured her until the symptoms began to ease after about 15 minutes.

*The next day, Aarohi visited a doctor. After routine tests ruled out heart disease, the physician explained that she had suffered a **panic attack**—a sudden episode of intense anxiety that can cause increased heart rate, sweating, breathlessness, and a sense of impending doom, without actual damage to the heart.*

*She was referred to a psychiatrist, who through **counselling and psychotherapy** helped her uncover the deeper triggers—the grief of her lost relationship, combined with exam stress and the absence of close family nearby. Over time, with therapy, relaxation techniques, and regular follow-up, Aarohi learned to manage her anxiety and rebuild confidence, recognizing that while panic attacks feel terrifying, they are not life-threatening.*

WHAT IS ANXIETY AND PANIC ATTACK?

- **Anxiety** is the body's natural response to stress. It often presents as worry, nervousness, or fear about everyday situations.
- **Panic attack** is a sudden surge of intense fear or discomfort, usually peaking within minutes, often accompanied by physical symptoms like palpitations, sweating, trembling, or breathlessness.
- While anxiety builds gradually, panic attacks come abruptly and can mimic serious medical conditions, making them frightening for both patients and families.

CAUSES OF ANXIETY

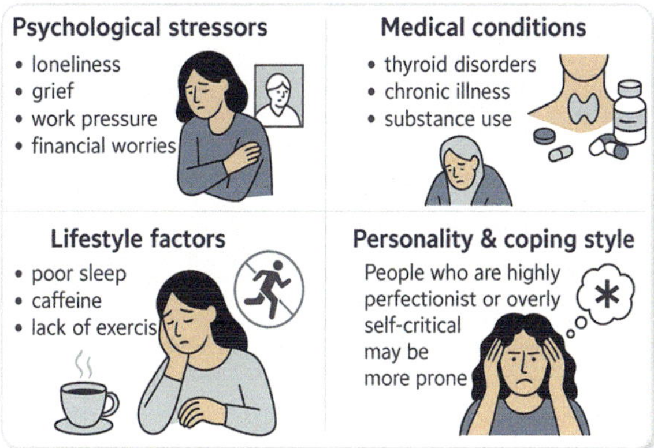

CAUSES OF PANIC ATTACKS

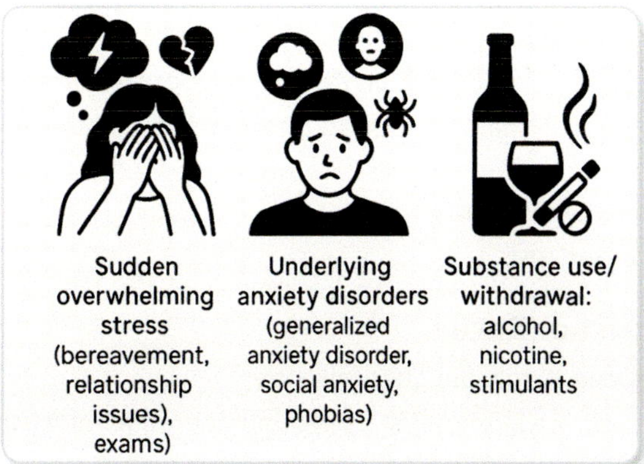

RED FLAG SIGNS YOU NEED TO SEE THE DOCTOR

- Palpitations lasting more than 15-20 minutes despite calming measures.
- Associated chest pain, fainting, or severe breathlessness
- History of heart disease, hypertension, diabetes, or thyroid disorder
- Panic attacks that are frequent, disabling, or interfere with daily life
- Thoughts of self-harm, hopelessness, or depression

WHEN TO ATTEND EMERGENCIES

- If palpitations are associated with **collapse, chest pain, or very low/high blood pressure**.
- If the person becomes **unconscious, unresponsive, or develops seizure-like activity**.
- If panic attack symptoms **cannot be differentiated from a possible heart attack** (better safe than sorry).
- In elderly patients or those with significant medical illnesses, always err on the side of caution and seek emergency care.

STEPWISE MANAGEMENT OF ANXIETY AND PANIC ATTACK: FROM HOME CARE TO EMERGENCY CARE

At Home

- Stay calm and reassure the patient that the episode will pass.
- Deep breathing exercises: Slow inhalation through the nose, exhalation through the mouth.
- Grounding techniques: Ask them to notice 5 things they see, 4 they feel, 3 they hear, 2 they smell, and 1 they taste.
- Avoid excess crowding or overstimulation.
- Encourage hydration and rest.

When Symptoms Persist or Recur

- Visit a **general physician** to rule out physical causes.
- If anxiety/panic is confirmed, referral to a **psychiatrist or psychologist** for counseling and therapy is essential.

In Emergency Room

- Doctors will assess **vital signs, ECG, blood tests** to rule out heart attack or arrhythmia.
- Short-acting medications may be given to relieve severe anxiety.
- Referral for long-term psychiatric follow-up (counseling, psychotherapy, medication if needed).

MYTHS AND FACTS

Myths	Facts
Panic attacks cause heart attacks	Panic attacks feel like a heart attack but usually do not damage the heart. Still, ruling out heart disease is important.
Anxiety means you are "weak-minded."	Anxiety is a medical condition, not a weakness. Anyone can develop it.
You can "snap out" of a panic attack by willpower.	Panic attacks are involuntary. Support, therapy, and sometimes medication are needed.
Psychiatric help is only for "serious mental illness."	Psychiatrists and psychologists help manage common issues like stress, anxiety, panic, and depression.

CONCLUSION

Anxiety and panic attacks are common but often misunderstood conditions. They may mimic dangerous emergencies, but not every palpitation or episode of fear is a heart problem. Recognizing the difference, knowing red-flag signs, and seeking timely medical and psychiatric help can prevent unnecessary suffering. Equally important is emotional support—patients who feel understood and cared for recover faster. Just as Aarohi's roommate stood by her, a calm presence and timely action from loved ones can make all the difference in turning fear into resilience.

Scan to watch Dr Lokendra's 1-minute reel on this emergency.

SECTION 4: BLOOD AND METABOLIC DISORDERS

Chapter 16

DIABETIC EMERGENCY (LOW AND HIGH SUGAR)

"WHEN SUGAR SWINGS": UNDERSTANDING DIABETIC EMERGENCIES (LOW AND HIGH BLOOD SUGAR)

Story: The Grocery Store Incident

Mrs Nirmala, a 58-year-old homemaker, had been living with diabetes for over 10 years. That morning she had been rushing to finish her household chores and decided to ***skip breakfast****, thinking she would grab something to eat after her shopping. It was also a day of religious fasting for her family, so she thought skipping one meal wouldn't hurt.*

While moving through the aisles of a busy grocery store, she suddenly felt strange. Her heart was pounding, her hands started trembling, and sweat poured down her face despite the cool air-conditioning. She felt lightheaded and confused and struggled to read the labels on products. A packet of biscuits slipped from her weakening grip.

A concerned shopper quickly came to her aid, offering a chair. Observing her pale face and shaky hands, someone asked, "Aunty, are you diabetic?" Mrs Nirmala, though confused, nodded faintly. Another kind customer rushed to get her a small ***pack of sweet fruit juice*** *from a nearby fridge.*

*Within **5–10 minutes of sipping the juice**, her color returned, her hands steadied, and her mind began to clear. By the time her son arrived in a panic, she was much better but still shaken.*

*At the doctor's clinic later that day, the cause was clear: **A hypoglycemic episode, a sudden dangerous drop in blood sugar.***

The doctor gently explained:

"This happened because you skipped breakfast and went shopping on an empty stomach. For people with diabetes, fasting, delayed meals, or skipping meals can easily lead to low sugar levels, especially if you are on medications like insulin or sulfonylureas."

*He emphasized that both **low and high blood sugars are dangerous** and can escalate quickly if not recognized.*

"Symptoms like sweating, confusion, trembling, and dizziness for low sugars and excessive thirst, frequent urination, and fatigue for high sugars must be recognized early. Never ignore them."

Role of the Glucometer at Home, Work, and While Out

The doctor also advised Mrs Nirmala and her son to always carry a glucometer at home, at work, and even while traveling.

"With a glucometer, you can instantly know whether your sugar is too low or too high. It removes guesswork and allows you to treat early. Sometimes just a glass of juice can save a life."

That evening her son bought a compact glucometer and glucose tablets. Now Mrs Nirmala checks her sugar regularly, carries a snack with her, and feels much more secure.

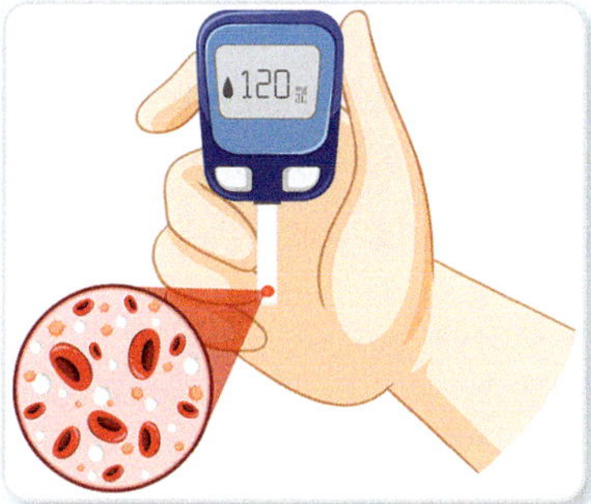

WHAT IS A DIABETIC EMERGENCY?

A diabetic emergency occurs when blood sugar levels become either too low (hypoglycemia) or too high (hyperglycemia), leading to life-threatening symptoms. Quick action is crucial to prevent complications like unconsciousness, coma, or even death.

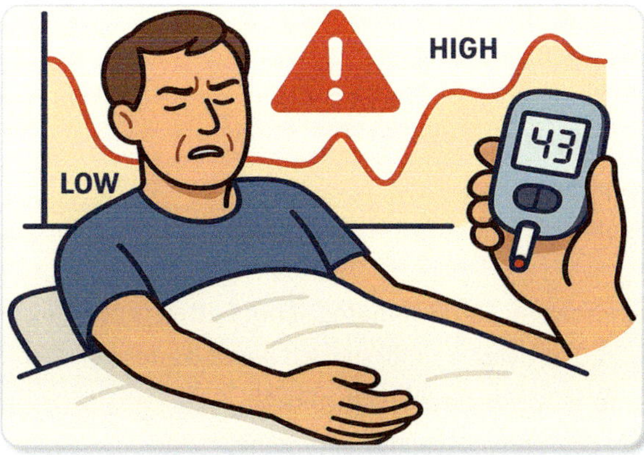

Signs and Symptoms

Low Blood Sugar (Hypoglycemia)

- Shakiness or tremors
- Sweating
- Dizziness or lightheadedness
- Confusion or irritability
- Rapid heartbeat
- Blurred vision
- Fainting or unconsciousness

High Blood Sugar (Hyperglycemia)

- Frequent urination
- Extreme thirst
- Dry mouth and skin
- Fatigue or drowsiness
- Fruity-smelling breath
- Nausea or vomiting
- Confusion or unconsciousness (in severe cases)

Causes/Risk Factors

- Skipping meals or irregular eating
- Overdose or missed dose of insulin or diabetes medications
- Intense physical activity without food intake
- Infections or illnesses
- Stress or emotional upset
- Excessive carbohydrate intake or sugary foods in diabetics
- Dehydration or missed medications in hyperglycemia

STEPWISE FIRST AID BEFORE REACHING A HOSPITAL

Identify the type of emergency and act quickly.

For Low Blood Sugar (Hypoglycemia)

- ***Step 1:*** Confirm symptoms (sweating, confusion, and trembling).
- ***Step 2****:* The 15-15 Rule: Eat 15 g of fast-acting carbs → Wait 15 minutes → Recheck sugar → Repeat if still low
- ***Step 3****:* Recheck symptoms in 10–15 minutes. If not better, repeat sugar intake.
- ***Step 4:*** Once recovered, provide a small snack if needed and seek medical help.
  - » If unconscious, do NOT give anything by mouth.
  - » Place in recovery position and call for emergency help.

For High Blood Sugar (Hyperglycemia)

- ***Step 1:*** Check for excessive thirst, urination, and fruity breath.
- ***Step 2:*** Encourage hydration (water, not sugary drinks).
- ***Step 3:*** If on insulin, follow doctor's advice on dose adjustment (if trained).
- ***Step 4:*** Seek urgent medical care to prevent diabetic ketoacidosis (DKA) or coma.

WHEN TO SEE A DOCTOR

- Any unconsciousness or seizure in a diabetic patient
- Blood sugar <70 mg/dL or >300 mg/dL and not improving
- Severe vomiting, confusion, or deep rapid breathing
- Multiple episodes of high or low sugar in a week
- Known diabetic with infection, fever, or dehydration

MYTHS AND FACTS

Myths	Facts
Give insulin to anyone with a diabetic emergency.	Insulin may worsen low sugar—never give unless sure and trained.
Only sweets cause high blood sugar.	Many factors such as stress, illness, and skipped medicines can raise sugar.
A fainting diabetic always has high sugar.	Most fainting spells in diabetics are due to low sugar.
If they are unconscious, give them food or drink.	This can cause choking—call for help and place them on their side.

PREVENTION TIPS

- Eat meals on time and do not skip them.
- Monitor blood sugar regularly.
- Carry glucose tablets or sweets when going out.
- Stay hydrated, especially during illness.
- Take medications as prescribed and avoid self-adjusting doses.
- Inform close contacts about your diabetes and first aid steps.

CONCLUSION

- "Diabetic emergencies are silent threats—knowing the signs and acting fast can save a life."
- *Always keep sugar within reach and ensure family and friends know what to do in an emergency.*

Scan to watch Dr Lokendra's 1-minute reel on this emergency.

Chapter 17

BLEEDING EMERGENCIES: SECONDS TO SURVIVAL

"WHEN EVERY SECOND COUNTS"—A PUBLIC AWARENESS CHAPTER ON HEMORRHAGE

Story: The Glass that Nearly Took a Life

It was a lazy Sunday afternoon when ***22-year-old Rohan*** *decided to help his mother clean the large windows of their living room. The day felt ordinary—until one sudden, life-threatening moment changed everything. As Rohan pressed against a stubborn pane, there was a sharp crack. Before he could react, a* ***jagged shard of glass sliced deep into his forearm.***

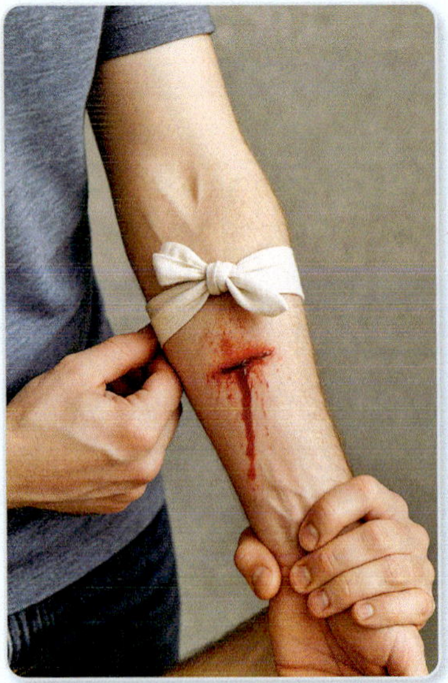

Within seconds, bright red blood began spurting out in powerful bursts—a frightening sign of arterial bleeding. His shirt was soaked almost instantly. Rohan stared in shock, his legs trembling, while his younger sister's panicked scream filled the house. His mother, terrified and unprepared, ***grabbed a towel and tried to wipe away the blood, but the bleeding wouldn't stop.***

Every second felt like an eternity. Just then, their neighbor, Mr Mehta—a retired army medic—heard the chaos and rushed over. Recognizing the danger, he immediately shouted, ***"Don't waste time wiping! We need to stop the bleeding now!"***

He quickly:

- *Tied a tight cloth tourniquet a few inches above the cut to slow the blood flow.*
- *Applied firm, continuous pressure directly on the wound using a clean cloth.*
- *Asked Rohan to lie down and remain calm, keeping his arm elevated above heart level.*

Within minutes, the ambulance arrived. Doctors later confirmed that Rohan had lost a significant amount of blood but was lucky—those few minutes of quick action likely saved his life. They explained that hemorrhage, especially from a major artery, can cause a ***person to go into shock or lose consciousness within 5–10 minutes, and death can occur if the bleeding is not controlled quickly.***

For Rohan and his family, this was an eye-opening moment. They realized how important it is to know basic first aid for bleeding emergencies—not just for accidents at home but in everyday life. Something as simple as ***pressing on a wound or using a piece of cloth as a makeshift tourniquet can be the difference between life and death.***

WHAT IS HEMORRHAGE (SEVERE BLEEDING)?

- Hemorrhage is *uncontrolled blood loss* from an injury. If not treated quickly, it can lead to *shock*, *organ failure*, or *death*.
- Hemorrhage can be *external* (visible from a wound) or *internal* (bleeding inside the body).

Shock is not just emotional distress. In medical terms, it means the body's organs are not getting enough blood or oxygen due to very low blood pressure.

Signs of Hemorrhage

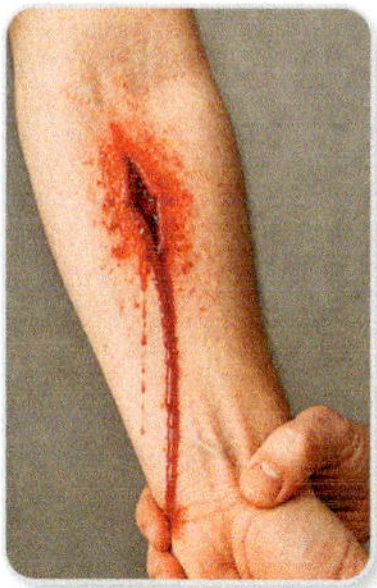

- *Blood spurting or gushing* from a wound
- *Soaking through clothing or bandages quickly*
- Pale, cold, or clammy skin
- *Weak or rapid pulse*
- *Dizziness, confusion*, or *fainting*
- Bleeding *not slowing* after 10 minutes of pressure

FIRST AID: STEP-BY-STEP BEFORE HELP ARRIVES

Act fast. Hemorrhage is a medical emergency.

For External Bleeding

- Call for emergency medical help immediately.
- *Protect yourself:* Use gloves if available, or cover hands with clean plastic to avoid contact with blood.
- *Apply direct pressure:*
    - » Use a clean cloth, gauze, or even a T-shirt.
    - » *Press firmly* on the wound with your hand.
    - » Do *not remove* soaked cloths; add more layers if needed.

- *Elevate the injured area* (if possible and there is no fracture) above heart level to reduce blood flow.
- *Apply a tourniquet* (only if bleeding is life-threatening and not controlled by pressure):
  - » Wrap a cloth/belt 2–3 inches above the wound.
  - » Tighten until bleeding stops.
  - » Note the time of application and inform medics.
- *Keep the person calm and lying flat.*
  - » Cover with a blanket to prevent shock.

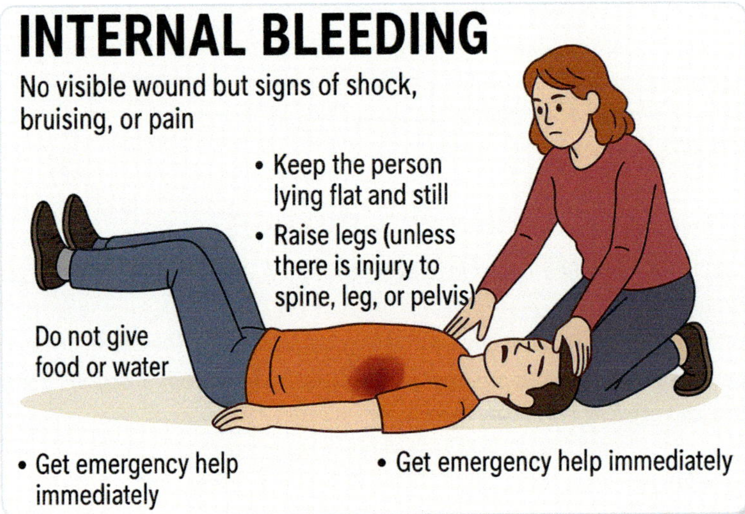

PREVENTION TIPS

- *Use safety gear* during work, sports, or driving.
- *Keep sharp tools* away from children.
- Install *antishatter film* on large glass panes/windows.
- *Handle knives and glass with care* in the kitchen.
- Learn *basic first aid*—it can save lives.
- Keep a *well-stocked first aid kit* at home, school, and workplace.

MYTHS AND FACTS

Myths	Facts
"Just wash the wound with water to stop bleeding."	Water alone will not stop hemorrhage. Apply direct pressure immediately.
"Removing the soaked cloth helps the blood drain."	Never remove soaked cloths—add layers and keep pressure.

Myths	Facts
"Tourniquets are too risky and should not be used."	When used correctly, a tourniquet can save a life in severe limb bleeding.
"Only deep cuts bleed a lot."	Even shallow cuts near arteries or veins can cause dangerous blood loss.

WHEN TO SEEK EMERGENCY HELP

Always call for medical help if:

- Blood is *spurting or gushing*.
- Bleeding does not stop after *10 minutes of pressure*.
- The wound is *deep*, *large*, or caused by a *dirty/rusty object*.
- There is *significant bruising or swelling*, possibly indicating *internal bleeding*.
- The injured person shows signs of *shock* (pale, dizzy, rapid pulse, or cold skin).

CONCLUSION

- "A life can be saved in minutes, if you act with knowledge—not panic."
- Hemorrhage looks scary, but the *right response can make all the difference*. With quick action and basic first aid, anyone—whether a friend, neighbor, or stranger—can become a lifesaver.

Scan to watch Dr Lokendra's 1-minute reel on this emergency.

SECTION 5: TRAUMA AND ACCIDENTS

Chapter 18

ROAD TRAFFIC ACCIDENTS: WHAT TO DO FIRST?

"WHEN SECONDS MATTER"—ROAD TRAFFIC ACCIDENTS: WHAT TO DO FIRST?

Story: The Highway Hero

It was late in the evening, Anil, a 42-year-old office worker, was driving home after another long, tiring day. The highway was nearly empty, the streetlights casting long shadows on the road. He was just a few kilometers from home when, in an instant, he saw it.

A small sedan ahead of him suddenly swerved, lost control, and ***smashed violently into the highway divider.***

For a brief moment, Anil froze. ***Should he stop? Should he intervene?*** *His heart raced, but his instincts took over. He pulled over safely, turned on his hazard lights, and ran towards the wreckage.*

Inside the car, chaos reigned. The driver, a young man, sat slumped, ***blood trickling down his forehead****. The passengers, dazed and trembling, was screaming for help. Neither of them seemed to understand what had just happened.*

Anil didn't panic. He remembered the first aid workshop he'd attended at his company last year—how those simple lessons could make the difference between life and death.

He ***called emergency services immediately. He gently reassured the conscious passengers, keeping them calm while carefully checking for any signs of more serious injuries. He made sure*** *not to move the injured driver unnecessarily—he knew spinal injuries are common in crashes. Meanwhile, he positioned his car strategically to block oncoming traffic, waving others to slow down and avoid a second accident. Minutes felt like hours. Finally, the ambulance arrived. The paramedics commended Anil's actions:* ***"Because you acted quickly and calmly, they'll get the care they need in time. You may have saved their lives."***

That night, Anil went home shaken but grateful—grateful for the awareness he had, and even more grateful he didn't assume "someone else will help."

The Lesson

You don't have to be a doctor to save a life. You just need to know what to do—and act without fear. ***Awareness, preparedness, and courage can turn any bystander into a hero.***

WHAT IS A ROAD TRAFFIC ACCIDENT?

A road traffic accident (RTA) involves any vehicle collision that leads to injury or damage. It can result in bleeding, fractures, head injuries, or even unconsciousness. Timely and appropriate first aid can save lives and prevent complications.

Signs and Symptoms

- Visible bleeding or wounds
- Deformities (fractures) or inability to move limbs
- Unconsciousness or confusion
- Breathing difficulties or chest injuries
- Vomiting, seizures, or abnormal pupils (head injury)
- Pain in neck, back, or abdomen

Causes/Risk Factors

- Overspeeding or reckless driving
- Drunk or distracted driving
- Poor road or weather conditions
- Not wearing helmets or seatbelts
- Pedestrian negligence
- Mechanical failure or tire burst

ESSENTIAL FIRST AID STEPS FOR THE GENERAL PUBLIC (SCIENTIFIC EVIDENCE-BASED)

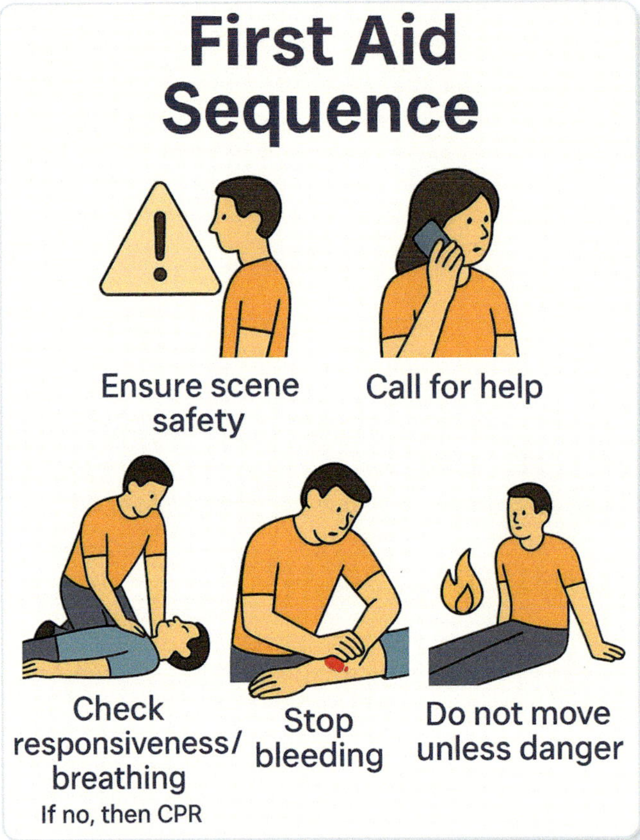

- **Ensure Your Safety First**
    - Before helping, **check for dangers** (traffic, fire, electricity, violence).
    - **Protect yourself** with gloves if available.
    - Do not become the second victim.
- **Call for Professional Help Early**
    - **Dial 112/108 immediately.**
    - Clearly state: **Location, type of incident, number of victims, condition of victims.**
    - Keep your phone on and follow dispatcher instructions.
- **Check Responsiveness and Breathing (Use "Look, Listen, Feel")**
    - Gently tap and speak to the person.
    - If **unresponsive and not breathing normally, begin CPR immediately.**
    - If breathing is normal but unconscious, place in **recovery position.**

- **Control Severe Bleeding ("Stop the Bleed")**
    - » Apply **firm, direct pressure** with a clean cloth or your hand.
    - » Use **compression only; avoid tourniquets unless trained.**
    - » Elevate the limb if no fracture is suspected
- **Do Not Move Victims Unnecessarily**
    - » If you suspect **spinal/head/neck injury**, keep the victim still.
    - » Move only if immediate danger exists (fire, flood, collapsing structure)
    - » Support head and neck if any repositioning is necessary.
- **Provide Basic Life Support (Hands-only CPR)**
    - » For an **unconscious, non-breathing and no neck pulse, begin chest compressions immediately.**
    - » Rate: **100–120 per minute**.
    - » Depth: **5–6 cm in adults.**
    - » No mouth-to-mouth unless trained and willing.
- **Comfort and Reassure the Victim**
    - » Keep the person **calm, warm, and still.**
    - » Do not give food or drink **(risk of aspiration or surgery delay).**
    - » Reassure until professionals arrive.
- **Handover to Emergency Responders**
    - » Clearly report what happened.
    - » First aid steps you provided.
    - » Any changes in the victim's condition.

Why these Steps Matter (Scientific Basis)

- Rapid bleeding control and CPR improve survival dramatically.
- Early calling of EMS shortens time to definitive care.
- Minimal movement prevents worsening spinal or internal injuries.
- Hands-only CPR is scientifically proven to save lives in cardiac arrest.

WHEN TO SEE A DOCTOR

- Any injury involving unconsciousness or confusion
- Severe bleeding, fractures, or breathing difficulty
- Abdominal pain or vomiting postaccident
- Head injury with dizziness or vision changes
- All RTA victims should be evaluated—even if injuries seem minor

PREVENTION TIPS

- Always wear helmets and seatbelts
- Do not use mobile phones while driving
- Avoid driving under the influence of alcohol or drugs
- Obey speed limits and traffic rules
- Keep emergency numbers and a first aid kit in the vehicle
- Encourage learning basic life support (BLS)

MYTHS AND FACTS

Myths	Facts
Move the victim immediately to help them.	Only move if there is fire or danger—spinal injuries worsen with movement.
Giving water or food will help the injured.	Never give anything orally—risk of choking or surgery delay.
If the person is talking, they are fine.	Internal injuries or shock can still be present—get medical help.
Only doctors can give CPR.	Bystander CPR saves lives—anyone can and should learn it.

CONCLUSION

- "In a road traffic accident, the right first steps can mean the difference between life and death."
- *Stay calm, stay safe, and be someone's reason to survive.*

Scan to watch Dr Lokendra's 1-minute reel on this emergency.

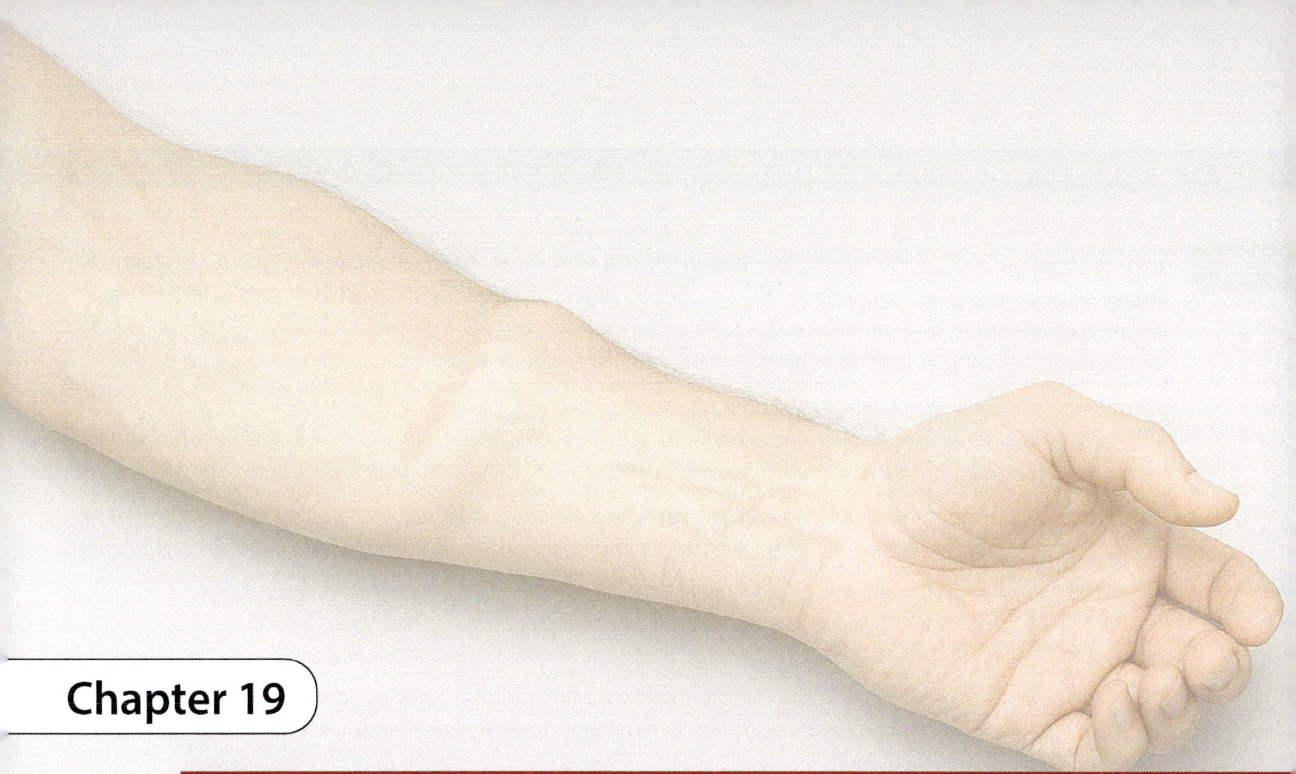

Chapter 19

FRACTURES AND BROKEN BONES

"WHEN BONES BREAK"—FRACTURE AND BROKEN BONES

Story: The Playground Fall

It was a bright afternoon at school, and the playground echoed with cheers as the students played an intense cricket match. Among them was 12-year-old Ayaan, an enthusiastic young player, who was determined to take the winning catch for his team. As the ball soared toward him, Ayaan made a daring dive to grab it—but instead of glory, the fall left him in excruciating pain.

He landed hard on his outstretched right arm. A sharp cry escaped his lips, and the game came to an abrupt halt. His forearm looked twisted at an unnatural angle, and within moments, swelling and bruising began to appear. Ayaan clutched his arm, tears streaming down his face, unable to move it.

His teacher, who had basic first aid knowledge, quickly recognized the signs of a possible fracture:

- *Severe pain and swelling.*
- *Inability to move the arm.*
- *An unusual bend in the forearm.*

Instead of panicking or attempting to ***straighten the arm—a dangerous mistake that can worsen the injury—she acted calmly and efficiently. She gently placed a rolled-up magazine along*** *Ayaan's forearm as a makeshift splint and tied it in place with a piece of cloth to keep the arm stable. She then created a temporary sling using a scarf to support the injured limb against his chest.*

Ayaan was rushed to the emergency room, where X-rays confirmed a fracture in his forearm. The doctor praised the teacher's quick thinking, explaining that her simple but correct first aid prevented further damage to the bone, surrounding muscles, and nerves.

With proper treatment—a plaster cast, rest, and follow-up care—Ayaan's arm healed completely. But for the young boy and his classmates, this incident became a lesson: knowing basic first aid and staying calm can make all the difference in emergencies.

WHAT IS A FRACTURE?

A fracture is a break or crack in a bone. It can be closed (skin intact) or open (bone pierces through skin). Fractures vary from hairline cracks to complete breaks, and they require proper immobilization and medical attention to heal correctly.

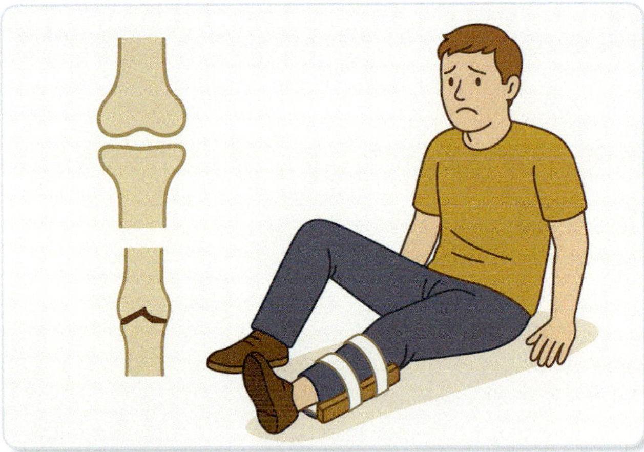

Signs and Symptoms

- Sudden pain at the site of injury
- Swelling, bruising, or tenderness
- Deformity or abnormal angle of the limb
- Inability to move or bear weight
- Numbness or tingling (if nerve involved)
- Open wound with bone visible (in open fracture)

Causes/Risk Factors

- Falls or direct trauma (sports, accidents)
- Road traffic collisions

- Osteoporosis (weak bones) in elderly
- High-impact injuries (industrial or construction sites)
- Overuse injuries (stress fractures in athletes)

STEPWISE FIRST AID BEFORE REACHING A HOSPITAL

Avoid moving the injured part unnecessarily. Immobilize and support.

- ***Step 1:*** Keep the person calm and still
  - » Encourage them not to move the injured area.
- ***Step 2:*** Immobilize the limb
  - » Use a splint (stick, rolled paper, or cardboard) and tie it gently to support the limb.
  - » Do not attempt to straighten a bent or deformed bone.
- ***Step 3:*** Elevate and support
  - » If possible, elevate the limb to reduce swelling (only if no severe pain or deformity).
  - » Use cloth or sling to support the arm or leg.
- ***Step 4:*** Control bleeding (if open fracture)
  - » Apply gentle pressure around—not directly—on the wound with a clean cloth.
- ***Step 5:*** Apply ice packs
  - » Wrap in cloth and apply near the injury to reduce swelling (avoid direct contact).
- ***Step 6:*** Call emergency services or go to hospital
  - » Seek immediate care, especially if signs of severe fracture or shock.

DO'S V/S DON'TS

- Never straighten
- Never apply heat
- Don't delay care

WHEN TO SEE A DOCTOR

- Obvious deformity or suspected broken bone
- Inability to move or bear weight
- Numbness or tingling below the injury
- Open wounds with exposed bone
- Severe swelling, pain, or bleeding
- Any fracture in children or elderly

MYTHS AND FACTS

Myths	Facts
You must straighten the bone before applying a splint.	Never try to realign—immobilize as it is to prevent further damage.
If you can move it, it is not broken.	Some fractures still allow movement—pain and swelling are key clues.
Applying heat helps.	Ice is best for reducing swelling and pain in early hours.
Open fractures should be cleaned with antiseptic.	Cover with a clean cloth and avoid applying anything until medical help arrives.

PREVENTION TIPS

- Use safety gear during sports, biking, or riding.
- Install railings and nonslip mats at home for elderly.
- Encourage calcium- and vitamin D-rich diet for bone strength.
- Teach children safe play and proper use of playground equipment.
- Avoid risky activities without proper training or protection.
- Exercise regularly to improve balance and prevent falls.

CONCLUSION

- "Broken bones can heal—but only if handled right from the start."
- Immobilize, support, and seek timely care. A calm response and proper first aid can prevent long-term damage.

Scan to watch Dr Lokendra's 1-minute reel on this emergency.

Chapter 20

BURNS AND SCALDS

"WHEN SKIN MEETS FIRE"—UNDERSTANDING BURNS AND SCALDS

Story: The Kitchen Spill

It was an ordinary evening in Rita's home. Like many mothers, ***35-year-old Rita*** *was multitasking—preparing dinner, tidying up, and keeping an eye on her 4-year-old son, Aarav, who was playing nearby. The delicious aroma of boiling lentils filled the kitchen. A towel hung loosely over the stove handle, something Rita had done countless times without thinking twice.*

But accidents don't ask for permission.

In a moment of innocent curiosity, little Aarav reached for the dangling towel, tugging on it playfully. In a terrifying instant, the ***pot of boiling water toppled over, splashing directly onto Rita's exposed forearm.***

The pain was immediate and intense. *Rita screamed as her skin turned an angry red and blisters began to form within seconds. Aarav stood frozen, wide-eyed and scared. Her husband, hearing the commotion, rushed in. Though alarmed, he remained calm and remembered what he had learned in a workplace safety session about burn first aid.*

Correct First Aid Saved Her Skin

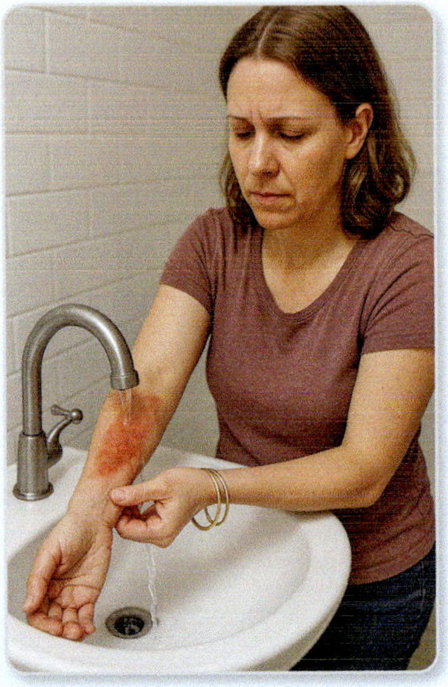

*Without wasting a moment, he guided Rita to the sink and placed her injured arm under **cool running water**—not ice water, just regular tap water—and kept it there for nearly **20 minutes.** He gently removed her **bangles** before swelling could trap them against her skin, a small but crucial step often forgotten in panic.*

*They didn't apply **ice, butter, toothpaste, or any home remedies. Instead, he lightly covered the burn with a clean, soft cloth** to protect it and immediately took her to the nearest clinic.*

*At the clinic, the doctor praised them. The burn was categorized as superficial to partial thickness—painful but treatable, and, most importantly, free from deeper complications because of the **quick, appropriate first aid.** Rita was prescribed a burn ointment and given advice on how to care for her wound at home. Over the next few weeks, her skin healed well, leaving no infection, no severe scarring—and a powerful lesson learned.*

Why this Story Matters to Every Household

*Burns and scalds can happen in any home, especially kitchens. Yet, **what you do in the first few minutes determines the outcome.** Prompt and proper first aid doesn't just reduce pain—it can prevent deeper damage, infection, long-term scarring, or even permanent disability.*

What Rita's Story Teaches Us All

- ***Prevention:*** *Keep children away from kitchen hazards. Avoid hanging towels near stoves.*
- ***First Aid Knowledge Saves Skin****: Quick, cool water treatment prevents deeper damage.*
- ***Act Fast, Act Right****: Correct steps make all the difference between recovery and complication.*

WHAT ARE BURNS AND SCALDS?

Burns are injuries caused by heat, electricity, chemicals, or radiation. Scalds are a type of burn caused specifically by hot liquids or steam. They damage the skin and underlying tissues, and the severity depends on the depth and extent of the burn.

Types of Burns

- *First-degree burn:* Redness, pain, dry skin (e.g., sunburn)
- *Second-degree burn:* Blisters, swelling, intense pain
- *Third-degree burn:* White, charred, or leathery skin, possibly painless due to nerve damage

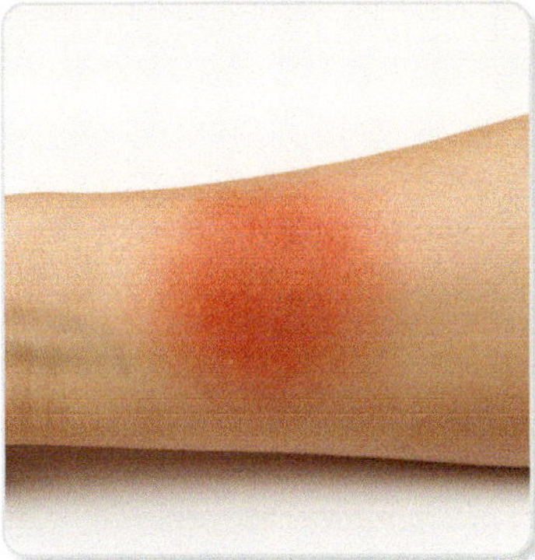

First Degree Burn

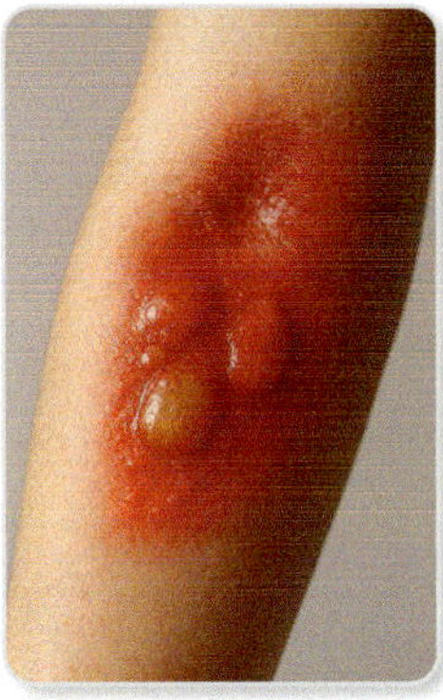

Second Degree Burn

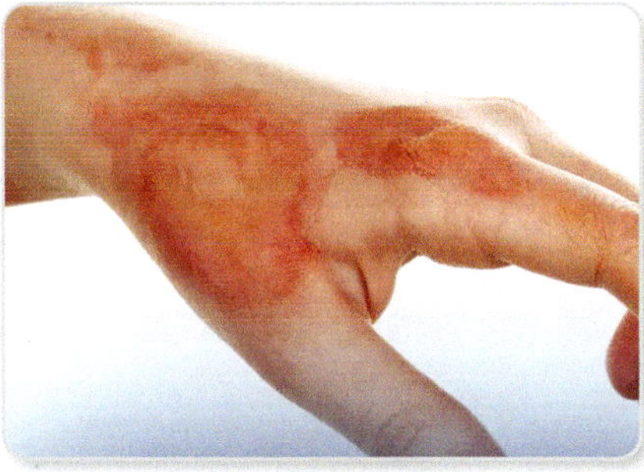

Third Degree Burn

Signs and Symptoms

- Swelling at the burn site
- Peeling or blistering skin
- Shock (pale, cold skin, rapid pulse) in severe cases

Causes/Risk Factors

- Contact with hot liquids (scalds) or flames
- Electrical injuries (open wires, shocks)
- Chemical spills (cleaners, acids, pesticides)
- Hot appliances (irons, geysers, stoves)
- Accidents in kitchens, bathrooms, or workplaces
- Lack of fire safety measures at home or in public

STEPWISE FIRST AID BEFORE REACHING A HOSPITAL

Early first aid limits damage and speeds healing.

- ***Step 1:*** Remove the Person from Danger
  - » Turn off the heat source, move away from fire, and ensure safety.
- ***Step 2:*** Cool the Burn Immediately
  - » Hold the burn under cool (not cold) running water for 20 minutes.
  - » Do not use ice, toothpaste, butter, or creams.
- ***Step 3:*** Remove Tight Items
  - » Gently remove rings, watches, or clothing near the burn site before swelling starts.
- ***Step 4:*** Cover the Burn
  - » Use a clean, nonstick cloth, or sterile gauze.
  - » Avoid breaking blisters or applying powders.
- ***Step 5:*** Seek Medical Help If:
  - » The burn is larger than a coin, on the face, hands, genitals, or joints.
  - » There are signs of infection or the burn looks white/charred.

WHEN TO SEE A DOCTOR

- Burn involves face, hands, feet, or genitals
- Blisters larger than a coin or deep tissue damage
- Electrical or chemical burns
- *Signs of infection:* Pus, increasing redness, or fever
- Difficulty breathing after inhaling smoke or steam

MYTHS AND FACTS

Myths	Facts
Apply toothpaste or butter on burns.	These can trap heat and increase infection risk.
Pop blisters to drain fluid.	Blisters protect the skin and should not be broken.
Use ice to cool burns quickly.	Ice can worsen tissue damage—use cool water instead.
Small burns do not need attention.	Burns on sensitive areas or deep skin still need care.

PREVENTION TIPS

- Keep hot liquids and appliances out of children's reach.
- Use back burners and turn pot handles inward while cooking.
- Test bath water temperature before use.
- Store chemicals safely and label them clearly.
- Install smoke detectors and fire extinguishers at home.
- Wear protective clothing while handling heat or chemicals.

CONCLUSION

- "Burns may happen in seconds, but with the right response, scars can be avoided."
- Cool it, cover it, and call for help—these three actions can save skin and lives.

Scan to watch Dr Lokendra's 1-minute reel on this emergency.

Chapter 21

ELECTRIC SHOCK AND LIGHTNING INJURY

"WHEN CURRENT STRIKES"—ELECTRIC SHOCK AND LIGHTNING INJURY

Story: The Rainy Day Jolt

The first drops of the monsoon had just begun to fall when ***28-year-old Ravi****, a young shopkeeper, noticed flickering lights in his house. Suspecting a* ***loose wire on the verandah****, he decided to fix it before the rains worsened. With the floor wet and his hands slightly damp, Ravi unknowingly touched a live wire. Suddenly, a powerful jolt of electricity shot through his body. He froze, unable to let go of the wire, as if his hands were glued to it. A loud crackle followed, and Ravi collapsed to the ground.*

His neighbor, hearing a heavy thud, rushed out. Instead of touching Ravi directly—which could have been fatal—he ***immediately switched off the main power supply*** *and called emergency services. Ravi was carefully moved to a safe area and placed on his side. When he regained consciousness, he was confused, his palm and chest bore burn marks, and his heart was racing.*

At the hospital, ***doctors treated his burns,*** *monitored his heart for dangerous rhythm disturbances (arrhythmias), and explained how electricity can silently damage the heart, brain, and muscles even if the victim looks fine from outside.*

The Lightning Strike

Just a few days later, in a nearby village, ***35-year-old Ramesh, a farmer,*** *was caught in a sudden thunderstorm while working in his paddy field. A blinding flash of light split the sky, followed by a deafening crack. Before he could react, a* ***bolt of lightning struck*** *the ground near him, throwing him several feet away. He was found lying unconscious, but still breathing.*

His family, ***aware of basic first aid,*** *avoided crowding around him and instead quickly carried him to the nearest hospital. The doctors explained that lightning can travel through the body like a massive electrical surge, often* ***stopping the heart or causing severe burns****. Fortunately,* ***Ramesh survived with supportive care, but the fear of that blinding strike stayed with him forever.***

WHAT IS AN ELECTRIC SHOCK OR LIGHTNING INJURY?

An electric shock occurs when electric current passes through the body, causing internal or external injuries. Lightning injury is a high-voltage natural electrical discharge that can cause similar or more severe damage. Both can affect the skin, muscles, heart, and brain.

Causes/Risk Factors

- Touching live wires or faulty appliances
- Handling electrical items with wet hands
- Broken or exposed electrical outlets
- Working outdoors during thunderstorms
- Standing under trees or near metal objects in storms
- Lack of safety gear while working with electricity

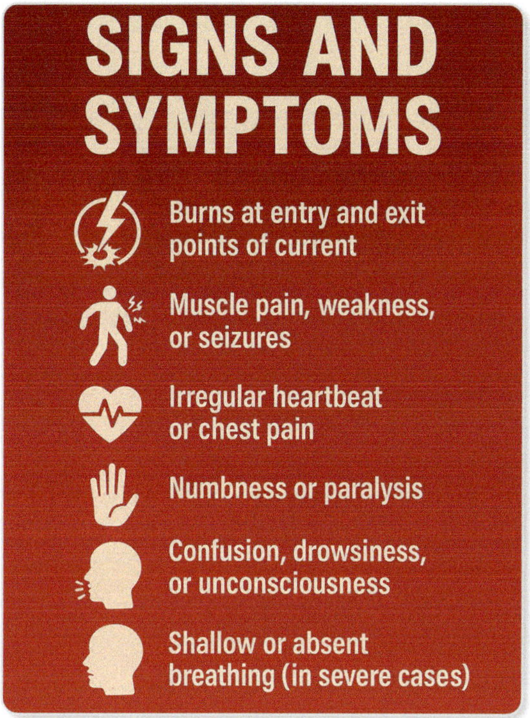

STEPWISE FIRST AID BEFORE REACHING A HOSPITAL

Act fast, but ensure your own safety first.

For Electric Shock

- ***Step 1:*** Switch Off the Power Source
    - » Do not touch the person until the source is off.
    - » Use a wooden stick or dry nonmetallic object to separate the person from the source if needed.
- ***Step 2:*** Check for Breathing and Pulse
    - » If unresponsive and not breathing, start cardiopulmonary resuscitation (CPR) immediately if trained.
    - » If breathing, lay the person on their back and monitor.
- ***Step 3:*** Look for Burns or Injuries
    - » Cover burns with a clean cloth, avoid using creams or ice.
    - » Keep the person warm and comfortable.
- ***Step 4:*** Call Emergency Services (112/108)
    - » Mention it is an electric shock and if CPR is in progress.

First Aid Flow: Electric Shock

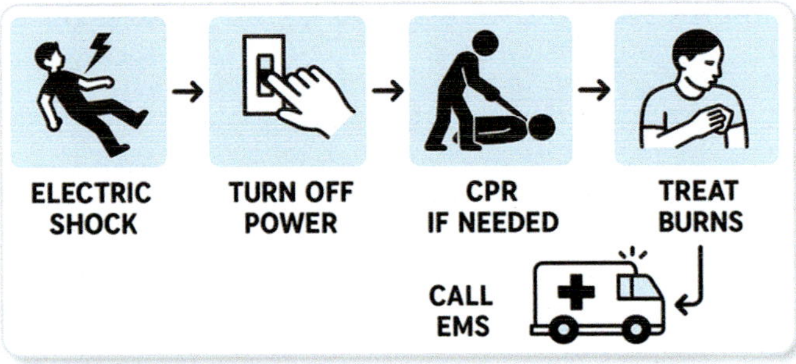

For Lightning Injury

- ***Step 1:*** Ensure Scene is Safe
  - » Move the person to shelter if lightning risk continues.
- ***Step 2:*** Start CPR Immediately if Unresponsive
  - » Lightning victims do not carry current—rescue is safe.
- ***Step 3:*** Check for Burns and Fractures
  - » Cover wounds and immobilize fractures gently.
- ***Step 4:*** Transport to Hospital Urgently
  - » Heart monitoring and supportive care are essential.

First Aid Flow: Lightening

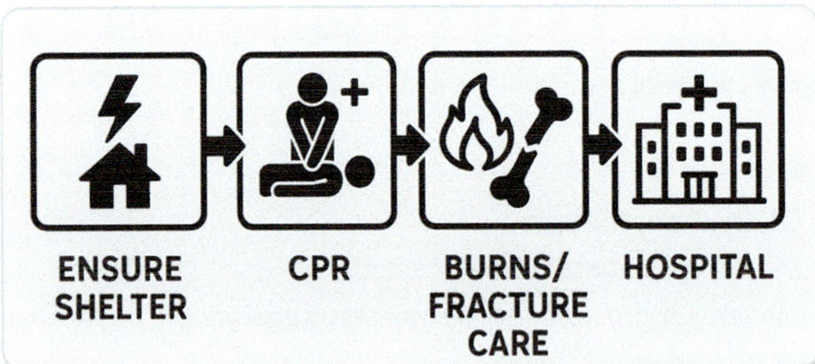

Golden Minute

For cardiac arrest after electric shock/lightning, survival drops 10% every minute without CPR—this drives urgency.

WHEN TO SEE A DOCTOR

- Any electric shock, especially with burns or unconsciousness
- Chest pain, confusion, or irregular heartbeat
- Loss of consciousness or seizure postshock
- Visible entry/exit wounds
- Anyone struck by lightning should be evaluated immediately

MYTHS AND FACTS

Myths	Facts
Victims of electric shock are dangerous to touch.	Safe to touch once power is turned off.
Lightning strike victims do not survive.	Many survive with timely CPR and care.
Small shocks do not need medical attention.	Internal damage or heart issues may occur without symptoms.
Rubber soles fully protect against lightning.	Lightning travels through air and ground—rubber offers minimal protection.

PREVENTION TIPS

- Keep electrical systems well maintained.
- Use insulated tools and wear rubber gloves for repairs.
- Avoid using electrical appliances with wet hands or feet.
- Stay indoors during thunderstorms; avoid water and wired devices.
- Do not take shelter under trees or near poles during lightning.
- Install circuit breakers and surge protectors at home.

CONCLUSION

- "Electricity gives life power—but mishandled, it can take it away."
- *Respect its force, take precautions, and act swiftly in emergencies. Know the risk—know the rescue.*

Scan to watch Dr Lokendra's 1-minute reel on this emergency.

SECTION 6: ENVIRONMENTAL EMERGENCIES

Chapter 22

HEAT STROKE AND DEHYDRATION

"WHEN THE BODY OVERHEATS"—HEAT STROKE AND DEHYDRATION

Story: The Summer Parade Collapse

The sun was blazing in the sky, and the streets shimmered with heat as the community parade made its way through the town. Among the participants was ***42-year-old Rajesh, a dedicated school teacher*** *who had been rehearsing with his students for weeks. It was only mid-morning,* ***but the temperature had already soared past 40°C.*** *Rajesh had barely eaten and had sipped only a small amount of water since morning, underestimating how harsh the summer heat could be.*

As the parade moved forward, ***Rajesh began to feel lightheaded and unsteady.*** *His vision blurred, and an intense wave of heat seemed to rise from inside his body. He tried to sit down but* ***collapsed to the ground.*** *Bystanders rushed toward him, realizing something was seriously wrong.*

One of them noticed the telltale signs of heat stroke—his skin was hot and dry to touch, his face flushed, and he wasn't sweating at all. Rajesh seemed confused and mumbled incoherently.

Fortunately, a retired nurse in the crowd stepped in. She quickly:

- *Moved Rajesh to a shaded, cooler area.*
- *Removed his shoes and loosened his clothes.*
- *Poured water over his body and fanned him to bring his temperature down.*
- *Placed cool, wet clothes on his neck and armpits, key areas where cooling is most effective.*
- *Asked someone to call an ambulance immediately.*

*By the time paramedics arrived, **Rajesh's condition had stabilized slightly,** but his pulse was still fast, and he was weak. At the hospital, doctors confirmed it was severe heat stroke, a life-threatening emergency where the body's core temperature rises dangerously high. They rapidly cooled him using ice packs and gave intravenous (IV) fluids to combat dehydration.*

Within 24 hours, Rajesh recovered, but the experience left a lasting impression. He later admitted, "I never thought skipping water could almost cost me my life". The summer heat is not just uncomfortable—it can be deadly.

WHAT IS HEAT STROKE AND DEHYDRATION?

Heat stroke is a life-threatening condition caused by prolonged exposure to high temperatures, where the body fails to regulate its temperature. Dehydration occurs when the body loses more fluids than it takes in. Both often occur together in hot, humid conditions, and require urgent intervention.

Signs and Symptoms: Dehydration

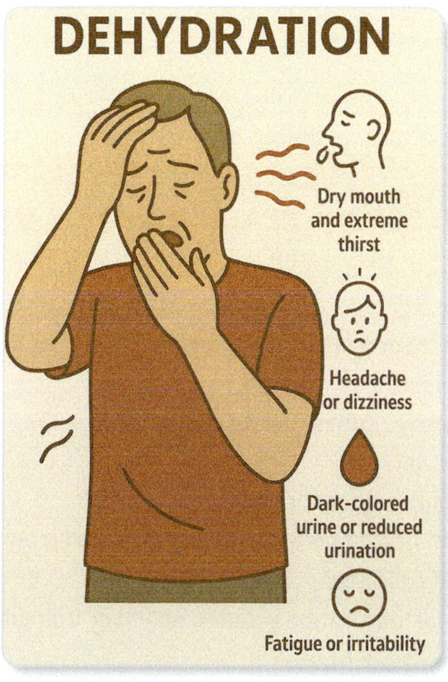

Signs and Symptoms: Heat Stroke (Severe)

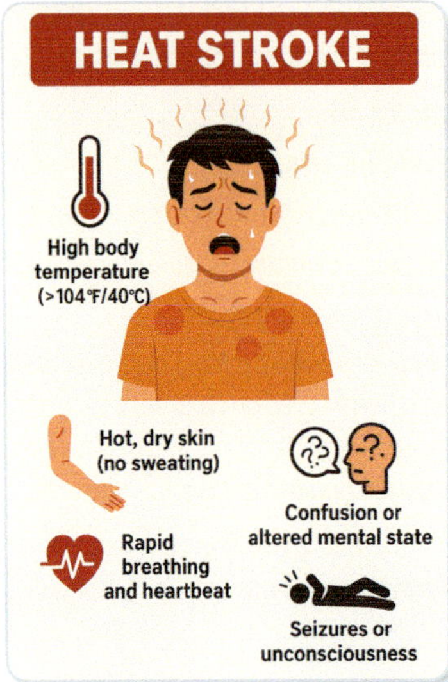

Causes/Risk Factors

- Prolonged exposure to high temperatures
- Strenuous activity under the sun
- Inadequate fluid intake
- Wearing heavy or dark clothing
- Elderly, infants, and those with chronic illness
- Alcohol use or certain medications

"Do NOT give oral fluids if the person is unconscious or unable to swallow safely." **(Important for laypersons)**

STEPWISE FIRST AID BEFORE REACHING A HOSPITAL

Heat stroke is a medical emergency. Act quickly to cool the person down.

- ***Step 1:*** Move to a cooler area
  - » Take the person to a shaded or air-conditioned space.
- ***Step 2:*** Remove excess clothing
  - » Loosen or remove heavy clothes to help heat escape.
- ***Step 3:*** Cool the body immediately
  - » Pour cool (not ice-cold) water over the body.
  - » Use wet clothes, fans, or cold packs (neck, armpits, and groin).
- ***Step 4:*** Offer oral fluids if conscious
  - » Give sips of water, oral rehydration solution (ORS), or fruit juice.
  - » Avoid sugary or caffeinated drinks.

- ***Step 5:*** Call emergency services (112/108)
  - » Especially if unconscious, confused, or not responding to cooling.
  - » Continue cooling while waiting for help.

WHEN TO SEE A DOCTOR

- High body temperature with altered mental state
- Seizures, unconsciousness, or chest pain
- Symptoms not improving with basic cooling
- Dehydration with vomiting or inability to drink fluids
- Any heat illness in children or elderly

MYTHS AND FACTS

Myths	Facts
Sweating always occurs in heat stroke.	In heat stroke, the body may stop sweating completely.
Drinking cold water too fast helps immediately.	Rapid cooling should be external—cold water may cause cramps.
Heat strokes only affect athletes.	Anyone in high temperatures is at risk, especially elderly and children.
You can wait for the person to cool down on their own.	Delay in cooling increases risk of brain and organ damage.

PREVENTION TIPS

- Stay hydrated—drink water regularly, even if not thirsty.
- Wear loose, light-colored, and breathable clothing.
- Avoid outdoor activities during peak heat (12 PM–4 PM).
- Use umbrellas, hats, and sunscreen when outside.
- Keep homes cool with fans, curtains, or cooling devices.
- Check on elderly neighbors and children during heatwaves.

CONCLUSION

- "Heat does not just exhaust—it can kill."
- Be alert to the early signs of dehydration and heat stroke. Stay cool, stay hydrated, and protect the vulnerable during peak heat.

Scan to watch Dr Lokendra's 1-minute reel on this emergency.

Chapter 23

COLD EXPOSURE AND HYPOTHERMIA

"WHEN THE COLD CREEPS IN"—COLD EXPOSURE AND HYPOTHERMIA

Story: The Trekker's Ordeal

The Himalayas are as unforgiving as they are beautiful. ***Aditya, a 29-year-old trekker****, learned this the hard way during a winter expedition. A sudden snowstorm reduced visibility to almost zero, and in the chaos, he became separated from his group.* ***With no immediate shelter, his wet clothes and icy wind accelerated heat loss from his body.***

Hours later, ***rescuers found him shivering uncontrollably,*** *his lips blue, and his speech slurred—classic signs of moderate hypothermia (core temperature between 28°C and 32°C). His confusion and clumsiness showed that his body was beginning to fail at keeping warm.*

The rescue team acted swiftly and correctly: They ***removed his wet clothing,*** *as wet fabric drains body heat 20–30 times faster than dry air.*

He was ***wrapped in multiple dry blankets*** *and a sleeping bag to provide insulation.*

*Once Aditya was alert enough to swallow, he was given **small sips of warm, sweet fluids to** help gently raise his energy and body temperature.*

They did not rub his skin or immerse him in hot water, as this could trigger dangerous heart rhythm disturbances in hypothermia patients.

*Aditya was carried to the base hospital, where he received active rewarming, including **heated IV fluids** and warm air therapy. Within 24 hours, he made a full recovery.*

*This chilling experience reinforced the fact that hypothermia can set in rapidly, even above freezing temperatures, when wet clothing and wind are involved. **Early recognition—shivering, slurred speech, confusion—and proper first aid can mean the difference between survival and tragedy.***

WHAT IS COLD EXPOSURE AND HYPOTHERMIA?

Hypothermia is a medical emergency that occurs when the body loses heat faster than it can produce it, causing the core temperature to fall below 35°C (95°F). Cold exposure from wind, wet clothing, or immersion in cold water increases the risk. Left untreated, it can lead to unconsciousness, organ failure, or death.

Signs and Symptoms

Mild hypothermia:

- Shivering
- Cold, pale skin
- Numb hands or feet
- Fatigue or slurred speech

Moderate-to-severe hypothermia:

- Confusion or disorientation
- Weak pulse or shallow breathing
- No shivering (a dangerous sign)
- Loss of coordination or consciousness

Causes/Risk Factors

- Prolonged exposure to cold weather without proper clothing
- Wet clothing or immersion in cold water
- Wind chill and high altitudes
- Elderly, infants, and those with chronic illness
- Alcohol or drug use impairing judgment or body heat regulation
- Mental health issues or homelessness

STEPWISE FIRST AID BEFORE REACHING A HOSPITAL

Handle the person gently—sudden movements can trigger cardiac arrest.

- ***Step 1:*** Move to a warm, dry place
  - » Shelter the person from wind, rain, or snow.
- ***Step 2***: Remove wet clothing
  - » Gently take off wet clothes and replace with dry, warm layers or blankets.
- ***Step 3***: Warm the core first
  - » Focus on chest, neck, and groin using warm compresses or body heat.
  - » Avoid direct heat like hot water bottles or electric blankets.
- ***Step 4:*** Offer warm fluids if conscious
  - » Give sips of warm, sweet fluids (not alcohol or caffeine).
- ***Step 5:*** Monitor breathing and response
  - » If unconscious or not breathing, begin cardiopulmonary resuscitation (CPR) and call emergency services (☎ 112/108).
- ***Step 6:*** Do not massage limbs or rub the skin
  - » This can cause cold blood to rush to the heart and worsen the condition.

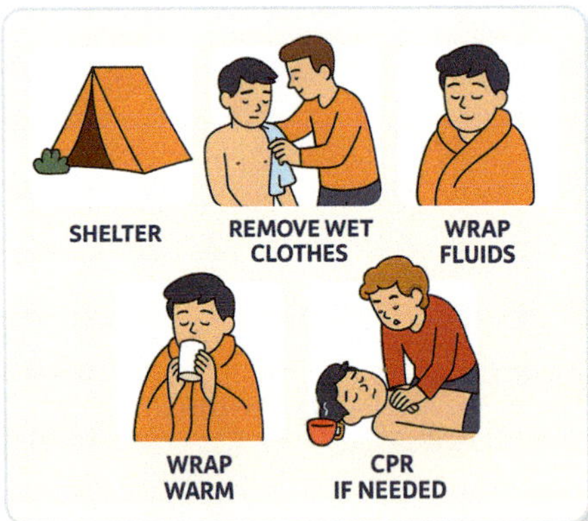

WHEN TO SEE A DOCTOR

- Any signs of confusion, slurred speech, or drowsiness in cold weather
- Shivering followed by sudden stillness (a sign of worsening hypothermia)
- Frostbite, bluish skin, or loss of consciousness
- After rescue from cold water or prolonged cold exposure

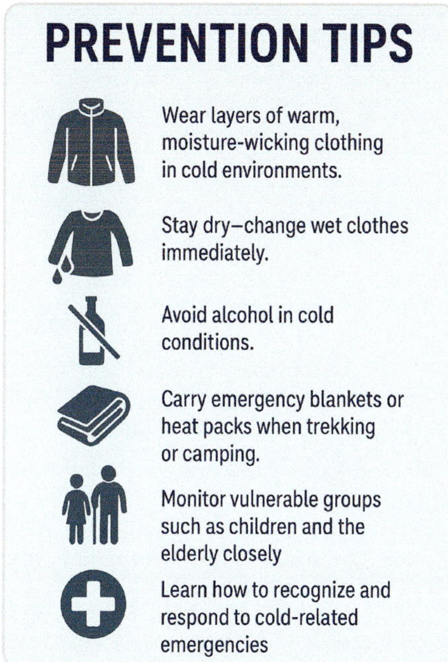

MYTHS AND FACTS

Myths	Facts
Alcohol warms you up in the cold.	Alcohol gives a false sense of warmth and increases heat loss.
Rubbing hands or feet vigorously helps.	It can damage cold tissues and send cold blood to vital organs.
Hypothermia only happens in freezing temperatures.	It can occur even in cool weather, especially if wet or windy.
Once they stop shivering, they are getting better.	Loss of shivering is a sign of worsening hypothermia.

CONCLUSION

- "Cold can kill quietly—know the signs, stay warm, and act fast."
- Prevention and prompt first aid are your best defense against hypothermia. Do not underestimate the chill.

Scan to watch Dr Lokendra's 1-minute reel on this emergency.

Chapter 24

DROWNING AND NEAR-DROWNING

"WHEN EVERY BREATH COUNTS"—NEAR-DROWNING AND DROWNING

Story: The Poolside Miracle

It was a bright Sunday afternoon at a family picnic in a resort. The poolside was full of laughter as children splashed around, while adults relaxed nearby. Amid the cheerful chaos, ***8-year-old Karan,*** *trying to keep up with his older cousins, wandered toward the deep end of the pool. One slip, and he was underwater—****his small hands flailing desperately,*** *but no one noticed right away.*

Within seconds, his playful splashes turned silent. Drowning makes no noise; it is quick and deceptive. By the time his cousin shouted, ***Karan had already sunk below the surface****. His uncle, realizing the danger, leapt into the pool without hesitation. He pulled Karan out, but the sight was terrifying—****the boy was limp, unconscious, and not breathing, his lips tinged blue.***

Panic swept through the family, ***but a resort staff member trained in CPR rushed forward.*** *Kneeling beside Karan, he checked his airway and breathing, finding none. He immediately began five rescue breaths, forcing life-giving air into the child's lungs. Then, with firm hands, he started chest compressions—****pushing down 30 times on the small chest, followed by 2 rescue breaths****—repeating the cycle. Each second felt like an eternity.*

*Suddenly, after a few tense minutes, Karan coughed—**a gush of water poured out from his mouth,** followed by a faint gasp. His chest rose with a shallow breath, and soon, tears of relief filled everyone's eyes.*

An ambulance arrived and rushed Karan to the hospital. Doctors confirmed it was a near-drowning incident, cautioning the family about the risk of secondary drowning, where water in the lungs can cause breathing difficulties hours later. Fortunately, Karan recovered completely.

*That day, the Sharmas learned a life-changing lesson: **Constant supervision around water and knowing CPR are as important as preventing accidents.** What could have been a tragedy turned into a miracle because someone knew what to do when every second mattered.*

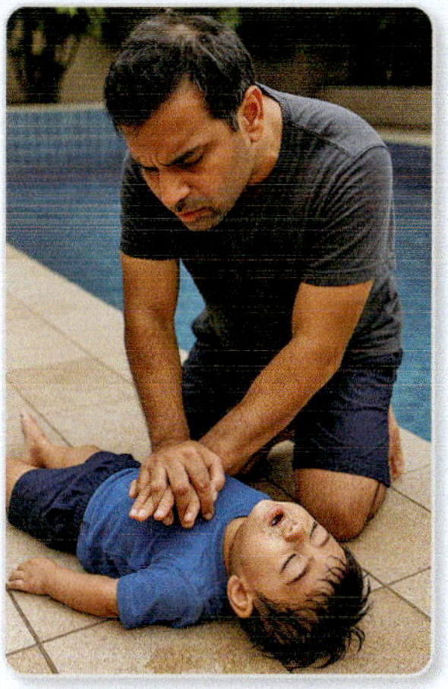

WHAT IS DROWNING AND NEAR-DROWNING?

Drowning is the process of experiencing respiratory impairment due to submersion in liquid. It can lead to death, injury, or survival with complications. "Near-drowning" refers to survival after a submersion incident, often requiring urgent medical care.

Signs and Symptoms

- Unconsciousness or drowsiness after being pulled from water
- Coughing, choking, or vomiting water
- Difficulty breathing or bluish lips/skin (cyanosis)
- Cold, pale, or clammy skin
- Confusion or irritability
- Seizures or limp body in severe cases

Causes/Risk Factors

- Lack of swimming ability or supervision
- Slipping into deep water (pools, lakes, or tubs)
- Swimming under the influence of alcohol or drugs
- Medical conditions like seizures or heart issues
- Absence of safety barriers or floatation devices
- Strong currents, tides, or exhaustion while swimming

STEPS TO GIVE RESCUE BREATHS

- Ensure Airway is Clear
- Lay the person on their back.
- Quickly check and clear the mouth of any obstruction (water, vomit, mud, etc.).
- Head-Tilt, Chin-Lift
- Place one hand on the forehead and gently tilt the head back.

- With the other hand, lift the chin upwards to open the airway.
- Pinch the nose closed with your thumb and index finger.
- Seal Your Mouth Over Theirs
- Take a normal breath.
- Seal your lips tightly around the victim's mouth (for infants, cover both the mouth and nose with your mouth).
- Give a Slow, Steady Breath
- Blow gently for 1 second, just enough for the chest to rise visibly (do NOT blow too hard, which can cause air to enter the stomach).
- Allow the chest to fall as the person exhales.
- Repeat
- Wait 1 second, then give the second breath (in CPR cycle).
- For drowning victims, start with 5 rescue breaths before chest compressions.

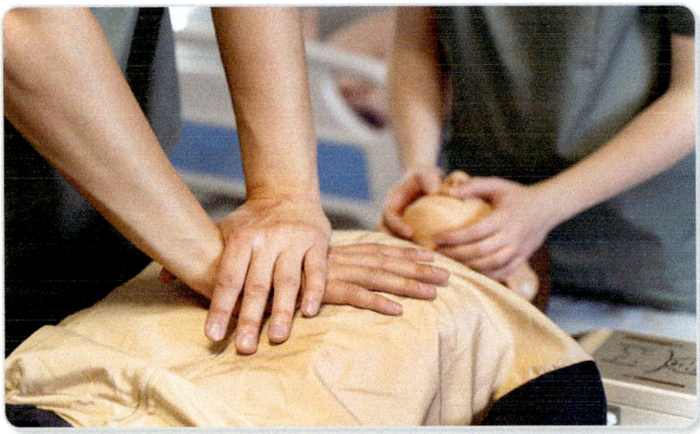

STEPWISE FIRST AID BEFORE REACHING A HOSPITAL

Act immediately—brain damage can begin within minutes of oxygen deprivation.

- ***Step 1:*** Ensure Your Own Safety First
  - » Do not enter water unless safe to do so.
  - » Use a pole, rope, or floatation device to pull the person to safety if needed.
- ***Step 2****:* Check for Breathing and Responsiveness
  - » If unresponsive and not breathing, begin CPR immediately.
  - » If breathing, lay them on their side (recovery position).
- ***Step 3****:* Start CPR if Not Breathing
  - » Begin with five rescue breaths, then alternate 30 compressions with two breaths.
  - » Continue until help arrives or the person starts breathing.
- ***Step 4:*** Remove Wet Clothing and Keep Warm
  - » Cover with a towel or blanket to prevent hypothermia.

- *Step 5:* Call Emergency Services (☎112/108)
  - » Inform them it is a drowning/near-drowning case.
  - » Transport to hospital even if the person seems fine—complications can be delayed.

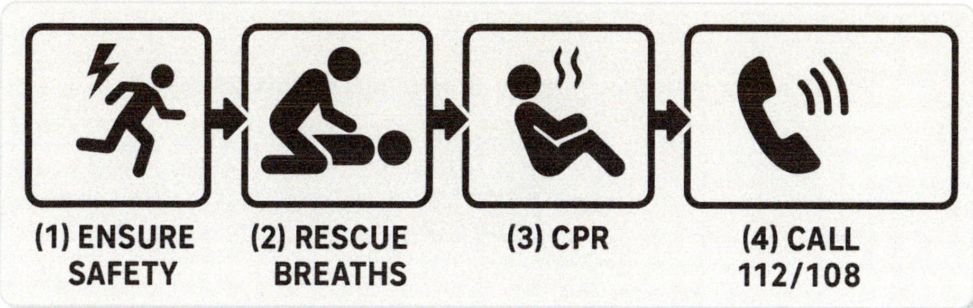

WHEN TO SEE A DOCTOR

- After any near-drowning incident—even if person appears okay
- Persistent cough, breathing difficulty, or drowsiness
- Vomiting, confusion, or seizures after submersion
- Water inhalation or unconsciousness at any time
- Any drowning involving infants, elderly, or underlying health issues

MYTHS AND FACTS

Myths	Facts
If someone coughs and stands, they are fine.	Secondary drowning can occur hours later—medical check-up is essential.
You should hang someone upside down to drain water.	This wastes valuable CPR time—focus on rescue breaths and compressions.
CPR should start only when ambulance arrives.	Immediate CPR improves survival dramatically.
Children drown with loud splashing.	Drowning is often silent and quick—vigilance is key.

PREVENTION TIPS

- Always supervise children near water—never leave them alone.
- Install pool fences and use life jackets.
- Learn swimming and basic water safety.
- Avoid alcohol or heavy meals before swimming.
- Never swim alone or in unfamiliar waters.
- Learn CPR—it can save a life before help arrives.

CONCLUSION

Drowning is swift, silent, and often invisible to bystanders. Constant vigilance, active supervision, and learning essential skills like swimming and CPR can transform ordinary individuals into lifesavers. Every second of awareness and timely action can turn a tragedy into a survival story. Let us remember: water can bring joy, but it demands respect. Stay alert, stay prepared, and protect every precious life around water.

Scan to watch Dr Lokendra's 1-minute reel on this emergency.

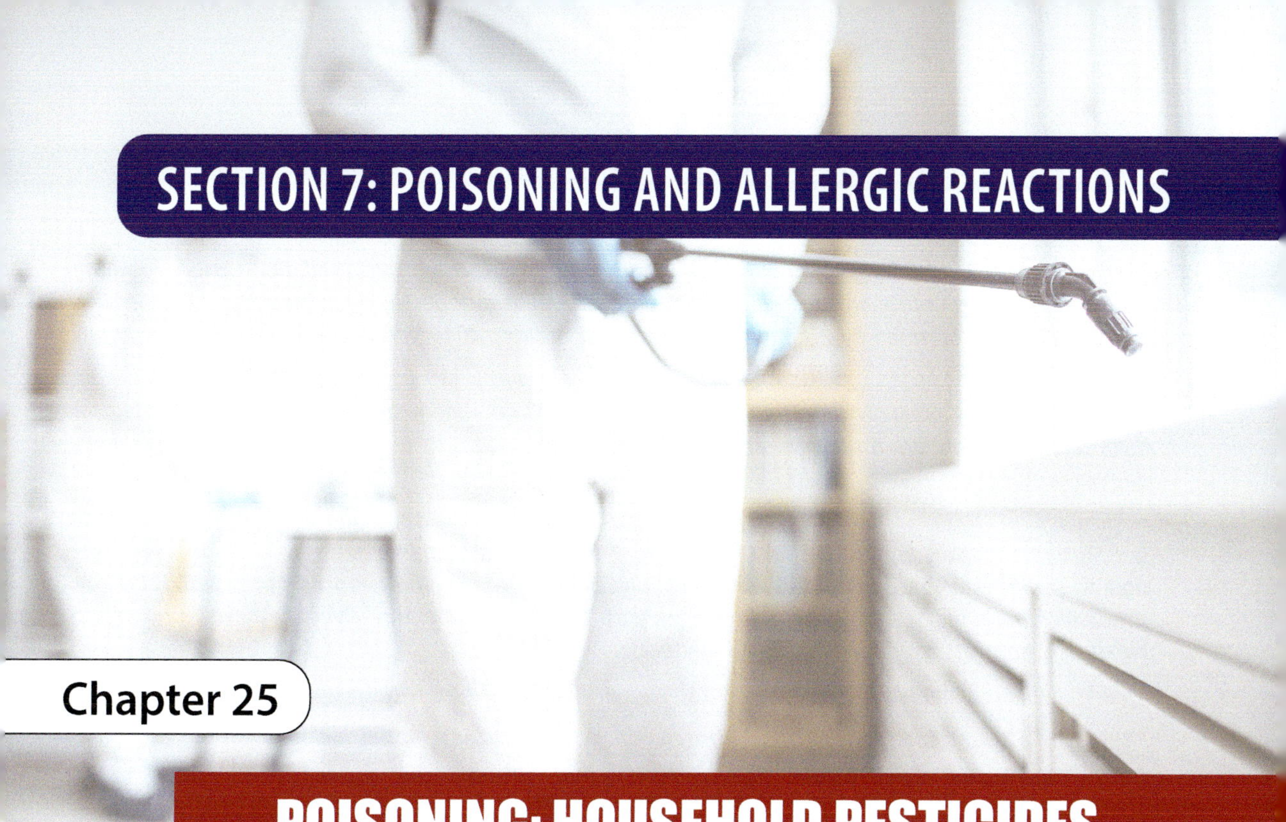

SECTION 7: POISONING AND ALLERGIC REACTIONS

Chapter 25

POISONING: HOUSEHOLD PESTICIDES

"WHEN THE CURE BECOMES A THREAT"—POISONING WITH HOUSEHOLD PESTICIDES

Story: The Mistaken Sip

It was an ordinary, sweltering ***summer afternoon*** *in a small town where* ***4-year-old Aarav*** *was playing with his toy cars near the kitchen. His grandmother, busy with her seasonal deep-cleaning routine, was scrubbing shelves and trying to rid the kitchen of ants. Like many others in her neighborhood, she had poured* ***leftover pesticide liquid into an old soft drink bottle****—planning to use the rest later. Without thinking much of it, she placed the bottle casually near the sink and got busy cleaning.*

Little Aarav, tired and thirsty from his play, spotted the familiar shape of the ***soft drink bottle*** *with its bright label still intact. Without hesitation, he grabbed it, unscrewed the cap, and took a big gulp—expecting the sweet fizz of cola.*

What happened next was terrifying.

*Within **minutes, Aarav began coughing violently. His face turned pale, and he started vomiting uncontrollably.** His breathing became labored, and his eyelids drooped as he grew increasingly drowsy. His grandmother, alarmed by his sudden collapse and noticing the open pesticide bottle, immediately understood the gravity of the mistake.*

*Instead of wasting precious time trying home remedies or panicking, she acted fast. She shouted for help, and the neighbors rushed in. Together, they whisked Aarav to the **nearest hospital emergency department.***

*At the hospital, the doctors quickly recognized the classic signs of organophosphate poisoning—a common but highly dangerous type of pesticide poisoning. Thanks to his grandmother's swift action, they were **able to stabilize his breathing, give antidotes, and begin decontamination procedures without delay.** Aarav was admitted to the Pediatric Intensive Care Unit for observation. Over the next 48 hours, his condition improved steadily under close monitoring.*

*Thankfully, Aarav made a **full recovery.** But the doctor's words stayed with the family:*

"This was preventable. Children are naturally curious. Pesticides should never be stored in bottles meant for food or drink. This could have ended very differently."

Why this Story Matters: A Reminder for Every Household

- *Never store pesticides or chemicals in soft drink bottles or food containers.*
- *Keep all chemicals locked away and out of reach of children.*
- *Label clearly and dispose of leftovers safely.*
- *Immediate medical care can save lives.*

Key Message for Parents and Caregivers

One careless moment can turn everyday household items into a silent threat. Prevention is always better than regret.

WHAT IS PESTICIDE POISONING?

Pesticide poisoning occurs when harmful chemicals used to kill pests are accidentally swallowed, inhaled, or absorbed through the skin. Many household pesticides, especially organophosphates, can be extremely toxic—even in small amounts—and require urgent medical attention.

Signs and Symptoms

- Vomiting, nausea, or abdominal pain
- Drooling or excessive salivation
- Sweating and muscle twitching
- Difficulty breathing or wheezing
- Pinpoint pupils
- Drowsiness, confusion, or seizures
- Unconsciousness or shock in severe cases

Causes/Risk Factors

- Improper storage in drink bottles or food containers
- Children playing unsupervised near chemical products
- Spraying pesticides in enclosed or poorly ventilated areas
- Lack of protective gloves or masks while handling pesticides
- Accidental ingestion, especially in children or elderly
- Suicidal ingestion (intentional poisoning)

STEPWISE FIRST AID BEFORE REACHING A HOSPITAL

For Suspected Pesticide Poisoning—Evidence-based Guidelines

Pesticide poisoning is a medical emergency. Act quickly but stay calm.

- ***Step 1****: Remove the Person from the Exposure Source*
  - » ***If inhaled:*** *Move the person immediately to* ***fresh air****, away from fumes.*
  - » ***If on skin:*** *Remove the person from the contaminated area.*
  - » ***Protect yourself:*** *Wear gloves or use cloth to avoid direct contact.*
- ***Step 2:*** *Check Responsiveness and Breathing*
  - » *If* ***unconscious but breathing, place the person in the recovery position.***
  - » *If* ***not breathing, begin CPR (if trained).***
  - » *Keep the airway clear and monitor for changes.*
- ***Step 3****: Do NOT Induce Vomiting*
  - » ***Do NOT make the person vomit.*** *Vomiting can worsen the condition, especially with corrosive or* oil-based pesticides.
  - » *Do not give anything to eat or drink unless advised by medical professionals.*
- ***Step 4:*** *Rinse Mouth and Skin (If Contaminated)*
  - » *If conscious and able to cooperate, rinse the mouth* ***thoroughly with clean water.***
  - » ***Remove contaminated clothing carefully.***
  - » *Wash exposed skin areas with* ***plenty of soap and running water.***
- ***Step 5:*** *Seek Emergency Medical Help Immediately*
  - » *Dial* ***112 or 108*** *without delay.*
  - » *Clearly inform responders: "****Suspected pesticide poisoning.****"*
  - » *If possible, take the* ***pesticide container, label, or name*** *to the hospital to assist doctors in identifying the poison.*

Why these Steps are Scientifically Recommended

- ***No vomiting****: Modern toxicology guidelines discourage home-induced vomiting.*
- *Quick decontamination:* ***Reduces further absorption through skin or lungs.***
- ***Early emergency care:*** *Rapid hospital care improves outcomes significantly*

WHEN TO SEE A DOCTOR

- After any suspected ingestion or exposure to pesticides
- Vomiting, drowsiness, or breathing difficulty
- Skin or eye contact with concentrated pesticide
- Seizures, confusion, or unconsciousness
- Persistent symptoms despite rinsing or removal from exposure

MYTHS AND FACTS

Myths	Facts
Give milk to neutralize poison.	Milk may delay treatment—seek medical care immediately.
Make the person vomit to remove poison after 3–4 hours.	Vomiting after 3–4 hours can cause aspiration or worsen chemical burns.
Washing the face is enough.	Full body exposure requires decontamination of skin and clothes.
Small amounts are harmless.	Even small sips or fumes of some pesticides can be deadly.

CONCLUSION

- "Household pesticides can kill—if misused or left within reach."
- *Store safely, act quickly, and never ignore early signs of poisoning. Awareness and preparedness can save a life.*

Scan to watch Dr Lokendra's 1-minute reel on this emergency.

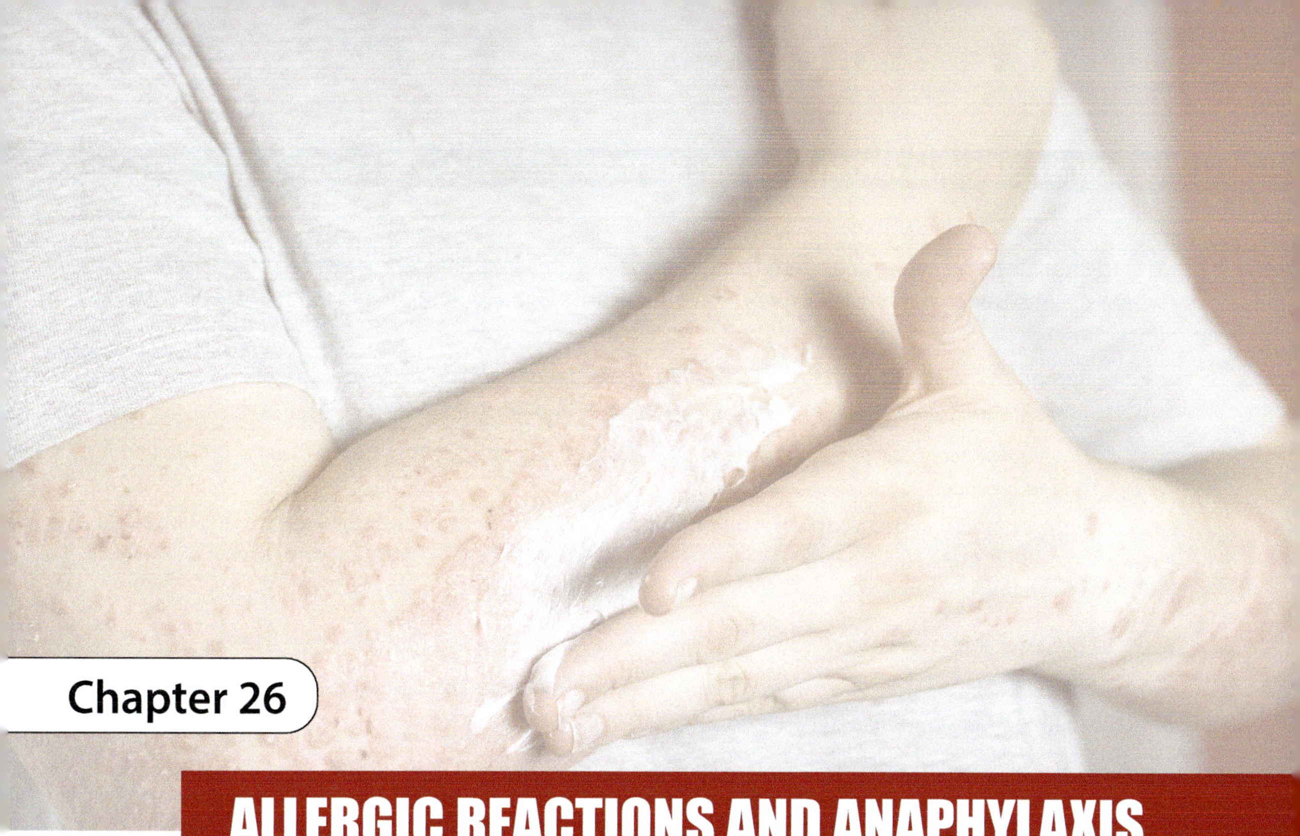

Chapter 26

ALLERGIC REACTIONS AND ANAPHYLAXIS

"THE HIDDEN DANGER"—PUBLIC AWARENESS ON ANAPHYLAXIS

The Cookie that Almost Killed

It was meant to be a fun-filled birthday celebration. **Ten-year-old Tanish** was laughing with his friends as he grabbed a chocolate cookie from the snack table. But within minutes, the joy turned to terror.

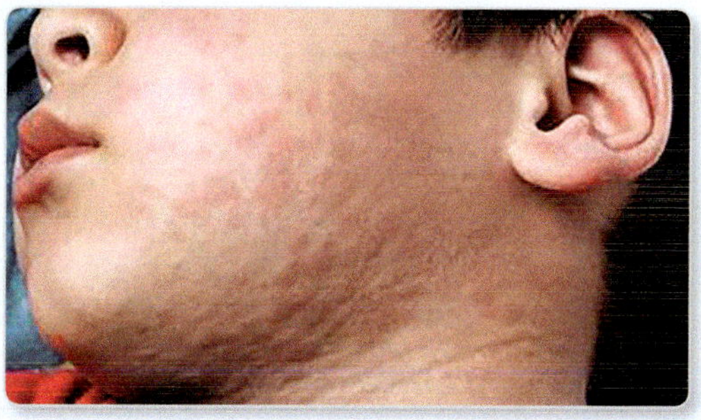

Tanish began **coughing violently, struggling to breathe.** His lips turned blue, his face became swollen, and red rashes appeared across his arms and neck. The room filled with panic—some adults thought he was choking, while others hesitated, unsure what to do.

One parent, realizing it was likely a **severe allergic reaction,** quickly laid Tanish down, called emergency services, and ensured his airway was clear. A teacher present at the party helped **keep him calm and positioned him on his side** when he began feeling faint. By the time the ambulance arrived, Tanish's condition was critical but manageable thanks to their prompt action.

At the hospital's emergency department, the doctors worked quickly—**giving oxygen, intravenous medications, fluids, and continuous monitoring.** Within a short time, Tanish was breathing steadily, his swelling reduced, and his skin color returned to normal. He was kept under observation for the next 24 hours to rule out a biphasic reaction, which can sometimes occur hours after the initial episode.

This frightening incident became a reminder for everyone present that anaphylaxis is a medical emergency where every second counts. **While preventive measures like avoiding allergens are vital, it is equally important to:**

- *Recognize the early signs (sudden swelling, rashes, breathing difficulty).*
- *Seek immediate medical help rather than trying home remedies.*
- *Have quick access to emergency departments that are well-prepared with trained teams and life-saving protocols.*

Tanish survived because **the people around him acted fast and because he received timely, expert care in a good emergency department.**

WHAT IS ANAPHYLAXIS?

Anaphylaxis is a severe, *life-threatening allergic reaction* that comes on suddenly and progresses rapidly. It affects multiple organ systems—*skin, airways, heart, and digestive system.*

It can occur *within minutes* of exposure to a trigger and *requires immediate treatment.*

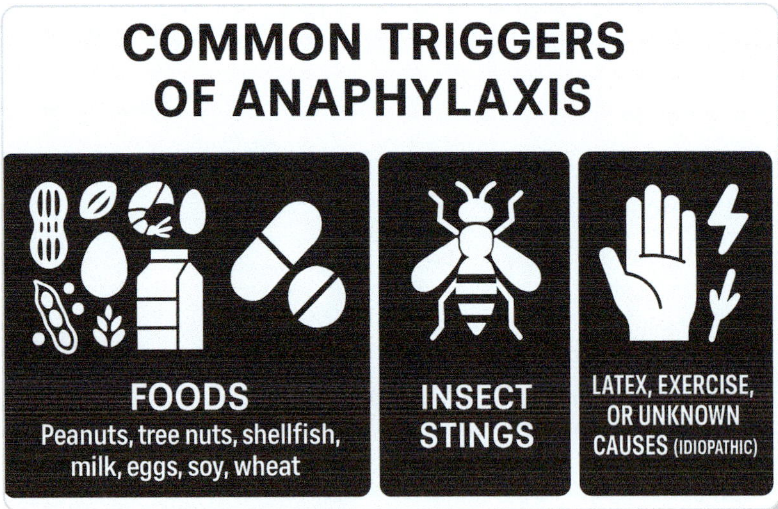

WARNING SIGNS AND SYMPTOMS

Usually appear within minutes to an hour after exposure.

Early Symptoms

- Itching, hives, skin flushing
- Swelling of lips, face, or eyes
- Tingling in hands or feet
- Anxiety or a feeling of "impending doom"

Life-threatening Symptoms

- Difficulty breathing (wheezing, throat tightness, hoarseness)
- Swelling of tongue or throat
- Drop in blood pressure (dizziness, fainting)
- Rapid heartbeat or weak pulse
- Nausea, vomiting, abdominal pain
- Loss of consciousness

WHAT TO DO IN CASE OF ANAPHYLAXIS: STEP-BY-STEP EMERGENCY RESPONSE

Time = Life. React quickly and confidently

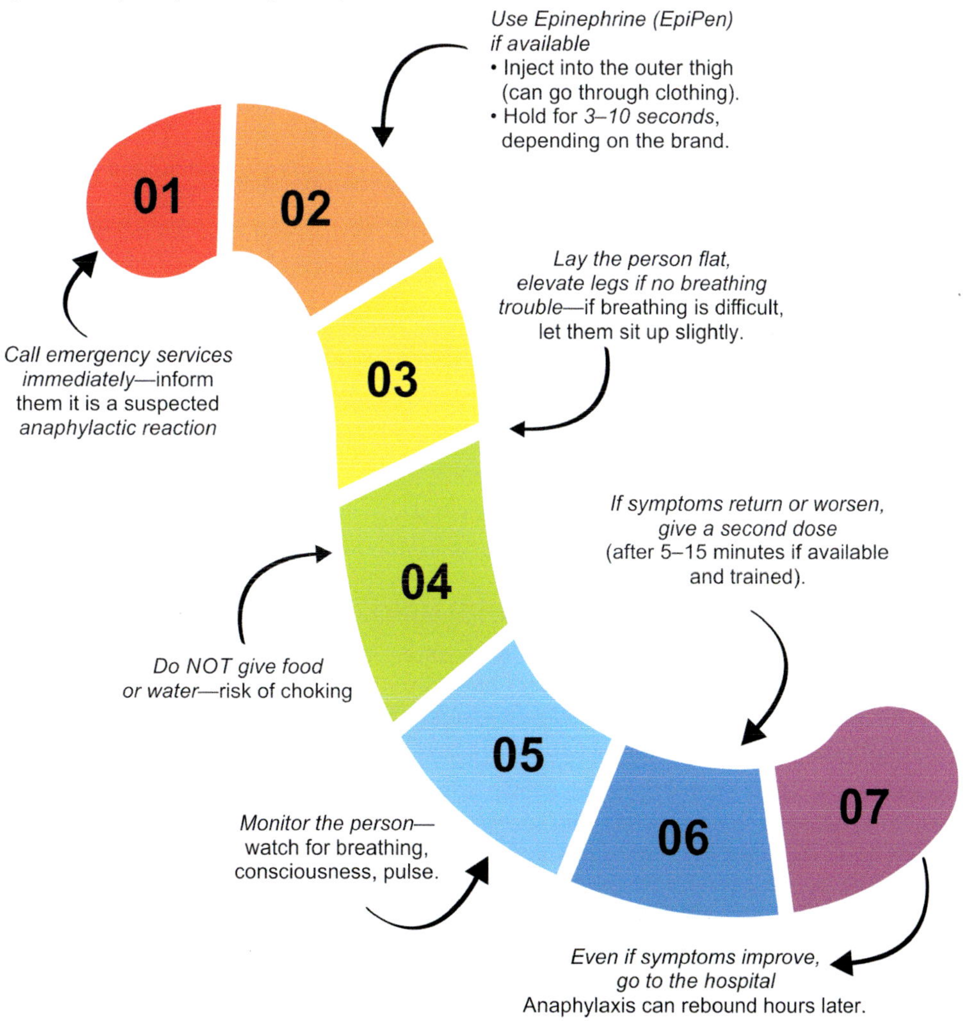

IMPORTANT: EPINEPHRINE SAVES LIVES

- *Do not wait* for symptoms to get worse.
- Epinephrine is *safe*—even if you are unsure, *it is better to give it than delay.*

ADVISORY ON EPINEPHRINE (EPIPEN)—FOR THE PUBLIC

Epinephrine (Epipen) is the only life-saving medicine for severe allergic reactions (anaphylaxis)

- It must be given immediately when someone develops
- Sudden difficulty in breathing
- Swelling of lips, tongue, or throat

PREVENTION TIPS

- *Identify and avoid triggers.*
  - » Read food labels carefully.
  - » Inform restaurants about allergies.
- *Always carry an epinephrine autoinjector* if you are at risk.
- *Wear a medical alert bracelet.*
- *Train friends, family, teachers, and coworkers* on how to recognize symptoms and use an EpiPen.
- *Have an emergency action plan* and keep it handy.

MYTHS AND FACTS

Myths	Facts
"It is just an allergy, not serious."	Anaphylaxis is *life-threatening* and needs *urgent care.*
"You should wait to see if it gets worse."	Never wait—*early epinephrine* is key to survival.
"Antihistamines like cetirizine can stop it."	Antihistamines may relieve *minor symptoms,* but *they cannot stop anaphylaxis.*
"Only children get severe allergies."	*Anyone, at any age,* can have a first-time severe reaction.

CONCLUSION

Anaphylaxis is a true medical emergency that can escalate rapidly and become fatal within minutes if not recognized and treated promptly. Awareness of its warning signs—ranging from skin rashes to life-threatening airway and circulatory compromise—is essential for timely action. Every suspected case must be treated as an emergency without delay, as hesitation can cost lives.

Equally important is prevention—avoiding known triggers, carrying auto-injectable adrenaline where prescribed, and educating family, friends, and caregivers on emergency response. By spreading knowledge and preparedness, we empower individuals and communities to act swiftly and confidently, turning a potentially fatal crisis into a survivable event.

Scan to watch Dr Lokendra's 1-minute reel on this emergency.

Chapter 27

SNAKE BITES

CLINICAL SCENARIO

A Life Saved: Sharp-witted Hariram

It was a bright sunny morning in Golf City. The air was fresh and crisp after the heavy rainfall from the night before. The sun glistened on the wet pavement as ***Vijay, the owner of a thriving construction company,*** *made his usual rounds at the site. A man of action, Vijay was always keen to ensure that projects stayed on track and that his team performed at their best.*

As he walked through the site, Vijay approached Hariram, one of his most trusted workers. "What is the progress, Hariram? Why is there so much delay in the project?" he asked, his brow furrowed with concern. Hariram began explaining the challenges they were facing when suddenly, Vijay felt a sharp pain in his ankle, followed by a burning sensation shooting up his leg.

"Sirji!" ***Hariram shouted in panic, his eyes wide with fear.*** *"It is a snake! A cobra!" He quickly crouched beside Vijay, who was now struggling to stay awake. The sight of the snake slithering away sent a chill down Hariram's spine, but he knew he had to act fast.*

"Do not worry, sir! Just lie down and do not move your leg," Hariram instructed, his voice steady despite the chaos around them. He could see the fear in Vijay's eyes but was determined to keep his boss calm. "Stay awake, sirji. I will call for help."

Hariram pulled out his mobile phone, dialing the ***emergency number for the Advanced Cardiac Life Support (ACLS) ambulance,*** *which he had saved for situations like this. "Help is on the way, sirji. Just breathe," he reassured Vijay, who was beginning to feel lightheaded.*

"Do not tie anything around your leg or try to suck out the venom," Hariram continued, recalling a similar episode he had witnessed years ago. He knew time was of the essence and that the right treatment was crucial. ***"The antivenom is the only thing that can save you now."***

Within 15 minutes, the sound of sirens filled the air as the ambulance arrived at the site. The paramedics rushed in, quickly assessing the situation. Hariram explained what had happened, showing them the pictures of the snake he had taken on his phone. The medical team wasted no time; ***they carefully transported Vijay to the emergency department*** *in the hospital, where a doctor was already waiting.*

In the emergency room, the doctor reviewed the images and immediately began administering the antisnake venom. The atmosphere was tense, but Hariram remained by Vijay's side, offering words of encouragement. "You are going to be alright, sirji. Just hold on," he said, his voice unwavering.

As the antivenom coursed through Vijay's veins, ***the burning sensation in his leg began to subside.*** *The doctor monitored his vitals closely, and after that felt like an eternity, he turned to Hariram with a reassuring smile. "We have got this under control. Your quick thinking saved his life."*

Vijay, still shaken but grateful, looked at Hariram with new found respect. "I owe you my life, Hariram. Thank you for staying calm and knowing what to do," he said, his voice filled with gratitude.

Hariram smiled modestly. "It is just part of the job, sirji. I am just glad you are okay."

As Vijay recovered, he realized that the bond between him and his foreman had deepened. Hariram's quick actions and knowledge had not only saved his life but also reinforced the importance of being prepared for emergencies. From that day onward, Vijay ensured all his workers received proper training in first aid and emergency response, knowing that in construction business, safety was paramount.

And so on, that bright sunny morning, amidst the chaos of a snake bite, a life was saved, and a lesson was learned—"Sometimes, the most unexpected heroes are those who act when it matters most."

DISCUSSION

Problem Statement

Snakebite is a medical emergency caused when venom (toxic substances) enters the body through a snake's bite. Venomous snakebites can lead to serious problems such as:paralysis (trouble breathing or moving).

- Severe bleeding and internal damage
- Muscle breakdown and kidney failure
- Painful tissue destruction, which may require amputation of a limb.

Globally, over 5.8 billion people are at risk, and snakebites kill 81,000–138,000 people every year. In India alone, snakebites cause about 58,000 deaths annually, with rural areas being the most affected.

EFFECTS OF SNAKE ENVENOMATION

Snakebite is often called a "disease of poverty," because it mostly affects:

- Farmers, fishermen, and outdoor workers
- Children and families living in rural areas.
- People who do not have quick access to medical care or antivenom (Only doctors at a hospital can give antivenom safely).

Most severe outcomes and deaths from snakebites are preventable with timely hospital treatment and antivenom. Lack of awareness and reliance on harmful home remedies increase risks.

In India, f**our main types of venomous snakes are responsible for most bites**. Identifying the snake is not necessary—what matters most is getting to a hospital immediately for proper treatment.

PREHOSPITAL MANAGEMENT OF SNAKE BITE CASE

Prehospital management of snake bite is crucial because timely and appropriate actions taken immediately after the bite can significantly impact the outcome, reducing complications and saving lives.

*The "**Do It Right**" approach to snakebite management is a simple first-aid guideline promoted in India and endorsed by the WHO. It helps community members remember what to do and what not to do after a snakebite.*

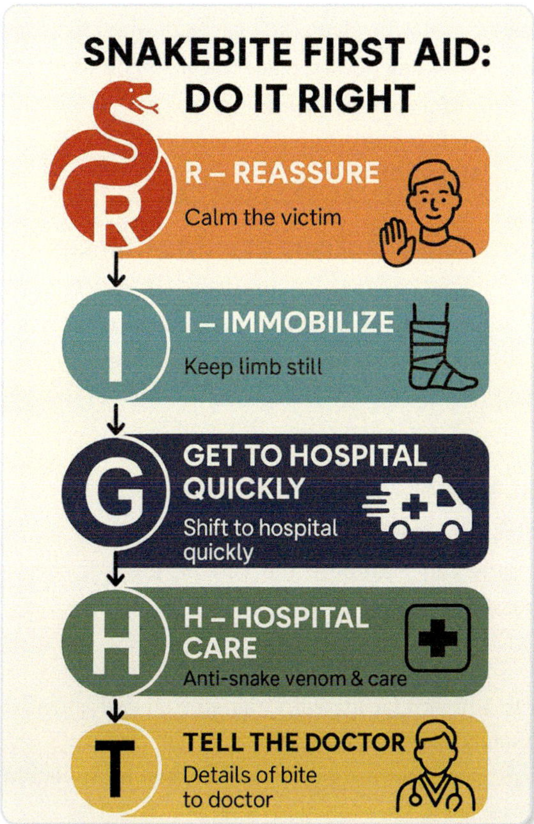

STEPWISE MANAGEMENT BEFORE REACHING HEALTHCARE FACILITY

If you suspect or come across a snake bite victim, then:

- ***Move to Safety:*** Immediately move away from the area where the bite occurred. If the snake is still attached, use a stick or tool to make it let go. Sea snake victims must be moved to dry land to avoid drowning due to lightheadedness after snake bite.
- ***Remove Tight Objects:*** Remove any tight objects around the bitten area (e.g., rings, anklets, bracelets) to prevent complications otherwise swelling occurs.
- ***Reassure the Victim:*** Reassure the victim. Many snake bites are caused by nonvenomous snakes, and even with venomous bites, the risk of immediate death is low.
- ***Immobilize the Victim:*** Completely immobilize the victim. Splint the bitten limb to keep it still, and use a makeshift stretcher to carry the person to transportation for a health facility. This is done to avoid spread of venom with blood stream.
- ***Avoid Tight Tourniquets:*** Never use a tight arterial tourniquet.
- Do not try any bandage unless guided by a doctor—just keep the person calm and still.
- ***Avoid Unsafe First Aid:*** Avoid traditional first aid methods, herbal medicines, and other unproven or unsafe practices.
- ***Seek Medical Help Quickly:*** Transport the victim to a health facility as soon as possible.
- ***Manage Pain:*** Paracetamol may be given for local pain, when the pain is severe.
- ***Position for Vomiting:*** If vomiting occurs, place the victim on their left side in the recovery position.
- ***Monitor Airway and Breathing:*** Closely monitor the airway and breathing, and be prepared to resuscitate, if necessary.

TREATMENT

When to Give Antivenom (Only Doctors at a Hospital can Give Antivenom Safely)

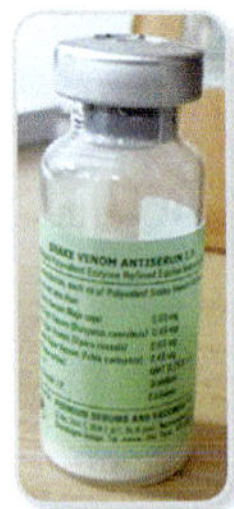

- If the victim shows signs of venom effects, such as uncontrolled bleeding, severe swelling, breathing difficulty, or paralysis, antivenom is required.
- Spontaneous bleeding (like bleeding from gums or wounds) is a key sign of serious envenoming.

Why Timely Treatment Matters

- The "golden hour" (first 1–2 hours) after a snakebite is critical.
- Administering ASV early can neutralize the venom, prevent complications like organ failure or paralysis, and save lives.

Role of Hospitals

- Immediate transfer to a health facility with trained staff and antivenom (Only doctors at a hospital can give antivenom safely) is essential.
- ASV is the only specific antidote that can reverse or stop most venom effects when given promptly and in the correct dose.
- Supportive care, like fluids, pain control, or breathing support, may also be required.

HOW TO AVOID SNAKEBITE

- Wear a closed pair of shoes while going out
- Always use a torch at night. Look where you put your hand or foot.
- Avoid sleeping on the floor and use a well tucked mosquito net.
- Keep home and surroundings clean and clutter free. Control rodent population.
- Create awareness in communities. Helps prevent snakebite.

DO'S & DON'TS

Traditional medicines and other treatments such as wound incision or excision, suction, or application of "black stones" should be avoided.

Do's		Don'ts	
Bitten by a snake, Call the ambulance.		Do not panic. Snakebite is a treatable condition.	
Immobilize the victim. Remove belt, jewelry, watch, rings, etc., as the bitten area may swell.		Say no to faith healing. Do not try to kill or capture the snake.	
If ambulance is delayed, rush to the nearest hospital using any mode of transport.		Do not cut or suck the bitten area.	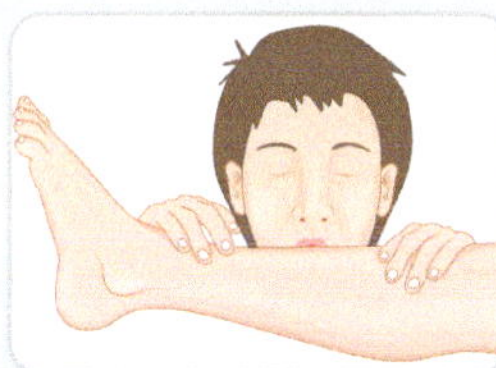
Transport the victim lying on left side, right leg bent, and hand supporting the face. Patient will breathe better and not choke on vomit.	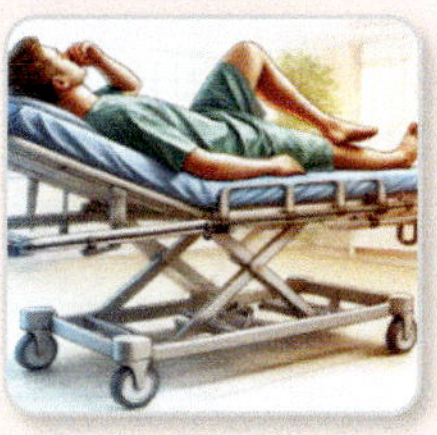	Do not tie a tourniquet, apply ice, or massage the bitten area as it causes further damage.	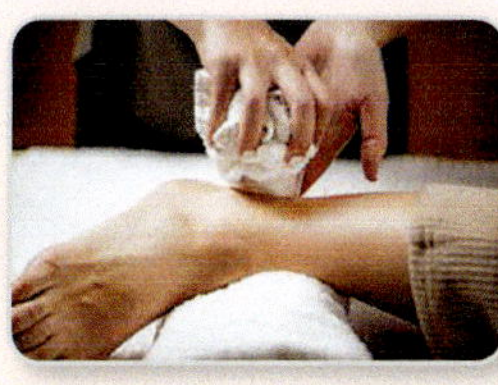

Do's	Don'ts
Inform the doctor details of the bite. Antivenom is the only cure. 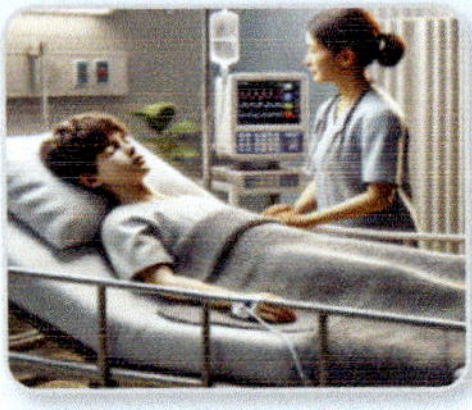	Do not self-medicate or apply any herbs or spices. Nothing helps. 

CONCLUSION

- Snakebite is a medical emergency—but it is treatable.
- Do not waste time on cutting, sucking, or home remedies.
- Stay calm, keep the victim still, and reach a hospital quickly.
- Every minute counts—the golden hour saves lives.

Scan to watch Dr Lokendra's 1-minute reel on this emergency.

Chapter 28

SCORPION BITE

"WHEN THE STING STRIKES": SCORPION BITE (STING) EMERGENCY

Story: The Midnight Sting

It was a humid summer night in rural Maharashtra when 7-year-old Kavya let out a sudden, piercing scream as she climbed into bed. Her bare foot had brushed against a scorpion hiding in a corner of the bed, and within seconds, ***she felt a sharp, burning pain shoot through her leg.***

Her parents rushed to her side and saw ***a red, swollen mark with severe pain****. Kavya began crying uncontrollably, clutching her foot. Instead of panicking, her parents recalled what they had learned during a village health camp:*

- **They did not tie a tourniquet** *(which can worsen tissue damage).*
- **They avoided home remedies** *like* ***applying oils, chemicals, or cutting the sting site.***
- *They immediately* ***wrapped her foot lightly*** *and rushed to the nearest health center.*

By the time they reached the clinic, Kavya was showing ***serious symptoms—drowsiness, sweating, fast heart rate, and difficulty breathing****. The medical team quickly recognized the signs of* ***scorpion envenomation*** *and started life-saving treatment, including antivenom and supportive care.*

Within hours, her pain reduced, her heartbeat stabilized, and she began to recover. Doctors later told her family that ***their quick action and avoidance of harmful practices saved valuable time and possibly her life.***

Kavya's midnight ordeal was a wake-up call for the entire village: ***Scorpion stings, though common in rural homes, can be deadly if not treated immediately by trained medical professionals****.*

WHAT IS A SCORPION BITE (STING)?

A scorpion bite is actually a sting that injects venom. While most stings cause only pain and swelling, some species—especially in India—can cause life-threatening symptoms such as heart and respiratory complications, particularly in children and the elderly.

Signs and Symptoms

Local Symptoms

- Immediate intense pain or burning at the sting site
- Swelling, redness, or numbness
- Tingling or twitching near the area

Severe (Systemic) Symptoms

- Excessive sweating or salivation
- Vomiting or abdominal pain
- Restlessness, anxiety, or drowsiness
- Fast heart rate, high or low blood pressure
- Breathing difficulty or chest tightness
- Seizures (rare but serious)

Causes/Risk Factors

- Sleeping on floors or in open areas without protection
- Storing bedding or clothes on the ground
- Reaching into dark corners, shoes, or under rocks
- Scorpions are more active during monsoon and warm seasons

STEPWISE FIRST AID BEFORE REACHING A HOSPITAL

Remain calm and prevent panic.

- ***Step 1:*** Reassure the Person and Limit Movement
  - » Keep the sting site at heart level or slightly lowered.
  - » Avoid unnecessary movement to slow venom spread.

- ***Step 2:*** Wash the Area Gently
  - » Use soap and water to reduce infection risk.
- ***Step 3:*** Apply a Cold Pack
  - » Wrap ice in a cloth and apply near the sting site to relieve pain.
  - » Avoid applying ice directly to skin or immersing in ice water.
- ***Step 4:*** Do NOT Use Tourniquets or Cut the Site
  - » These can cause further injury or worsen the condition.
- ***Step 5:*** Rush to the Nearest Hospital
  - » Especially if the victim is a child or shows systemic symptoms. Note the time of sting and description of the scorpion if possible.

WHEN TO SEE A DOCTOR?

- Any scorpion sting in children, elderly, or pregnant women
- Signs of sweating, vomiting, or abnormal heart rate
- Breathing difficulty, seizures, or unconsciousness
- Intense pain not relieved by simple measures

PREVENTION TIPS

MYTHS AND FACTS

Myths	Facts
Tying a tight band above the sting prevents venom spread.	It reduces blood flow and can cause more damage.
Sucking out the venom helps.	Ineffective and potentially dangerous.

Myths	Facts
Home remedies like turmeric or herbs can treat it.	Only medical care and antivenom (if needed) can help.
Scorpion bites are always fatal.	Most are not—but prompt care is key to survival.

CONCLUSION

Scorpion bites, though often feared, can be effectively managed with timely recognition and appropriate medical care. Most stings are mild and self-limiting, but some can cause life-threatening complications, especially in children and vulnerable individuals. The key lies in early first aid, rapid transfer to a hospital, and administration of specific treatment when required. Public awareness about what to do—and equally, what not to do—after a sting is vital in preventing unnecessary deaths. By combining community education, prompt medical response, and access to antivenom where indicated, the burden of scorpion envenomation can be greatly reduced. Ultimately, empowering people with knowledge and ensuring timely care transforms a potentially fatal event into a survivable one.

Scan to watch Dr Lokendra's 1-minute reel on this emergency.

Chapter 29

ANIMAL BITES (DOG, MONKEY, ETC.)

ANIMAL BITES: PREVENTION, AWARENESS, AND EFFECTIVE TREATMENT

Story: Bobby's Encounter with Rabies

*It was a warm afternoon when **14-year-old Bobby** went to the local park to play with his friends. While chasing after a ball, an aggressive stray dog suddenly appeared and bit his leg, leaving deep puncture wounds. Bobby cried out in pain, and the scene quickly drew the attention of nearby adults.*

*One alert bystander immediately **washed the wound with running water and soap for nearly 15 minutes**—a crucial first step to reduce the risk of infection. They then covered the wound with a clean cloth and rushed Bobby home.*

*Bobby's parents, having attended a recent community health session, knew that rabies is a deadly but preventable disease. They were aware that timely rabies vaccine and rabies immunoglobulin (antibodies) are essential after any animal bite. They also knew **where these life-saving treatments were available** and insisted on receiving them as soon as they reached the hospital.*

At the emergency department, doctors quickly assessed Bobby's injury and confirmed the parents' decision. He was given:

- *Rabies vaccine (post-exposure prophylaxis),*
- *Rabies immunoglobulin injections around the wound*
- *A tetanus booster,*
- *Antibiotics to prevent infection.*

Thanks to this swift response and the parents' awareness, Bobby's risk of rabies was completely eliminated. His experience became an important lesson in his community:

Never delay first aid or vaccination after an animal bite.

Knowing where rabies treatment is available can save critical time and save lives.

PROBLEM STATEMENT

In India, human rabies is still endemic, and 20,000 people are thought to die from the disease annually, according to recent estimates. Dog bites are responsible for the majority of these deaths (about 97%), although normal surveillance systems do not report or notify animal bites. Consequently, due to a subpar surveillance and reporting system, the country's data on animal bites is sparse, erratic, and contentious.

It was found that:

- Dogs were the main biting animal, affecting mostly the children and men from poor communities.
- The pet dog care and management were not satisfactory.
- The bite victims did not do proper wound care and mostly depended on Government Hospitals for antirabies vaccination and majority did not complete the full course.
- The use of life saving rabies immunoglobulins (RIGs) was abysmally low.
- The indigenous treatment including harmful applicants to wounds was quite prevalent.
- All these call for concerted efforts for a mass awareness campaign.

STEPWISE APPROACH TO MANAGE ANIMAL BITE

Wound Preparation

Washing immediately with soap and water for 15 minutes is essential to facilitate detailed examination, ensure the full extent of the injury is visible, and minimize the risk of infection. Proper management of the wound is crucial for preventing infection and is of utmost importance in the prevention of rabies. Apply direct pressure to the wound if it is actively bleeding, to control the bleeding.

Do's		
Physical	• Wash with running water 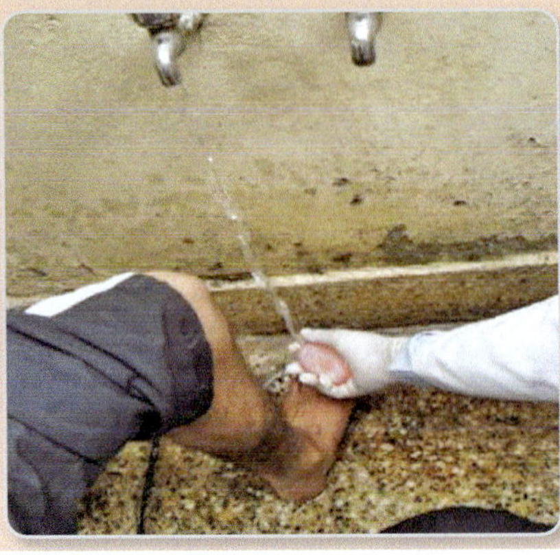	• Mechanical removal of virus from the wound(s)

Contd...

Contd...

Chemical	• Wash the wound(s) with soap and water • Apply disinfectant 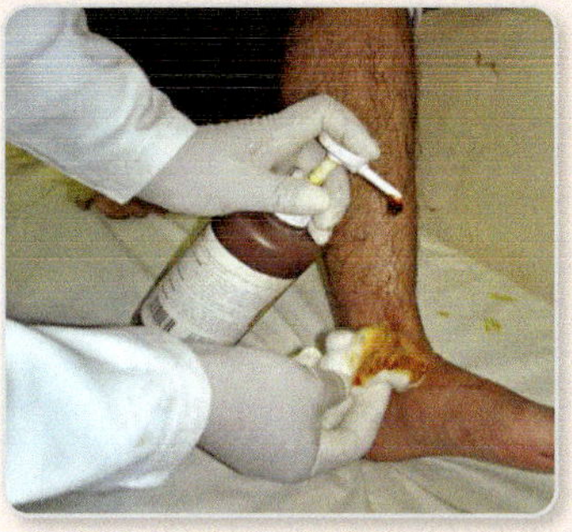	• Inactivation of the virus
Biological	• Infiltrate immunoglobulin into the depth and around the wound(s) in Category III exposures 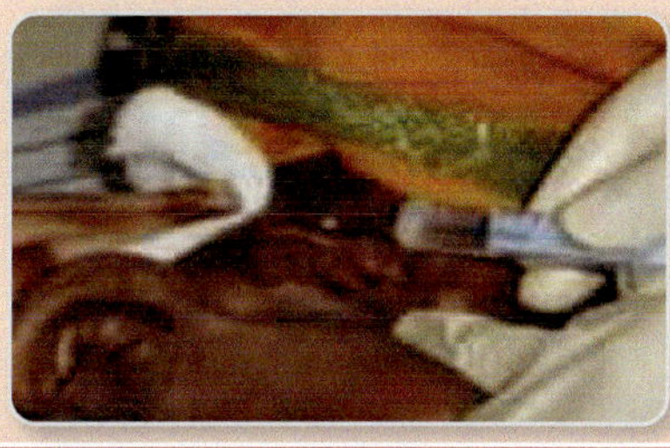	• Neutralization of the virus
Dont's		
• Touch the wound(s) with bare hand. • Apply irritants like soil, chilies, oil, lime, herbs, chalk, betel leaves, etc.		

Courtesy: National Rabies Control Program.

Wound closure: For the majority of individuals with bite wounds that are not infected, we recommend allowing these wounds to heal naturally through secondary intention, rather than opting for primary closure.

The decision on how to manage the closure of a bite wound—whether to opt for immediate primary closure, allow for natural healing through secondary intention, or consider delayed primary closure—should be tailored to the specific characteristics of the wound and will be decided by the emergency physicians.

Wounds that require specialized referral to a tertiary care center are:

- Facial wounds due to cosmetic concerns.
- Bites where there is a possibility of a foreign body in the wound.
- Wide gaping wounds which would benefit from closure.
- Devitalized wounds where debridement is required.
- Bites where the severity of the injury is difficult to assess.
- People with severe cellulitis, or with infected bite wounds that are not responding to treatment, or who are systemically unwell.

- People with an increased risk of infection—including those with diabetes or cirrhosis, those who are immunocompromised.
- Bites that might need reconstructive surgery.
- Any wound where an underlying bony fracture is considered (e.g., children with scalp wounds requiring radiological assessment).
- Bites to poorly vascularized areas, e.g., ear cartilage/nose cartilage.

Rabies Vaccine and Immunoglobulin

Postexposure prophylaxis will be decided by an emergency physician on the basis of category of wound (as shown in the table given in the following text).

- *Rabies vaccine:* The Essen regimen (1-1-1-1-1) which is a five-dose intramuscular schedule is followed in India. Five doses are given on the arm (deltoid region) on days 0, 3, 7, 14, and 28. In infants and young children anterolateral aspect of the thigh is preferred.
- *Rabies immunoglobulin:* Refer to emergency physician to get the patient administered rabies immunoglobulin which will provide passive immunization and immediate protection from the bite.

Category	Type of contact	Recommended post-exposure prophylaxis
I	• Touching or feeding of animals • Licks on intact skin • Contact of intact skin with secretions/ excretions of rabid animal/human case	• None, if reliable case history is available
II	• Nibbling of uncovered skin • Minor scratches or abrasions without bleeding 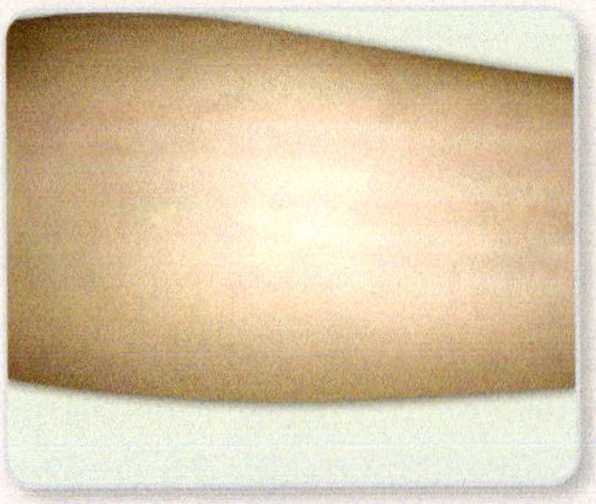	• Wound management • Antirabies vaccine
III	• Single or multiple transdermal bites or scratches, licks on broken skin 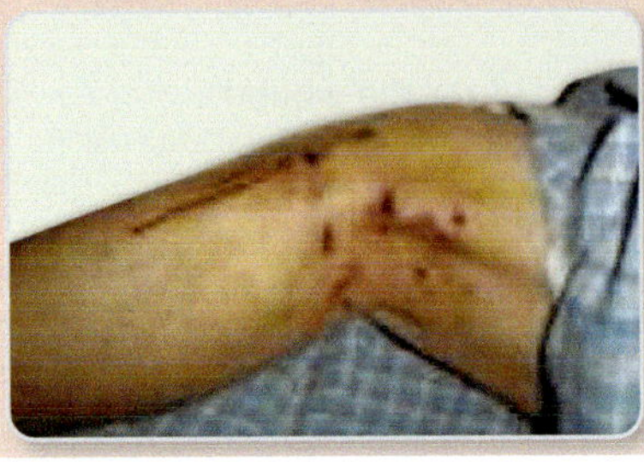	• Wound management • Rabies immunoglobulin • Antirabies vaccine

Contd...

Contd...

Category	Type of contact	Recommended post-exposure prophylaxis
	• Contamination or mucous membrane with saliva (i.e., licks) 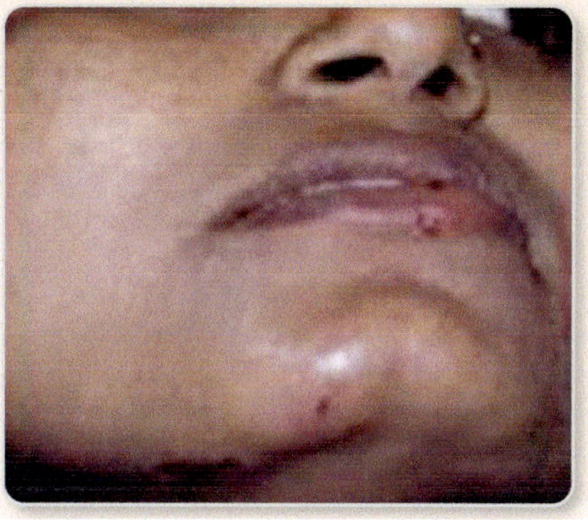	

Courtesy: National Rabies Control Program.

STEPWISE APPROACH AFTER AN ANIMAL BITE

MYTHS AND FACTS

Myths	Facts
Immediate wound closure is best.	Immediate closure can trap rabies virus in the wound, increasing the risk of infection. It is often better to clean and leave the wound slightly open, especially for puncture wounds.
All dog bites need antibiotics.	Not all dog bites require antibiotics. The decision depends on the wound's severity, location, and the victim's health status. High-risk wounds, however, may need prophylactic antibiotics.
Applying alcohol or hydrogen peroxide is the best way to clean a bite.	Using alcohol or hydrogen peroxide can actually irritate and damage the tissue. Cleaning with mild soap and water is recommended for initial wound care.
Dog bites do not require medical attention if the dog is known and vaccinated.	All dog bites should be evaluated by a healthcare professional to assess the risk of infection and determine if further treatment, such as a tetanus booster or rabies prophylaxis, is necessary.
Suturing dog bite wounds is always recommended.	Suturing is not always recommended, especially for puncture wounds or wounds with a high risk of infection. Each case should be evaluated individually.
Rabies shots are needed for every dog bite.	Rabies prophylaxis is recommended based on the dog's vaccination status, the bite's location, and the local prevalence of rabies. Not every dog bite necessitates rabies shots.
A tetanus shot is unnecessary if you have had one in the past.	Tetanus booster shots may be necessary if the last vaccination was >5 years ago and the wound is deep or dirty.
Dog saliva has healing properties.	Dog saliva contains viruses and bacteria that can cause infections. It is a myth that it has healing properties for human wounds.
Only large or deep bites are at risk of infection.	Even small scratches or puncture wounds from dog bites can become infected. All dog bites should be properly cleaned and monitored for signs of infection.
If the wound stops bleeding on its own, it does not need any medical attention.	Bleeding is just one aspect of the wound. All dog bites require evaluation for infection risk, potential for rabies or tetanus, and appropriate wound care.

CONCLUSION

Bobby's story shows us why quick action after an animal bite can save lives.

A dog bite can spread rabies, a deadly disease—but it is 100% preventable with timely treatment.

What to do immediately:

- Wash the wound with soap and water for at least 15 minutes.
- Visit a doctor right away—do not wait.
- Start the anti-rabies vaccine series as advised.

Why it matters:

- Rabies has no cure once symptoms appear.
- Early vaccination after a bite can save your life.

How communities stay safe:

- Vaccinate pet dogs and cats.
- Report stray dog bites quickly.
- Spread awareness—saving one life saves many.

Remember: Quick treatment + vaccination = Protection from rabies.

Scan to watch Dr Lokendra's 1-minute reel on this emergency.

Chapter 30

INSECT STINGS

"WHEN THE SMALLEST STING STRIKES": COMMON INSECT STINGS (NONALLERGIC REACTIONS)

Story: The Garden Sting

It was a bright morning when 9-year-old Aarav joined his grandfather in the garden to help water the plants. As he reached near a flowering bush, he suddenly cried out in pain—a ***wasp had stung his arm. Within minutes, the skin around the sting turned red, swollen, and itchy.***

Fortunately, Aarav showed no signs of breathing difficulty, dizziness, or severe allergic reaction. His grandfather, staying calm, followed simple first aid steps:

- ***Washed the sting site thoroughly*** with soap and water to prevent infection.
- *Applied a* ***cold compress*** *(a wet cloth with ice) to reduce swelling and pain*
- *Aarav was kept under observation for the next hour to ensure there were no serious symptoms, such as* ***facial swelling, vomiting, or breathing issues.*** *Soon, the redness and swelling began to subside, and he was playing again by afternoon.*

The family realized that ***most insect stings are harmless and can be treated at home*** *with calm, prompt action. Knowing the difference between a* ***mild reaction*** *and a* ***severe allergic reaction (anaphylaxis)*** *is key to avoiding unnecessary panic.*

WHAT ARE COMMON INSECT STINGS (NONALLERGIC REACTIONS)?

Insect stings from bees, wasps, or ants usually cause local pain, redness, and swelling. Most people experience only minor reactions that can be managed at home with simple first aid. These stings are not life-threatening unless symptoms worsen.

Signs and Symptoms

- Sharp, immediate pain at the sting site
- Redness and mild swelling
- Itching or burning sensation
- Small raised bump or welt
- Tenderness lasting a few hours to a day

Causes/Risk Factors

- Outdoor activity in gardens, parks, or fields
- Disturbing insect nests (wasps, bees, and ants)
- Wearing bright colors or sweet scents
- Going barefoot or handling plants and soil

STEPWISE FIRST AID BEFORE REACHING A HOSPITAL

Most stings improve with simple steps.

- ***Step 1:*** Remove the stinger (if visible)
  - » Gently scrape with a card or blunt edge—avoid squeezing.
- ***Step 2:*** Wash the area with soap and water
  - » Prevents infection and soothes irritation.
- ***Step 3:*** Apply a cold compress
  - » Reduces pain and swelling. Use for 10–15 minutes.
- ***Step 4:*** Give an antihistamine (if advised)
  - » Helps relieve itching and minor swelling.
- ***Step 5:*** Avoid scratching the site
  - » Scratching can cause further irritation or infection.

WHEN TO SEE A DOCTOR?

- Pain or swelling persists beyond 2–3 days
- *Signs of infection:* Pus, warmth, or spreading redness
- Sting near the eye or inside the mouth
- Multiple stings in children or elderly

- Pain or swelling persists beyond 2–3 days
- Signs of infection: pus, warmth, or spreading redness
- Sting near the eye or inside the mouth
- Multiple stings in children or elderly
- Difficulty breathing, dizziness, chest tightness, or swelling of lips/tongue—may indicate anaphylaxis
- Rapidly spreading swelling

MYTHS AND FACTS

Myths	Facts
You must suck out the venom.	Sucking the site is ineffective and can introduce infection.
Home remedies like turmeric are enough.	Washing, cooling, and antihistamines are more effective.
All stings are dangerous.	Most are harmless and heal with basic care.
You must always visit a hospital.	Most mild stings do not need medical care unless symptoms worsen.

PREVENTION TIPS

- Wear covered clothes and shoes while outdoors.
- Avoid disturbing nests or hives.
- Use insect repellent when necessary.
- Shake out clothes and shoes before wearing them.
- Teach children to avoid playing near flowering plants or trash bins.

CONCLUSION

- "Most stings just sting—but they do not have to scare."
- Stay calm, follow simple steps, and know when to watch for signs. Nature's little bites can be managed with a little knowledge and care.

Scan to watch Dr Lokendra's 1-minute reel on this emergency.

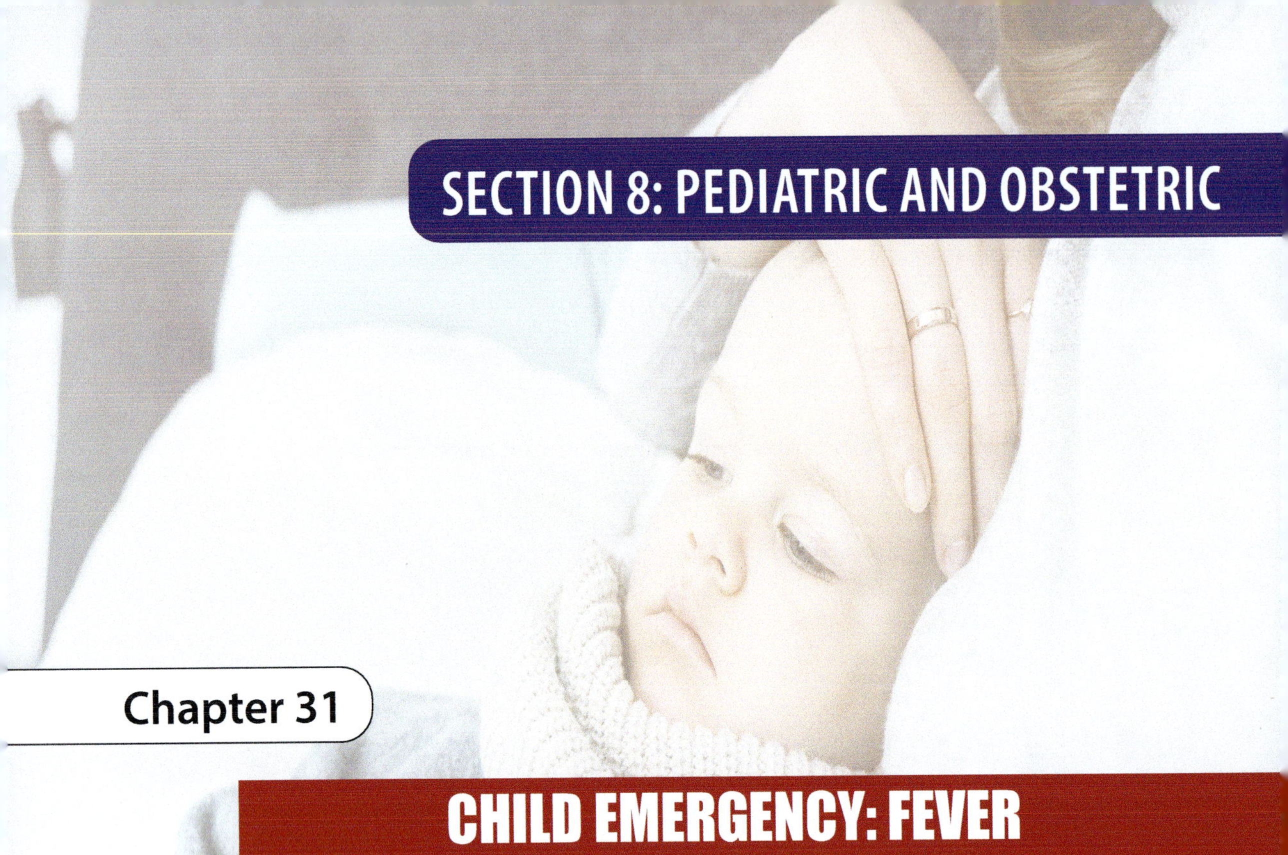

SECTION 8: PEDIATRIC AND OBSTETRIC

Chapter 31

CHILD EMERGENCY: FEVER WITH CONVULSIONS

"WHEN FEVER SPARKS FITS"—CHILD EMERGENCY: FEVER WITH CONVULSIONS

Story: The Mother's Midnight Scare

It was past midnight when Meera noticed that her ***2-year-old son****, Aarav, was restless and unusually warm. As she prepared to sponge him, the thermometer beeped—his fever had spiked to 103°F. Just as she reached for the medicines, Aarav* ***suddenly stiffened. His tiny body arched, his eyes rolled back, and he began to jerk violently in repeated convulsions.***

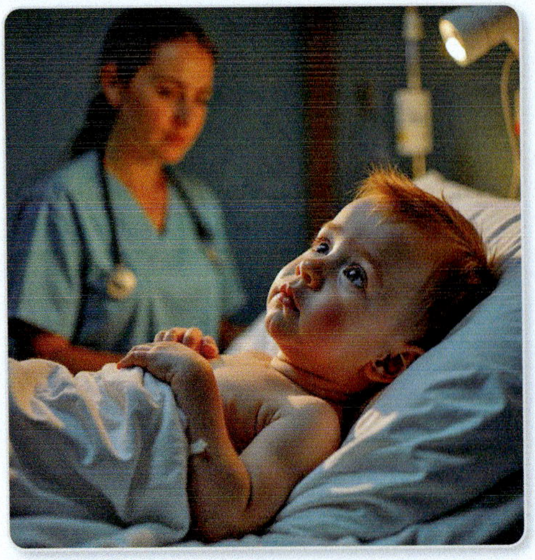

For a moment, Meera froze in terror. She had heard of febrile seizures but never imagined seeing one happen to her own child. Yet, ***she recalled her pediatrician's advice and resisted the urge to panic.***

She placed Aarav on his side on a flat, safe surface, ensuring there were no hard or sharp objects nearby.

She made sure his airway was clear and kept ***his head slightly tilted to allow saliva or vomit to drain out.*** *Most importantly, she did not put anything in his mouth, knowing this could cause choking or injury.*

She timed the seizure, staying calm, and after a tense minute, the jerking stopped on its own.

Meera ***sponged Aarav with room temperature water to bring down his fever*** *and rushed him to the nearest emergency department. There, doctors confirmed it was a febrile seizure—a common but frightening condition in toddlers, usually* ***triggered by a sudden spike in body temperature.*** *Aarav was monitored, treated for his fever, and discharged with clear guidance on what to do if it ever happened again.*

Later, the pediatrician praised Meera's quick and correct response, explaining that parents' actions during those first few minutes of a seizure can prevent complications and injuries. Meera, still shaken but relieved, said, ***"I realized that staying calm and knowing what to do made all the difference that night."***

WHAT IS FEVER WITH CONVULSIONS (FEBRILE SEIZURE)?

Febrile seizures are convulsions triggered by a sudden rise in body temperature, commonly seen in children aged 6 months–5 years. Although scary to witness, most febrile seizures are harmless and do not indicate epilepsy or brain damage.

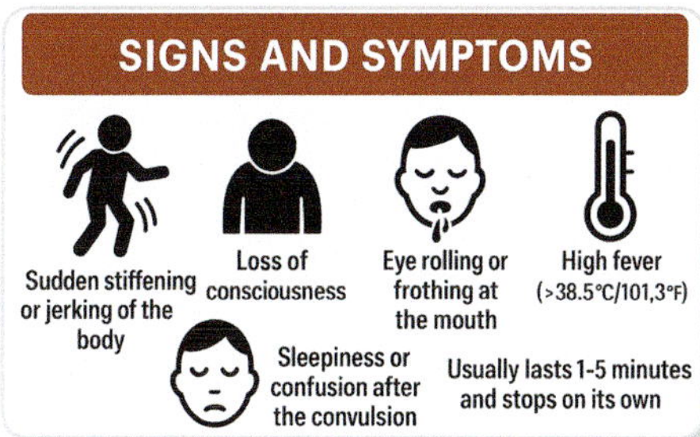

Causes/Risk Factors

- Rapid rise in temperature (due to viral or bacterial infections)
- Family history of febrile seizures
- Recent vaccinations (rarely)
- Common in age group 6 months–5 years

STEPWISE FIRST AID BEFORE REACHING A HOSPITAL

Stay calm and protect the child from injury.

- ***Step 1****:* Place the child on their side
  - » On a flat, safe surface to prevent choking.
  - » Turn their head to one side to let saliva drain.
- ***Step 2****:* Do not restrain or shake the child
  - » Allow the seizure to run its course.
  - » Remove nearby hard or sharp objects.

- ***Step 3:*** Do not put anything in the mouth
  - No spoon, finger, or liquid—this may cause choking.
- ***Step 4:*** Time the seizure
  - Most last <5 minutes.
  - If it exceeds 5 minutes, seek emergency help immediately.
- ***Step 5:*** Lower the fever after seizure ends
  - Sponge the child with lukewarm water. ***Never use ice water or alcohol rubs.***
  - Administer fever medicine (e.g., paracetamol) as prescribed.
- ***Step 6****:* Visit a hospital for evaluation
  - Even if the child seems well afterward. ***Hospital visit is mandatory after first seizure***

WHEN TO SEE A DOCTOR?

- First-time seizure in a child
- Seizure lasting >5 minutes
- Child not waking up or breathing properly after the seizure
- Stiff neck, persistent vomiting, or abnormal behavior
- Repeated seizures in a short time

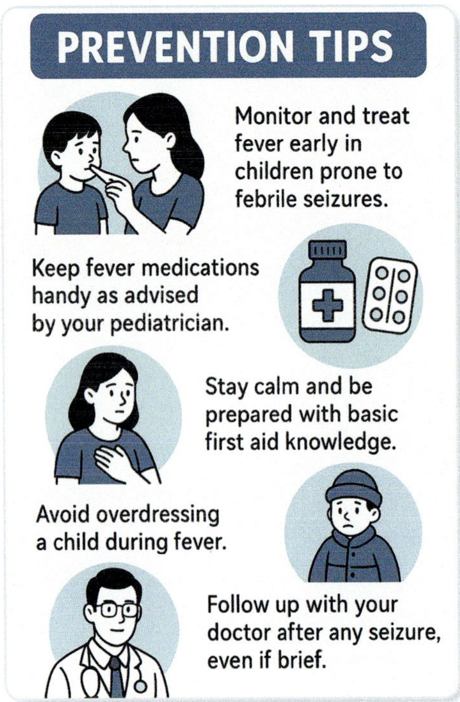

MYTHS AND FACTS

Myths	Facts
Child can swallow their tongue during a seizure.	This is not true—never put anything in their mouth.
You should give fever medicine during the seizure.	Wait until the seizure stops, then manage fever.
All seizures mean epilepsy.	Febrile seizures are not epilepsy and usually resolve with age.
Pouring water on a seizing child helps.	Focus on safety and side positioning instead.

REMEMBER (FOR PARENTS)

Most febrile seizures are short and harmless. Stay calm, follow first aid, and see a doctor immediately. Panic can cause more harm than the seizure itself.

CONCLUSION

- "Fever fits can be frightening—but they are often harmless when handled right."
- Knowing what to do in the moment can protect your child from injury and give you the confidence to stay calm. Be prepared, not panicked.

Scan to watch Dr Lokendra's 1-minute reel on this emergency.

Chapter 32

PREGNANCY EMERGENCIES: BLEEDING AND LABOR PAINS

"WHEN EVERY MINUTE COUNTS"—PREGNANCY EMERGENCIES: BLEEDING AND LABOR PAINS

Story: The Unexpected Labor

It was a peaceful afternoon when ***Ritika, in her eighth month of pregnancy****, sat on the couch reading. Suddenly, she felt an intense, stabbing pain low in her abdomen, followed by a warm gush of blood. Fear gripped her as she realized this wasn't normal.*

Her husband, Raj, ***immediately sprang into action.*** *He carefully helped Ritika lie down on her left side, with her legs slightly elevated, ensuring minimal movement to avoid worsening the bleeding. He avoided giving her food or water, knowing that* ***she might need emergency surgery.*** *While keeping her calm and speaking reassuringly, he dialed emergency services.*

*Within minutes, an ambulance arrived and rushed Ritika to the hospital. The medical team acted swiftly, diagnosing placental detaching—****a dangerous complication where the placenta partially or completely detaches***

from the uterus *before delivery. This condition can cut off oxygen and nutrients to the baby and cause severe bleeding in the mother.*

An emergency delivery was performed, and fortunately, both Ritika and her baby survived. The doctors praised Raj's prompt actions—keeping Ritika still, ***controlling panic, and calling for rapid transport****—as key factors that prevented a tragedy.*

For the couple, ***this was a life-changing reminder that pregnancy emergencies can occur without warning, and every minute truly counts.***

WHAT ARE PREGNANCY EMERGENCIES: BLEEDING AND LABOR PAINS?

Bleeding or abdominal pain during pregnancy may be signs of serious complications, especially in the second or third trimester. It may indicate miscarriage, placental detaching, or preterm labor. Recognizing these symptoms early and seeking emergency care can save the life of both mother and baby.

Signs and Symptoms

Emergency warning signs in pregnancy:

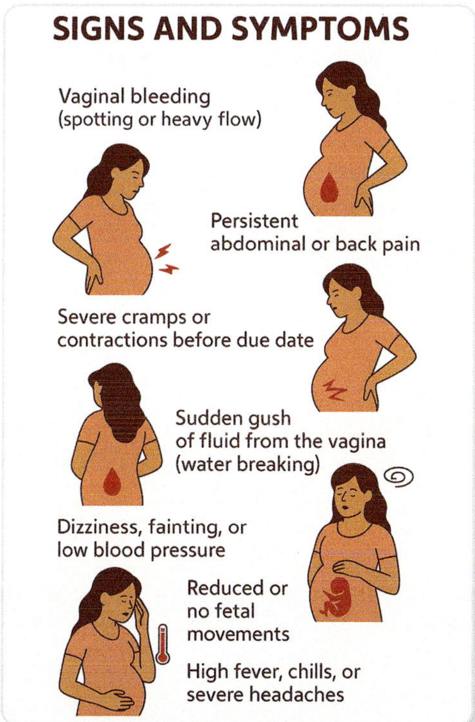

Causes/Risk Factors

- Placental detaching
- Preterm labor
- Infections or urinary tract issues

- Ectopic pregnancy or miscarriage
- High blood pressure or preeclampsia
- Trauma or fall during pregnancy
- Multiple pregnancies or past obstetric complications

STEPWISE FIRST AID BEFORE REACHING A HOSPITAL

Keep the mother calm and minimize movement.

- ***Step 1:*** Help her lie down on her side (left preferred)
  - » This improves blood flow to the uterus and baby.
- ***Step 2:*** Do not insert anything vaginally
  - » Avoid internal examination or sanitary products—wait for doctors.
- ***Step 3:*** Avoid giving food or water
  - » In case emergency surgery is needed.
- ***Step 4:*** Call for an ambulance (112/108)
  - » Clearly state that it is a pregnancy emergency and provide gestational age.
- ***Step 5:*** Note key details
  - » Gestation weeks, onset of symptoms, and previous complications.
  - » Amount and type of bleeding or discharge.
- ***Step 6:*** Reassure and monitor
  - » Keep the environment quiet and calm.
  - » Continue to observe her consciousness and breathing.

WHEN TO SEE A DOCTOR?

- Any bleeding during pregnancy
- Painful or premature contractions
- Water breaking before 37 weeks
- Reduced fetal movements
- Symptoms of high blood pressure (headache, swelling, and blurred vision)

MYTHS AND FACTS

Myths	Facts
Spotting in pregnancy is always normal.	Any bleeding should be evaluated to rule out complications.
Labor pain always begins near the due date.	Preterm labor can happen any time after 20 weeks.
You can wait and watch for a few hours.	Delay in care may risk both mother and baby's life.
Eating or drinking is fine in early labor.	Emergency surgery may require an empty stomach—avoid food until seen by a doctor.

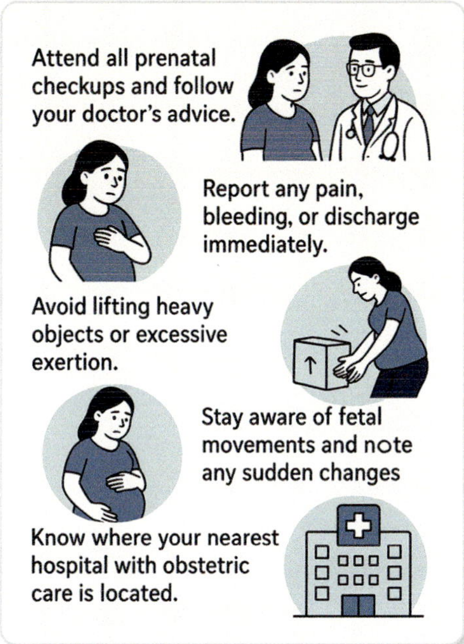

CONCLUSION

Bleeding or severe pain during pregnancy is never normal and should not be ignored. It can sometimes mean danger for the mother or the baby. Whether it happens early or late in pregnancy, it is always safest to see a doctor right away.

If pains start too early, it could be a sign of preterm labor; if bleeding occurs, it might be due to serious problems like miscarriage or issues with the placenta. Quick action—calling for help, reaching a hospital, and not waiting at home—can save lives.

Remember: In pregnancy, whenever there is unexpected bleeding or strong pains, act fast and seek medical care immediately.

Scan to watch Dr Lokendra's 1-minute reel on this emergency.

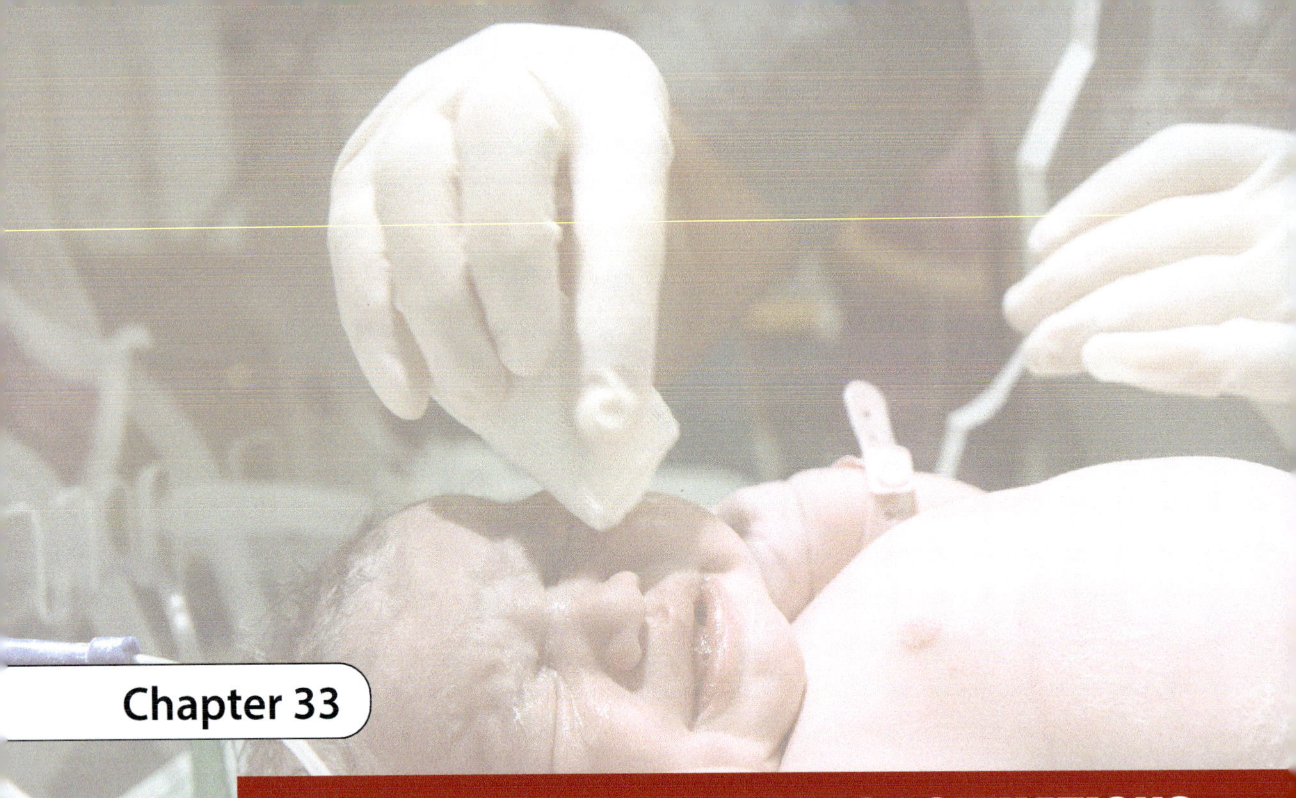

Chapter 33

CHILDBIRTH IN EMERGENCY SITUATIONS

CHILDBIRTH IN EMERGENCY SITUATIONS

Real Story: Gauri's Near-disaster Delivery

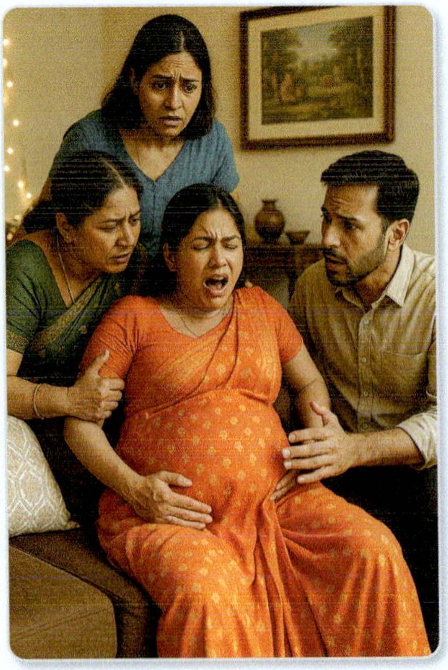

It was a festive evening in Gauri's home, filled with excitement. At 26 years old and 37 weeks pregnant, she was carrying her first child after years of waiting. Suddenly, she screamed in pain—her water had broken and heavy bleeding started. She was in severe labor with complications.

Panic spread in the house. The nearest hospital was 16 kilometers away, and Gauri's contractions were coming every two minutes. Her mother-in-law cried, "What if we don't reach on time? What if she bleeds too much?"

At that critical moment, Rekha, a trained auxiliary nurse midwife (ANM), rushed in. She immediately recognized the signs of danger.

"Do not panic," Rekha said firmly. "We must reach the hospital as quickly as possible—both mother and baby's lives depend on it."

She quickly:

- *Checked Gauri's pulse, blood pressure, and bleeding.*
- *Applied clean pads to reduce infection risk and control bleeding.*

- *Instructed the family to call an ambulance immediately and prepare the car for transport.*
- *Repeatedly reminded the family that hospital care is the safest option.*

During transport, Gauri's condition worsened. Her pain grew unbearable, and the baby's head began to crown before they could reach the hospital. In that rare, life-threatening emergency, Rekha—an experienced healthcare worker—was forced to assist with the delivery inside the vehicle.

With her skills, she managed to guide the baby out safely, clear the airway, and wrap him in clean cloth. But she continued urging, "We must reach the hospital quickly for proper care".

At the hospital, doctors immediately provided oxygen, IV fluids, blood transfusion support, and specialist care—interventions that no one could provide outside. Only then were both mother and baby out of danger.

Key Message

- *Childbirth should always take place in a hospital under trained doctors and nurses.*
- *Only in extreme emergencies, and only if an experienced healthcare worker is present, should delivery be attempted outside.*

STEPWISE MANAGEMENT BEFORE REACHING A HOSPITAL

- ***Step 1***: *Stay calm*
  - » Panic helps no one.
  - » Stay calm and speak reassuringly to the mother.
- ***Step 2***: *Call for help*
  - » Contact a nearby ANM, ASHA worker, or ambulance service (e.g., 102 or 108 in India).
- ***Step 3***: *Position the mother*
  - » Lay her on her back with knees bent and legs apart.
  - » Use clean towels or bedsheets.
- ***Step 4:*** *Maintain hygiene*
  - » Use clean hands, gloves if available.
  - » Ensure the mother's private area is clean.
- ***Step 5***: *Monitor labor*
  - » If pains are coming very quickly, less than 3 minutes apart.
- ***Step 6:*** *Prepare for delivery (if imminent)*
  - » Hold the baby's head carefully as it comes out. Never pull.
  - » Once born, clean the baby, tie/cut the cord only with sterile tools.
  - » Keep the baby warm.

- ***Step 7***: *Transport safely*
  » Even after delivery, both mother and child must go to the hospital for further care.

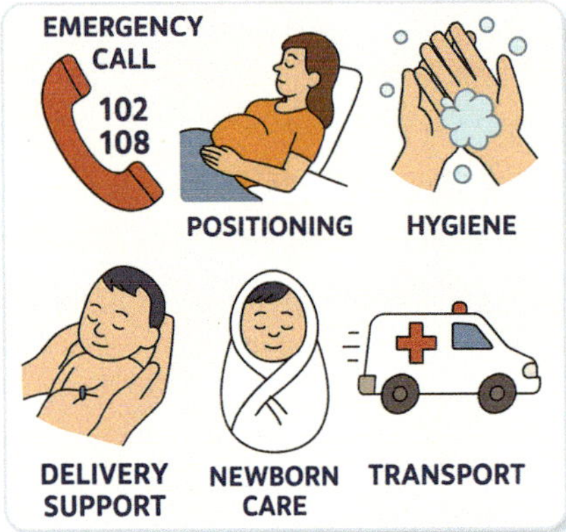

MYTHS AND FACTS

Myths	Facts
"Water breaking means there is still time."	Water breaking can mean delivery is near; delay can risk infection.
"It is dangerous to move the mother during labor."	With proper support, movement is often essential for getting medical help.
"The umbilical cord must be cut immediately."	It is best to wait for a few minutes or until professional care is available, unless necessary.
"Emergency deliveries are always harmful."	With correct steps and hygiene, even emergency births can be safe.

CONCLUSION

- Emergencies do not knock before arriving. Gauri's story teaches us that preparedness, basic knowledge, and trained community health workers can make the difference between life and death.
- Let us spread awareness, train more hands, and never let distance or fear stop a safe delivery. Every life counts—and every minute matters.

Scan to watch Dr Lokendra's 1-minute reel on this emergency.

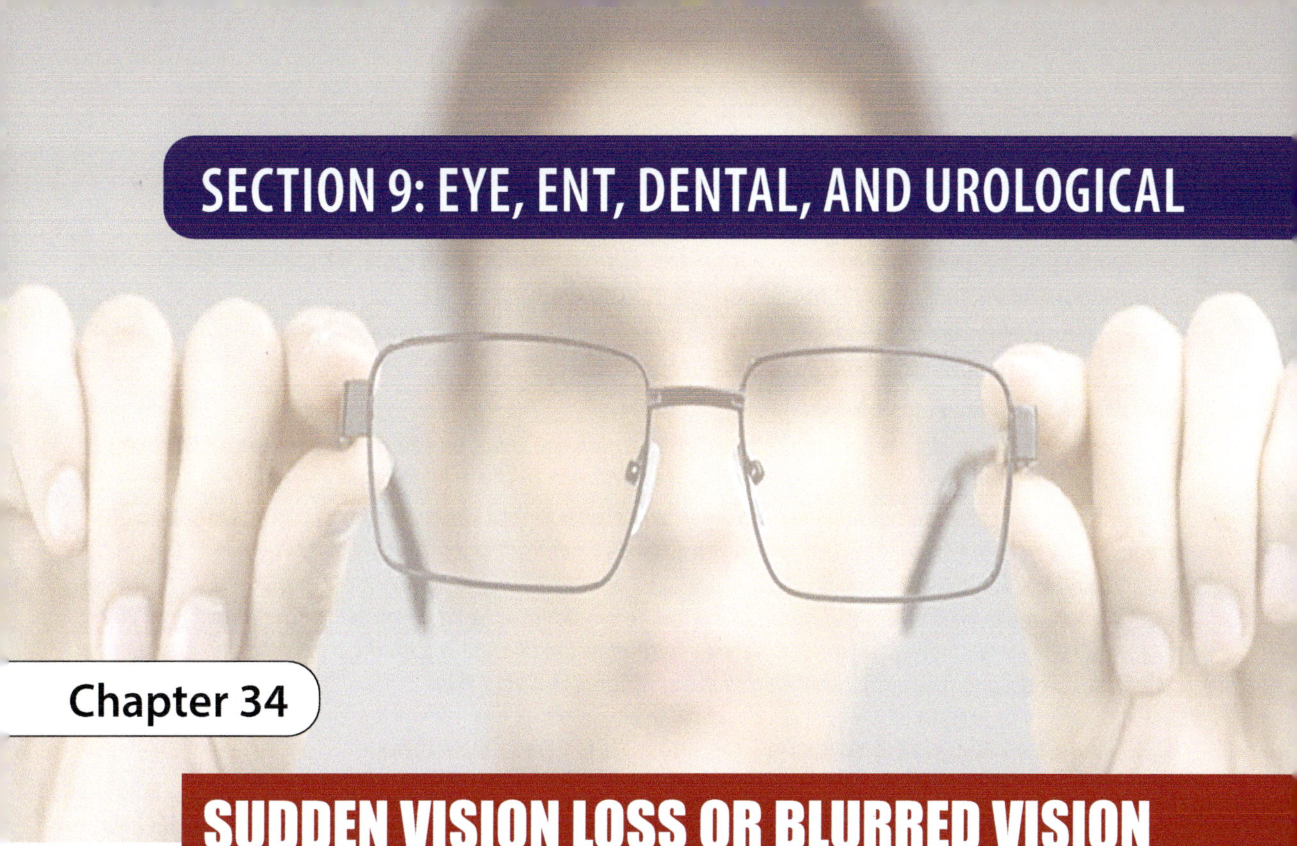

SECTION 9: EYE, ENT, DENTAL, AND UROLOGICAL

Chapter 34

SUDDEN VISION LOSS OR BLURRED VISION

"WHEN SIGHT SLIPS AWAY": SUDDEN VISION LOSS OR BLURRED VISION

Story: The Eye that Went Dark

*It was a pleasant evening, and 58-year-old Mr Rakesh had just finished his tea before heading out for his routine walk in the park. As he strolled down the familiar path, he suddenly felt something was wrong—**his right eye dimmed, as if someone had pulled down a curtain over his vision**. At first, he rubbed his eye, thinking it was dust or fatigue, but the blurring worsened within minutes.*

*Papa, what happened? his daughter Neha asked as he returned home looking unsettled. When he explained what he was experiencing, Neha's mind flashed back to a health awareness session she had attended—**sudden vision loss can be as urgent as a stroke.** Without wasting a second, she grabbed the car keys and drove him straight to the nearest emergency hospital.*

*In the hospital, the triage team acted quickly. An on-call ophthalmologist was alerted immediately. After a rapid eye examination and imaging tests, the doctor broke the news: **Mr Rakesh had central retinal artery occlusion (CRAO), often referred to as an "eye stroke."** This occurs when the artery supplying blood to the retina gets blocked, starving the eye of oxygen and leading to rapid, permanent vision loss if not treated urgently.*

Fortunately, Mr Rakesh had arrived ***within the critical golden hour****—just 90 minutes after the first symptoms.* ***The doctors immediately began emergency measures:***

- **Ocular massage** to dislodge the blockage.
- **Medications to lower eye pressur**e and improve blood flow.
- **Oxygen therapy** to boost retinal oxygen supply.

The next 30 minutes were tense. While some of his vision could not be saved, ***the prompt action allowed partial restoration of sight, preventing complete blindness in the affected eye.***

Further evaluation revealed that ***uncontrolled hypertension and cholesterol had caused tiny clots*** *that blocked the artery. For Rakesh, this was not just an eye emergency but a wake-up call to take his overall health seriously.*

"Had we delayed even by another hour, the damage would have been permanent," the doctor told Neha. That day, the family learned a vital lesson: ***any sudden vision change is a medical emergency****. Rakesh now keeps his blood pressure under control and never ignores warning signs.*

WHAT IS SUDDEN VISION LOSS OR BLURRED VISION?

Sudden loss or blurring of vision can signal a medical emergency. It may affect one or both eyes and range from partial to complete loss. Causes include retinal detachment, optic nerve issues, stroke, glaucoma, or even uncontrolled diabetes. Immediate evaluation is essential to prevent permanent vision damage.

Signs and Symptoms

- Blurred or dim vision (sudden or progressive)
- Loss of vision in part or whole of one eye
- Flashes of light or floaters
- Dark curtain-like shadow in visual field
- Eye pain or redness (in some cases)
- Double vision or vision distortion

Causes/Risk Factors

- Stroke or transient ischemic attack (TIA)
- Retinal detachment or retinal artery occlusion
- Optic neuritis (inflammation of optic nerve)
- Acute glaucoma (sudden rise in eye pressure)
- Diabetic or hypertensive retinopathy
- Head trauma or eye injury
- Migraine with aura (transient visual loss)
- High blood pressure and diabetes can silently damage the tiny blood vessels of the eye
- Eye injuries or sudden rise in pressure inside the eye can also lead to vision loss

STEPWISE FIRST AID BEFORE REACHING A HOSPITAL

Time is critical—early treatment improves outcomes.

- ***Step 1:*** Stay calm and do not rub eyes
    - » Avoid applying pressure or trying home remedies.

- ***Step 2:*** Ask about additional symptoms
  - » Check for headache, weakness, slurred speech, or imbalance (signs of stroke).
- ***Step 3:*** Cover the affected eye gently
  - » If painful or red, loosely cover with a clean cloth without pressure.
- ***Step 4:*** Reassure and support the person
  - » Keep them seated or lying down calmly.
- ***Step 5:*** Seek immediate medical care (112/108)
  - » Request an ambulance or rush to the nearest emergency department or eye hospital.
  - » Inform doctors of any recent trauma, illnesses, or chronic conditions like diabetes or high blood pressure (BP).

WHEN TO SEE A DOCTOR?

- Any sudden loss of vision in one or both eyes
- Blurred vision not improving within minutes
- Flashes, floaters, or dark shadows in vision
- Painful red eye with visual disturbance
- Vision changes after head injury or trauma
- Even if vision comes back in a few minutes, don't ignore it. It can be a warning sign of a bigger stroke

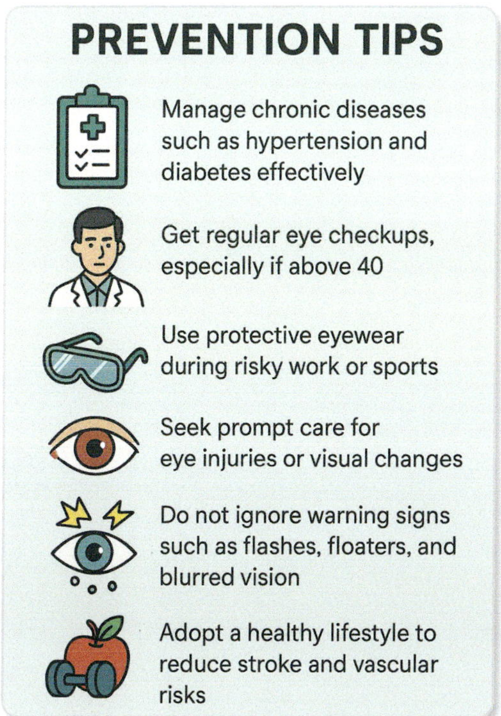

MYTHS AND FACTS

Myths	Facts
Vision loss will go away on its own.	Delay in treatment may result in permanent blindness.
Eye drops or rest are enough for blurred vision.	Some causes need urgent intervention like injections or surgery.
Vision problems are only due to spectacles.	Sudden vision loss often relates to the brain, nerves, or circulation.
Only elderly get serious eye issues.	Strokes, optic neuritis, or trauma can affect all age groups.

CONCLUSION

- "When vision dims, danger may loom—act swiftly."
- Eyes are not just windows to the world, they are mirrors of your health. Recognize early, respond fast, and preserve sight for a lifetime.

Scan to watch Dr Lokendra's 1-minute reel on this emergency.

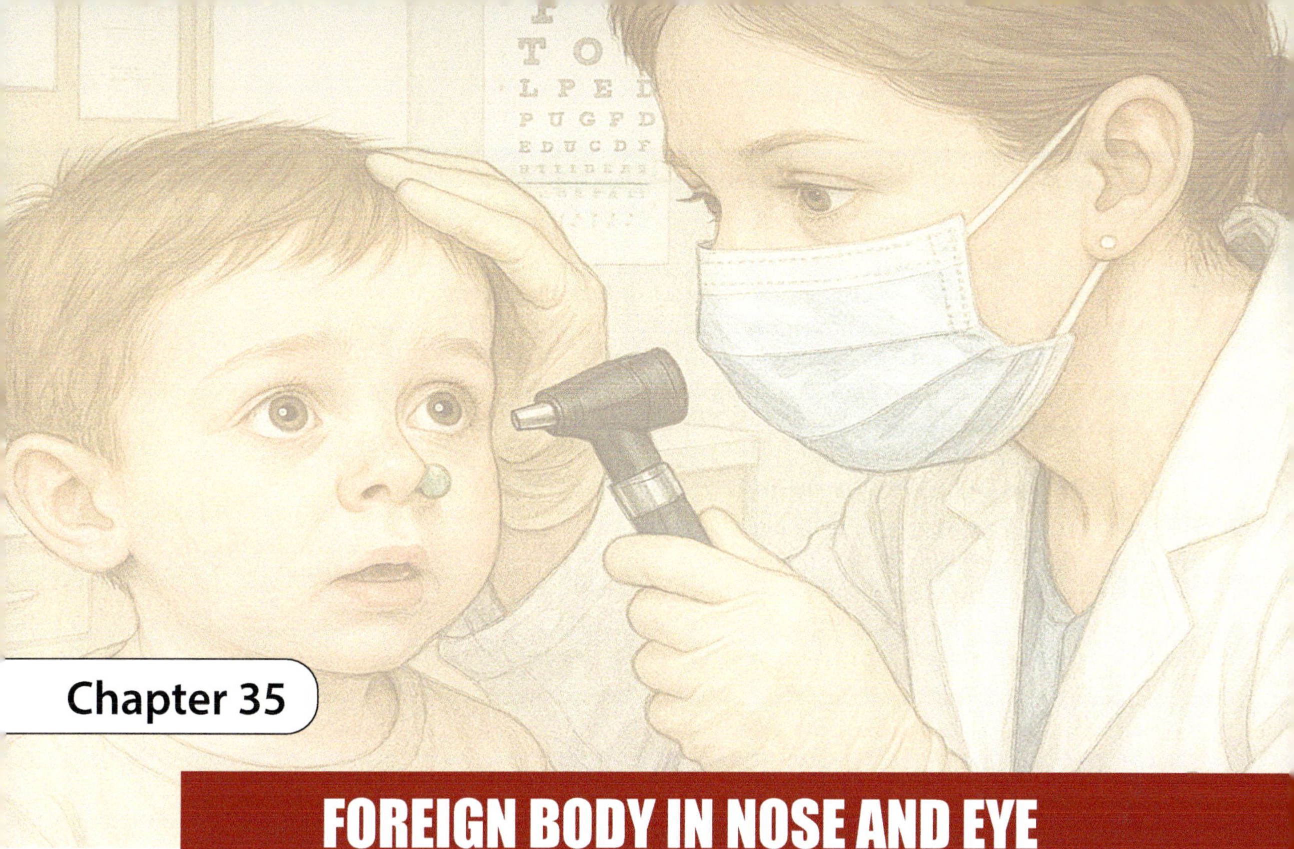

Chapter 35

FOREIGN BODY IN NOSE AND EYE

"TINY TROUBLE, BIG PANIC": PUBLIC AWARENESS ON FOREIGN BODY IN NOSE AND EYE

Story 1: The Curious Explorer (Foreign Body in the Nose)

It was a quiet afternoon when 4-year-old Aarav, full of curiosity, was playing alone in the living room. His eyes caught sight of a **shiny green bead** *that had rolled out of his sister's craft box. With the innocent logic of a toddler, he thought, "This would fit perfectly in my nose!"*

A few minutes later, Aarav's mother noticed something was off. He was **sniffling repeatedly, one nostril slightly swollen, and his face looked uncomfortable.** *When she asked what was wrong, Aarav covered his face and began to cry, afraid of getting scolded.*

Realizing this might be something serious, the parents rushed him to a nearby clinic. There, the doctor confirmed that a bead was stuck deep in his nostril. Rather than using force, the doctor demonstrated a safe and effective method called **"The Mother's Kiss."** *Aarav's mother placed her mouth over his,* **blocked his other nostril, and blew a quick, gentle breath.**

With a tiny pop, the stubborn bead shot out, much to Aarav's surprise and relief! The family laughed nervously, but the doctor explained the **dangers of inserting objects into the nose**—*such as choking, infections, or even damage to nasal passages.*

Aarav was perfectly fine, but the incident taught his parents an important lesson: **Always supervise toddlers, keep small objects out of reach, and never use sharp tools or pins to remove foreign bodies—leave it to a trained doctor.**

Story 2: The Dusty Playground (Foreign Body in the Eye)

One breezy evening, 6-year-old Ria was running around in the playground with her friends. As she slid down the swing, a sudden gust of wind blew fine dust and tiny sand particles into her eye. She stopped immediately, rubbing her eye furiously while crying in discomfort.

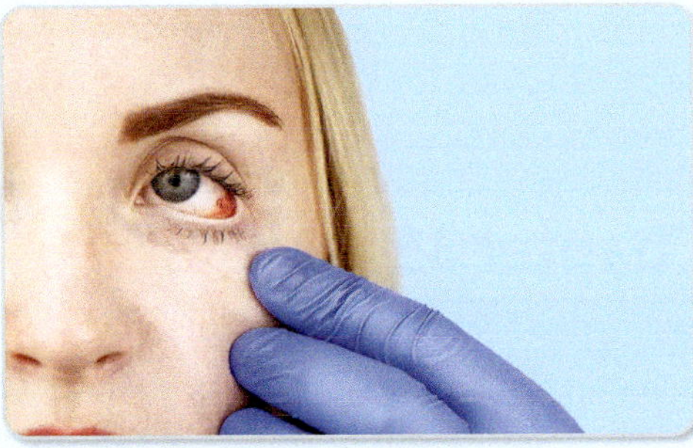

Her father, who was watching nearby, rushed over. Instead of panicking or trying to remove the particle with his fingers (which could scratch the eye), he calmly reassured Ria and **stopped her from rubbing her eyes further.**

At home, he gently washed her eye with clean, lukewarm water, letting it flush out the dust naturally. When Ria continued to feel a pricking sensation, they decided to visit an eye clinic.

The doctor examined her eye with a light and carefully removed a tiny grain of sand stuck under her eyelid. A soothing lubricating eye drop was prescribed to help with redness and irritation.

The doctor explained that **rubbing the eye or trying to remove an object with nails or cotton buds can cause scratches or infections.** *In more serious cases—like if something sharp, chemical, or metallic enters the eye—***immediate hospital care is vital.**

That evening, Ria's family learned a valuable lesson: or any foreign body in the eye, stay calm, rinse gently, and always seek medical help if the discomfort persists.

FOREIGN BODY IN THE NOSE

Signs and Symptoms

- One-sided nasal discharge (often foul-smelling)
- Sneezing, nosebleed, discomfort
- Swelling or redness around one nostril
- Breathing difficulty (if the object is large)

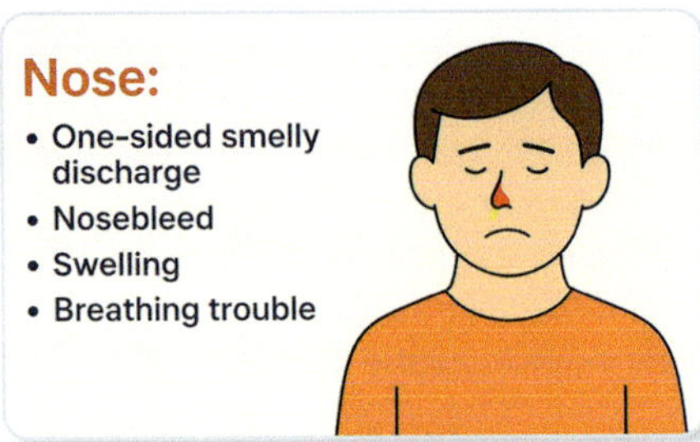

First Aid for Nasal Foreign Body

- *Keep the child calm* and upright.
- Avoid using cotton swabs, pins, or trying to dig the object out at home.
- Try the *Mother's Kiss technique* (explained in the following text) *if you are comfortable* and the object is not sharp.
- If the object does not come out easily, go to an *Ear, Nose, and Throat (ENT) doctor or emergency department.*

Mother's Kiss Technique

A simple and safe method that parents can try *before going to the hospital.*

How to do it?

- Explain to your child that you are going to help them "blow it out."
- *Block the clear nostril* with your finger.
- Seal your lips over the child's mouth *like giving a kiss.*
- Give a *quick, firm puff of air* into their mouth.
- The pressure will often *force the object out of the blocked nostril.*

This method works best with small, *nonsharp*, recently inserted objects like beads or food.

When not to Use

- If the object is *sharp or metallic*
- If the child is *uncooperative or distressed*
- If there are *signs of bleeding, swelling, or infection*

In those cases, go to a doctor *immediately*.

FOREIGN BODY IN THE EYE

Signs and Symptoms

- Redness, tearing, irritation
- Pain, blinking difficulty
- Feeling of something stuck
- Blurry vision or light sensitivity

First Aid for Eye Foreign Body

Do's

- Rinse the eye gently with clean water or saline.
- Blink repeatedly to try flushing it out.
- Cover the eye and visit a doctor if pain persists.

Don'ts

- Do not rub the eye—it can scratch the cornea.
- Do not try to remove sharp or stuck objects.
- Do not use unclean water or home remedies like rosewater.

PREVENTION TIPS

MYTHS AND FACTS

Myths	Facts
"The child will sneeze it out."	Not always—some objects stay stuck and cause infection.
"Rubbing helps remove things from the eye."	Rubbing can worsen the injury. Always flush or rinse.
"Pouring oil or water in the nose will help."	It can push the object deeper and cause aspiration.
"All red eyes are due to dust."	Could be serious. Always have it checked.

CONCLUSION

- "Small objects, big lessons. Calm action, quick thinking, and knowing simple methods like the *Mother's Kiss* can save a lot of trouble."
- Early first aid plus timely medical help is the safest route for both nose and eye foreign body incidents. Be prepared, not panicked.

Scan to watch Dr Lokendra's 1-minute reel on this emergency.

Chapter 36

BLEEDING FROM NOSE

"WHEN THE NOSE SPEAKS": UNDERSTANDING EPISTAXIS (NOSEBLEED)

Story: The Exam Day Surprise

It was just another cold Monday morning for Anaya, a 17-year-old student. Exhausted from a sleepless night cramming for her board exams, she dragged herself out of bed, her head pounding with ***anxiety and fatigue*** *The heater had been on full blast all night, leaving the air dry as a desert.*

*As she stood up to revise one last time before leaving for her exam, she suddenly felt something odd—****a warm, wet trickle sliding down from her nose to her upper lip****. Startled, she wiped it with her hand and was horrified to see bright red blood.*

"Maa!" she called out, panicked. Her mother rushed in and immediately ***told her to tilt her head back****, while her grandmother stuffed cotton balls up her nostrils—old home remedies passed down like gospel. But despite their best efforts, the blood stubbornly kept dripping.*

The clock was ticking, and so was Anaya's anxiety—"What if I faint? What if I miss my exam?" The family hurried her to the nearest clinic.

The doctor greeted them with a calm smile. "Don't worry. ***This is very common, especially in winter. And the good news is—it's easy to control."***

He patiently explained:

"The first mistake people make is tilting the head back—that only sends the blood down your throat. The right way? Lean slightly forward and pinch the soft part of your nose for 10–15 minutes. ***Breathe through your mouth. No cotton, no lying down."***

He demonstrated the correct steps. Within minutes, the bleeding stopped. Anaya and her family were relieved—and a little wiser.

As they left, the doctor smiled and said, ***"Remember, when the nose speaks, listen with calm, not panic."***

WHAT IS EPISTAXIS?

Epistaxis is the medical term for a nosebleed. It happens when the tiny blood vessels inside the nose burst, causing bleeding from one or both nostrils. It can be alarming, but most nosebleeds are *not dangerous* and can be treated at home.

Signs and Symptoms

- Sudden bleeding from one or both nostrils
- A sensation of liquid flowing at the back of the throat
- Nasal congestion or irritation after the bleed
- Blood-tinged mucus or clots

Causes/Risk Factors

- *Dry weather* or heated indoor air
- *Nose picking*, forceful sneezing, or blowing
- *Injury* or trauma to the nose
- *High blood pressure*
- *Use of blood thinners (aspirin, etc.)*
- *Nasal allergies,* infections, or structural problems
- In some cases—*bleeding disorders*

STEPWISE FIRST AID BEFORE REACHING A HOSPITAL

Stay calm—most nosebleeds can be stopped at home with the right approach.

- ***Step 1***: Stay calm and sit upright
    - » This reduces blood pressure in nasal vessels and minimizes bleeding.
- ***Step 2***: *Lean forward slightly*
    - » This prevents blood from flowing down the throat (which can cause nausea or vomiting).
- ***Step 3***: *Pinch the soft part of the nose.*
    - » Use thumb and index finger to squeeze the soft lower half of the nose (just below the bony bridge).
    - » Hold for *10–15 minutes* continuously, no peeking.

- ***Step 4:*** *Breathe through your mouth*
- ***Step 5:*** *Apply a cold compress to the nose or forehead.*
    - » This can help constrict blood vessels and slow the bleeding.
- ***Step 6:*** *Avoid lying down or tilting the head backward*
- ***Step 7:*** If bleeding continues beyond 20 minutes, or is heavy, or followed by fainting or trauma → *seek medical attention immediately*.

WHEN TO SEE A DOCTOR?

- Nosebleeds lasting longer than *20 minutes*
- Occurring *frequently* without clear cause
- Associated with *high blood pressure,* head injury, or blood-thinner medication
- Bleeding from *both nostrils* or alongside *bruising or gum bleeding*

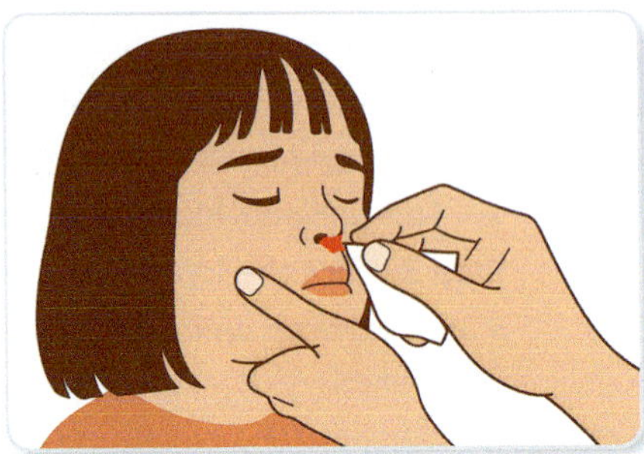

Special Advice for Children (Since Nosebleeds are Common in Kids)

"Children often get nosebleeds from nose picking or minor trauma. Teach them not to insert objects into their nose and keep nails short."

PREVENTION TIPS

Keep nasal passages moist with saline sprays or gels

Use a humidifier in dry environments.

Avoid nose picking or blowing too hard.

Keep fingernails trimmed, especially in children.

Wear protective gear during sports to avoid trauma.

Monitor blood pressure regularly, especially in the elderly.

Speak to a doctor before using aspirin or anticoagulants regularly

MYTHS AND FACTS

Myths	Facts
Tilt your head back to stop the bleed.	Tilting back can cause blood to enter the throat and lead to choking or vomiting.
Only hot weather causes nosebleeds.	Dry or cold air, especially indoor heaters, also increase the risk.
Nosebleeds are always serious.	Most are minor and stop with proper first aid. But recurring or severe cases need evaluation.
Stuffing tissue or cotton inside helps.	This can irritate the lining and worsen bleeding when removed.
Children outgrow nosebleeds completely.	Some may, but frequent bleeds could indicate allergies or nasal issues.

CONCLUSION

- *"A nosebleed can speak volumes about your body—do not panic, just listen and respond smartly."*
- With the right first aid knowledge, you can manage most nosebleeds at home. But if they keep coming back, do not ignore them—they might be your body's way of saying "get me checked."

Scan to watch Dr Lokendra's 1-minute reel on this emergency.

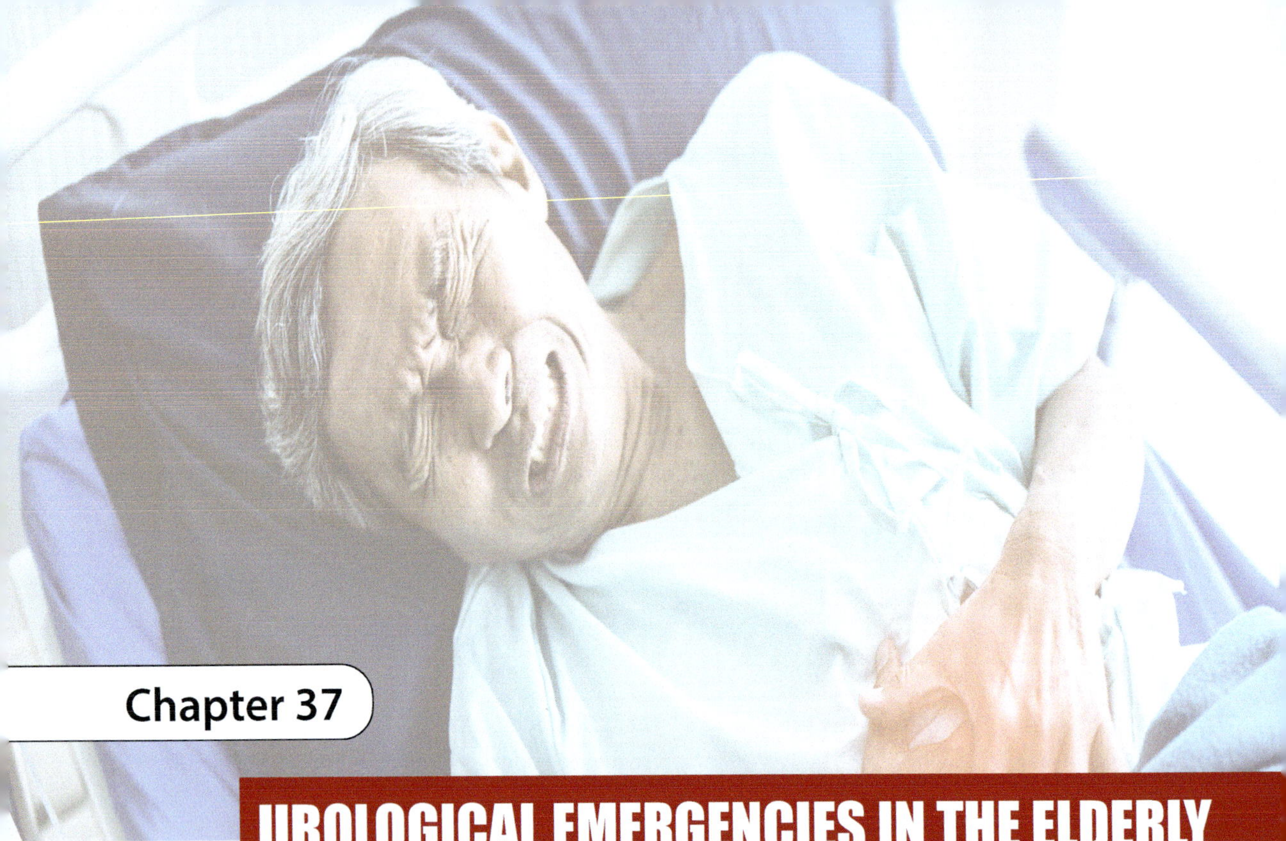

Chapter 37

UROLOGICAL EMERGENCIES IN THE ELDERLY

"WHEN WATERWAYS GET BLOCKED": UROLOGICAL EMERGENCIES IN THE ELDERLY

Story: The Painful Wait

Mr Sharma, a 74-year-old retired banker, had enjoyed a peaceful evening with his family. But late at night, he suddenly began to feel **severe, cramping pain in his lower abdomen**. *He repeatedly went to the washroom, feeling a strong urge to urinate, but* **not a single drop came out.**

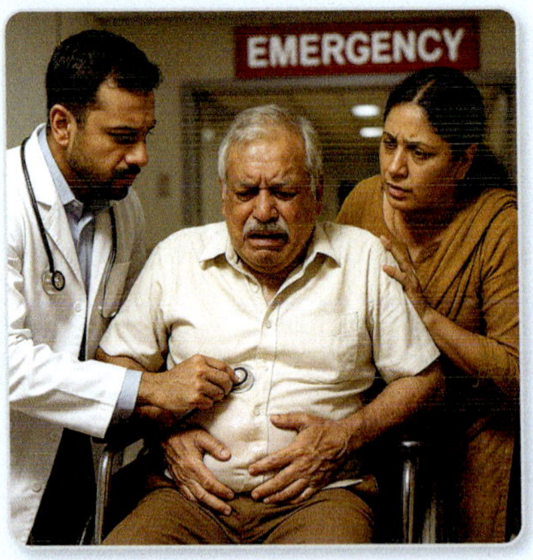

As the hours passed, the pain worsened, his abdomen appeared bloated, and he grew restless and sweaty. His worried family realized this was **not a minor problem but an emergency** *and rushed him to the nearest hospital.*

In the emergency department, the doctor quickly examined Mr Sharma and diagnosed **acute urinary retention**—*a condition where urine gets trapped in the bladder and cannot pass out, often caused by an enlarged prostate in elderly men.*

A **urinary catheter** *was inserted, and to everyone's surprise,* **nearly a liter of urine drained out instantly** *giving Mr Sharma immense relief. He was monitored for a few hours, and his condition stabilized. Further tests later confirmed* **benign prostatic hyperplasia (BPH),** *a common but treatable condition in older men.*

The doctor explained that if his family had delayed seeking help, **the back pressure could have damaged his kidneys or caused severe infection.**

This incident taught Mr Sharma and his family an important lesson:

Persistent difficulty in passing urine, especially with pain and swelling, should never be ignored. Timely medical attention can prevent serious complications.

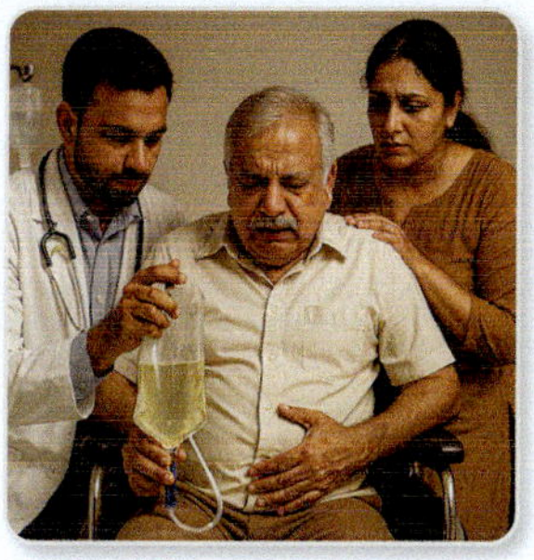

WHAT ARE UROLOGICAL EMERGENCIES IN THE ELDERLY?

Urological emergencies in elderly individuals include sudden urinary retention, severe urinary tract infections (UTIs), catheter blockages, and hematuria (blood in urine). These require immediate care as they can cause pain, kidney injury, sepsis, or confusion in older adults.

Signs and Symptoms

- Inability to pass urine despite urge
- Lower abdominal pain or swelling
- Fever, chills, or burning during urination
- Foul-smelling or cloudy urine
- Confusion or sudden behavioral changes
- Blood in urine
- Leakage of urine around catheter site

Causes/Risk Factors

- Enlarged prostate (BPH) or prostate cancer
- Constipation compressing the bladder
- Neurogenic bladder (due to diabetes, stroke, or Parkinson's disease)
- Chronic catheterization and infections
- Dehydration or immobility
- Medications like antihistamines or anticholinergics

STEPWISE FIRST AID BEFORE REACHING A HOSPITAL

Never delay care in elderly patients with urinary complaints.

- ***Step 1:*** Assess for symptoms
    - » Ask about the last time urine was passed.
    - » Check for pain, restlessness, or visible abdominal swelling.
- ***Step 2:*** Do *not* give excess fluids
    - » Avoid forcing water intake—it may worsen retention.

- ***Step 3:*** Do *not* attempt to insert a catheter at home
  - » Catheterization should only be done by trained professionals.
- ***Step 4:*** Help them sit or lie comfortably
  - » Keep them warm and reassure them to reduce anxiety.
- ***Step 5:*** Visit the nearest emergency center
  - » Especially if pain, fever, or mental confusion is present.
  - » Carry prior urology or medical records if available.

WHEN TO SEE A DOCTOR?

- Sudden inability to urinate
- Fever with urinary symptoms
- Catheter not draining or leaking
- Blood in urine or foul-smelling urine
- New onset confusion or drowsiness in elderly

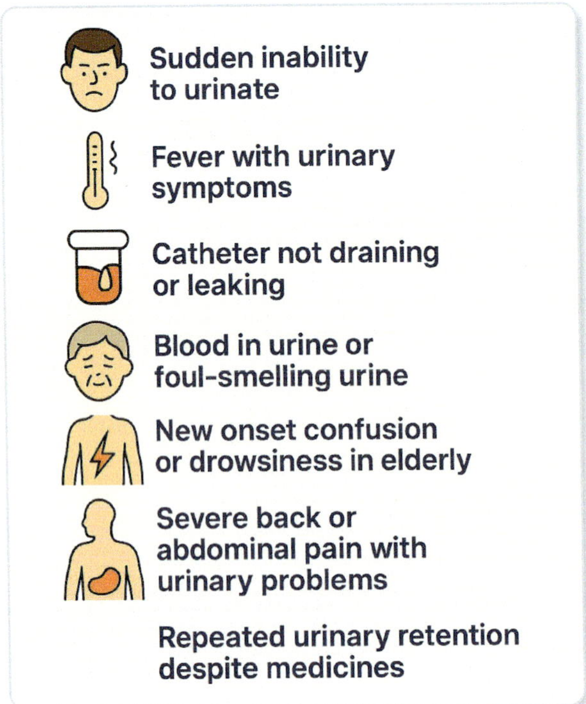

PREVENTION TIPS

Regular prostate and bladder checkups for men above 50.

Good catheter hygiene and timely change (if used).

Monitor urine output and color daily.

Keep them active and mobile to promote bladder function.

MYTHS AND FACTS

Myths	Facts
Elderly people urinate less, so retention is normal.	Inability to urinate is an emergency and may cause kidney failure.
Catheters do not need regular monitoring.	Catheter care is crucial to prevent infections and blockage.
Confusion in elderly is always dementia.	UTIs can cause sudden confusion (delirium) in older adults.
Drinking more water solves all urinary problems.	Overhydration during urinary blockage may worsen symptoms.

CONCLUSION

- "A blocked bladder can quickly become a blocked life—act fast."
- Urological symptoms in elderly are not just discomfort—they are warning signs.
- Early recognition and quick treatment can prevent complications and restore dignity.

Scan to watch Dr Lokendra's 1-minute reel on this emergency.

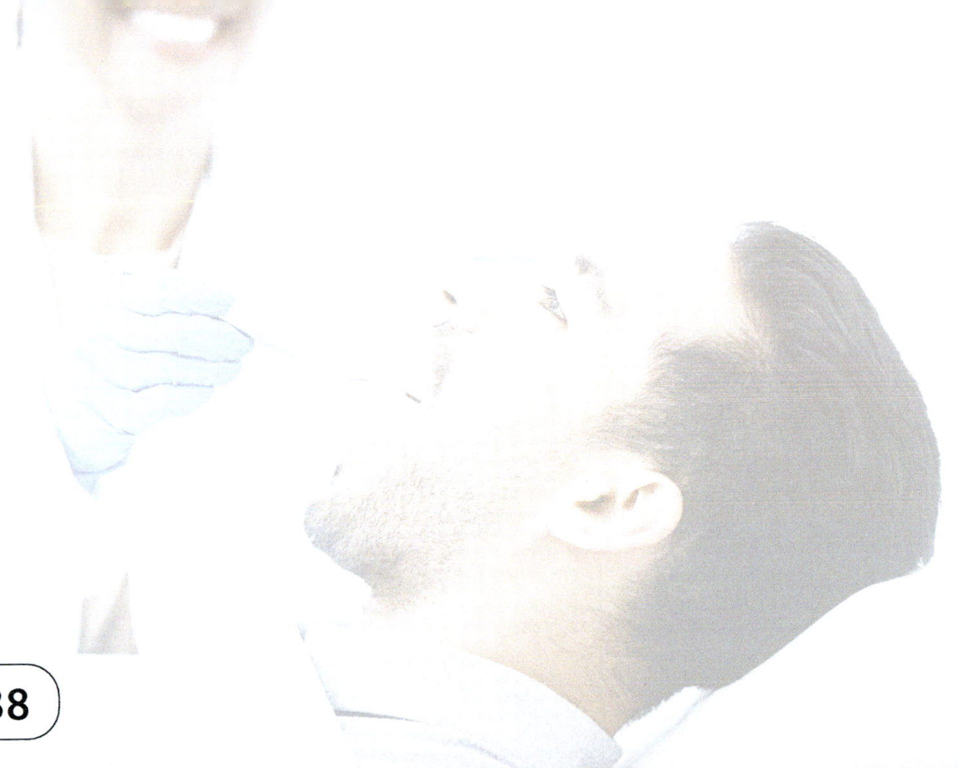

Chapter 38

DENTAL EMERGENCIES (TOOTH INJURY, SEVERE PAIN, BLEEDING)

FROM SWEET TOOTH TO SERIOUS THREAT

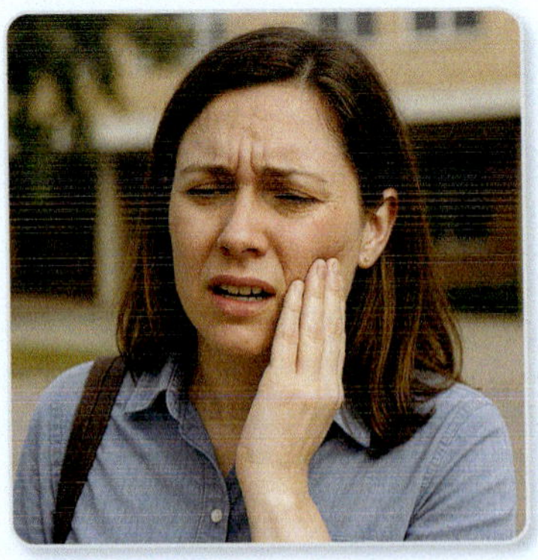

Meena, a 32-year-old schoolteacher, had been suffering from a nagging toothache for several weeks. Initially, she thought it was just due to eating sweets and ignored it. But one night, the pain became unbearable—throbbing, radiating to her ear, and keeping her awake. She tried clove oil and painkillers at home, but by morning, her face was swollen, and she could barely open her mouth. Alarmed, her husband rushed her to the dentist, where she was diagnosed with a severe tooth infection that needed urgent treatment. The doctor explained that ignoring dental pain can lead not only to abscesses but also to serious infections spreading to the neck or even bloodstream. With proper antibiotics, drainage, and later dental care, Meena recovered well and learned an important lesson: dental pain should never be neglected.

WHAT ARE DENTAL EMERGENCIES?

Dental emergencies are **sudden, painful, or dangerous problems** involving the teeth, gums, or surrounding tissues that require urgent care. They can cause:

- Severe pain
- Swelling of face or jaw

- Bleeding from mouth
- Difficulty opening mouth, chewing, or swallowing

Causes of Dental Emergencies

- **Severe toothache**—untreated cavities, pulp infection.
- **Dental abscess**—pus collection due to infection.
- **Fractured or broken tooth**—trauma, biting hard objects.
- **Knocked-out tooth (avulsion)**—accidents, sports injuries, falls.
- **Bleeding gums**—trauma, gum disease, post-extraction bleeding.
- **Impacted wisdom tooth**—swelling, pain, infection.
- **Jaw fracture or dislocation**—accidents, fights, road traffic injuries.
- **Foreign body lodged in gums/teeth**—food particles, splinters.

RED FLAG SIGNS: YOU MUST SEE A DOCTOR/DENTIST

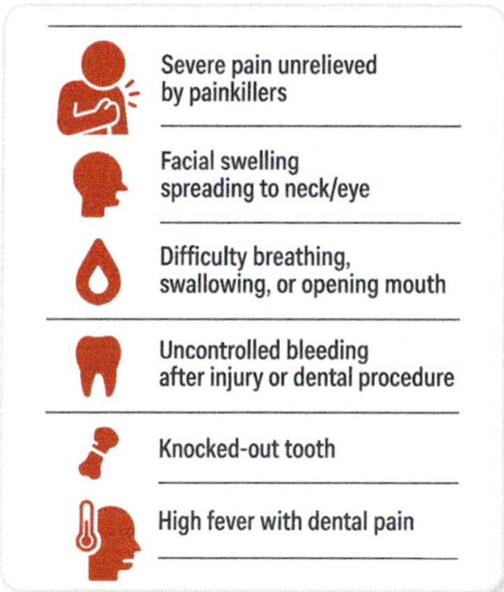

WHEN TO ATTEND EMERGENCIES

- Broken or knocked-out tooth after trauma.
- Sudden severe toothache with swelling.
- Bleeding that doesn't stop after 15–20 minutes of pressure.
- Infection spreading to face/neck.
- Jaw fracture/dislocation.

STEPWISE MANAGEMENT OF DENTAL EMERGENCIES: FROM HOME CARE TO EMERGENCY CARE

At Home (First Aid)

- Rinse mouth gently with warm salt water.
- Apply a cold pack on cheek for swelling.

- For bleeding: bite on clean gauze or cloth for pressure.
- Take paracetamol/ibuprofen for pain (if not allergic).

At Doctor's Clinic/Dentist

- Detailed examination, X-rays.
- Drainage of abscess if needed.
- Filling, root canal treatment, or extraction.
- Sutures for gum injuries.
- Antibiotics and tetanus prophylaxis in case of trauma.

In Hospital Emergency

- IV antibiotics, pain relief.
- Drainage of severe infections.
- Maxillofacial surgeon consultation for fractures or deep infections.
- Admission if airway is threatened.

MYTHS AND FACTS

Myths	Facts
Clove oil or home remedies can cure dental emergencies	They may help temporarily but definitive dental care is essential.
Dental abscesses heal on their own	Untreated abscesses can spread to brain or chest—life-threatening
Bleeding after tooth extraction is normal even if it continues for hours.	Persistent bleeding is dangerous and needs urgent attention

CONCLUSION

Dental emergencies are painful, frightening, and potentially life-threatening if ignored. Simple measures like prompt first aid, safe transport of knocked-out teeth, and early dental consultation can save teeth and lives. Remember: **never ignore dental pain, swelling, or bleeding—the mouth is the gateway to your body, and infections can spread quickly.**

Scan to watch Dr Lokendra's 1-minute reel on this emergency.

SECTION 10: SPECIAL SITUATIONS

Chapter 39

HANGING AND NEAR HANGING

"WHEN EVERY SECOND MATTERS": EMERGENCY RESPONSE TO HANGING

Story: The Timely Rescue

*It was a quiet evening in the hostel when Neha's phone buzzed with a call from her best friend, Riya. Her voice was trembling, filled with distress and despair. Alarmed, Neha ran to Riya's room, only to be met with a heart-stopping sight—**Riya was hanging from the ceiling fan,** unconscious, a dupatta tied around her neck.*

*For a split second, Neha froze. But instinct took over. **She screamed for help, rushed to support Riya's body,** and shouted for someone to bring a knife or scissors. With trembling hands but unwavering focus, she lifted Riya's weight to relieve pressure on her neck and carefully cut the dupatta.*

*Riya collapsed onto the bed, still breathing but barely. Her lips were bluish, and she was unresponsive. By then, the hostel warden had arrived. Recognizing the urgency, she checked Riya's pulse and airway. When Riya's breathing grew shallow, the warden started rescue breaths and **chest compressions (CPR)** to keep oxygen flowing to the brain. Meanwhile, another student called the ambulance and kept the crowd away to give space for first aid.*

Within minutes, the ambulance arrived, and Riya was rushed to the hospital. ***Doctors praised the quick intervention that had prevented brain damage or death****. After a few days in the ICU, Riya survived and during her hospital stay she was referred to a psychiatrist for counselling and emotional support.*

This close call left everyone shaken but also aware of two vital truths:

1. *Immediate first aid and CPR can save a life, even in hanging cases where every second is critical.*
2. *Mental health awareness, emotional support, and early intervention are just as important as physical rescue.*

WHAT IS HANGING AND NEAR HANGING?

Hanging

This means when a person puts a rope or cloth around their neck and their body weight pulls it tight. The pressure on the neck blocks breathing and blood flow to the brain. This can happen if the whole body is hanging or even if part of the body is still touching the ground.

Near-hanging

This means the person was found alive after a hanging attempt. They may still be breathing or can be revived. Such people may look fine at first but can develop serious problems later, like swelling in the throat, breathing trouble, brain damage due to lack of oxygen, or injuries to the voice box and neck bones.

In Simple Terms

Hanging = the act of choking due to suspension by the neck.

Near-hanging = when someone survives (at least for some time) after being hanged.

Signs and Symptoms

- Unconsciousness or unresponsiveness
- Bluish lips, fingertips
- No breathing or abnormal gasping
- Weak or absent pulse
- Neck marks, swelling, or bruising
- Dilated pupils, seizures, or frothing
- Incontinence or body limpness

Causes/Risk Factors

- Suicidal attempt due to depression or trauma
- Mental health disorders (anxiety, schizophrenia)
- Drug or alcohol use
- Sudden emotional crisis or abuse
- Social isolation or bullying

STEPWISE FIRST AID BEFORE REACHING A HOSPITAL

Every second counts. Act quickly but safely.

- ***Step 1:*** Cut down the person immediately
  - » Support their weight while cutting the rope or cloth.
  - » Avoid jerky movements to reduce spinal injury risk.
  - » Support the neck gently while cutting, as cervical injury may occur in some cases.
- ***Step 2:*** Loosen clothing around neck and chest
  - » Remove any tight clothing to help breathing.
- ***Step 3:*** Check for breathing and pulse
  - » If not breathing or no pulse, begin CPR immediately.
  - » If breathing, place the person in the recovery position.
- ***Step 4:*** Call emergency services (112/108)
  - » Clearly state it is a hanging case and if CPR is ongoing.
- ***Step 5:*** Monitor continuously
  - » Continue CPR if unresponsive until professional help arrives.
  - » Stay calm and provide emotional support if the person regains consciousness.

WHEN TO SEE A DOCTOR?

- Immediately, after any hanging or attempt
- Even if the person appears conscious or unharmed
- To assess for brain injury, airway trauma, or internal damage
- For mandatory psychological and psychiatric evaluation

MYTHS AND FACTS

Myths	Facts
If they are breathing, they do not need a doctor.	All hanging survivors need full evaluation and mental health support.
Cutting the rope is dangerous.	Cutting quickly while supporting the body can save a life.
They will recover with rest at home.	Complications like airway swelling or delayed brain damage can occur.
Talking about suicide increases risk.	Open conversations reduce stigma and save lives.

CONCLUSION

- "In a hanging emergency, seconds mean survival."
- Act fast, offer help, and remember—saving a life today may heal a soul tomorrow. Let us break the silence around mental health.

Scan to watch Dr Lokendra's 1-minute reel on this emergency.

Chapter 40

THE GOLDEN HOUR IN MEDICAL EMERGENCIES: A QUICK OVERVIEW

"WHEN THE BRAIN BEGS FOR TIME": STROKE EMERGENCY

Case Story: Rajesh's Missed Golden Hour

Rajesh, a 50-year-old respected school headmaster, was in the middle of a staff meeting when he suddenly collapsed, **his speech slurred, and his right side became weak.** *His colleagues, unsure of what was happening, delayed calling for emergency help. Instead, they tried home remedies and lost precious time.*

By the time Rajesh was finally transported from his remote village to a city hospital, **12 hour** *had passed—far beyond the* **"golden hour," the first 4.5 hours** *when clot-busting medications are most effective.*

Doctors confirmed an **ischemic stroke** *but explained that due to the long delay,* **life-saving treatment** *could no longer restore his brain function. Rajesh was left with* **permanent paralysis and speech difficulties,** *requiring months of rehabilitation.*

The Golden Hour: Why Every Minute Matters?

- *For* ***stroke****, treatment within 4.5 hours (preferably within the first 60–90 minutes) offers the best chance of reversing brain damage.*
- *Every minute lost means* ***1.9 million brain cells die.***
- *For heart attacks, trauma, or severe bleeding, early care during the golden hour can prevent death or lifelong disability.*

P.S.: *Some advanced stroke centers offer mechanical thrombectomy (a procedure to remove clots) up to 6–24 hours after onset, but the success rate decreases significantly with time. Early recognition and hospital arrival remain critical.*

The **"Golden Hour"** is the first crucial window (usually the first 60–120 minutes) after a medical emergency or trauma. Quick recognition and immediate care during this period can **save lives and prevent permanent disability.**

Stroke (Brain Attack)

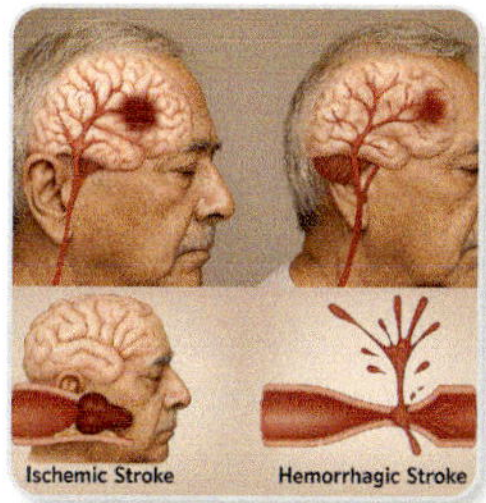

- **Best treatment window**: Intravenous clot-busting drugs (thrombolysis) are most effective within **4.5 hours** of stroke onset.
- **Why speed matters:** Every **15-minute delay** reduces the chance of full recovery and increases the risk of long-term paralysis.
- **Fact:** Every minute of untreated stroke kills **1.9 million brain cells**.

Trauma (Road Traffic Accidents and Injuries)

- **Why critical:** Rapid bleeding control, airway management, and surgery can save lives.
- **Impact**: Early care within the first hour can reduce preventable deaths by up to 25%.
- **Examples**: Head injuries, major fractures, severe bleeding.

Cardiac Arrest (Heart Stopping)

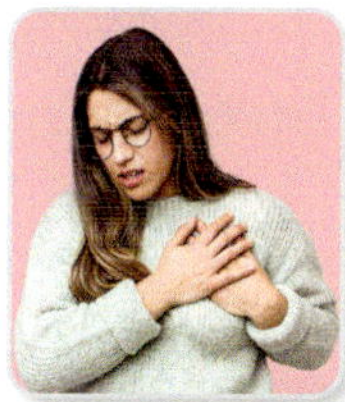

- **Time is heart and brain**: Survival drops by **7–10% every minute** without CPR or defibrillation.
- **Fact:** Immediate CPR and use of an automated external defibrillator (AED) **can double or triple survival rates.**

Heart Attack (Myocardial Infarction)

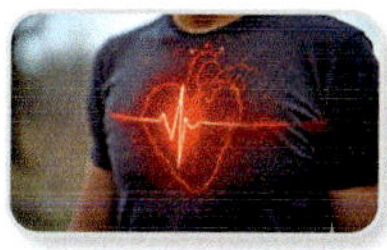

- **Golden window:** Immediate treatment with angioplasty or clot-busting drugs saves heart muscle.
- **Fact**: Most permanent heart damage happens within the first 1–2 hours after symptoms start.

Severe Bleeding and Shock

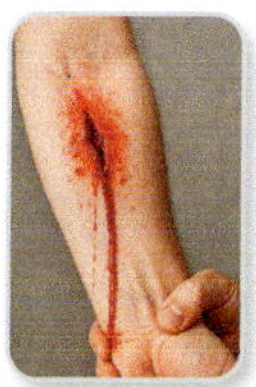

- **Why critical:** Uncontrolled bleeding can cause death within **30–60 minutes.**
- **Immediate steps:** Apply direct pressure, keep the person flat, and seek emergency care.

Snakebites and Poisoning

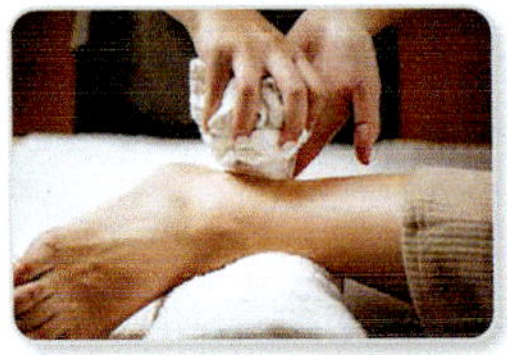

- **Golden period:** Antivenom or antidote should be given as soon as possible, ideally within **2–4 hours** to prevent organ failure or death.
- **Delay increases complications** like kidney damage or respiratory failure.

Obstetric Emergencies (Pregnancy-related)

- **Examples:** Heavy bleeding during pregnancy, eclampsia (fits), or obstructed labor.
- **Why urgent:** Both **mother and baby's survival** depends on reaching a hospital during this critical period.

Burns and Major Scalds

- **First hour care:** Immediate cooling of the burn, pain relief, and fluid management **reduce complications and infections.**

Seizures (Prolonged or Repeated)

- **Danger:** Seizures lasting more than 5 minutes (status epilepticus) can cause brain damage.
- **Action:** Immediate medical intervention is crucial.

Drowning and Electric Shock

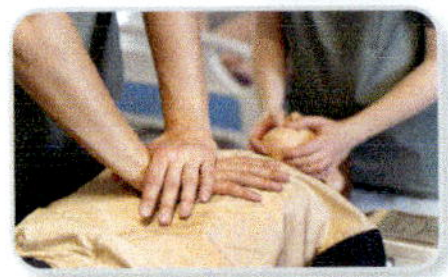

- **Why immediate response matters:** Quick CPR and oxygen delivery within minutes can **prevent brain death.**

Diabetic Emergencies (Hypoglycemia/Hyperglycemia)

- **Golden minutes: Low blood sugar can cause seizures or coma; rapid correction with glucose can save the brain.**

WHY GOLDEN HOUR MATTERS FOR EVERYONE

- **Recognizing early warning signs** (chest pain, stroke symptoms, severe bleeding) is vital.
- **Emergency care within this critical window often determines survival and long-term recovery.**

MYTHS AND FACTS IN EMERGENCY MEDICINE

Myths	Facts
Waiting a few hours would not affect the outcome of a medical emergency.	Most critical conditions (e.g., stroke, myocardial infarction, sepsis) require intervention within minutes to hours to prevent irreversible organ damage or death.
Only hospitals can provide life-saving interventions.	Immediate bystander actions [e.g., cardiopulmonary resuscitation (CPR), bleeding control, airway positioning] significantly improve survival outcomes before hospital care begins.

Myths	Facts
Stroke only affects the elderly.	Stroke can occur at any age, including young adults and children, and rapid thrombolysis or thrombectomy is time-dependent.
All medical conditions can wait for transportation to a major center.	Delays in initial stabilization, such as securing airway or controlling hemorrhage, can result in rapid deterioration or death during transit.
Having no visible injury means there is no emergency.	Internal injuries (e.g., brain hemorrhage, internal bleeding, cardiac arrhythmias) may not show immediate external signs but can be fatal if not recognized quickly.
Emergency care begins when the doctor sees the patient.	The "chain of survival" begins at the scene—recognition, activation of emergency medical services (EMS), early intervention, and rapid transport are all part of the golden hour.
Home remedies are safe initial responses.	Inappropriate or delayed interventions (e.g., giving oral fluids during altered consciousness) can worsen outcomes or cause aspiration.

CONCLUSION

The golden hour is a cornerstone of emergency medicine. Optimizing outcomes during this period requires public awareness, trained first responders, efficient emergency medical services, and equipped healthcare facilities. A coordinated approach involving communities, policymakers, and healthcare providers is vital to minimize preventable deaths and disabilities in both medical and surgical emergencies.

Scan to watch Dr Lokendra's 1-minute reel on this emergency.

Index

A

Accidents 76
Adrenal crisis 14
Advanced cardiac life support ambulance 116
Alcohol 52
- use 169
  - excessive 9
- withdrawal 43

Allergic reaction 14, 111
- severe 48, 133

Anaphylaxis 14, 48, 111-114, 133
Anemia 23
Angiotensin-converting enzyme inhibitors 11
Animal bite 125, 126, 129
Antibiotics 125
Anxiety 22, 56, 60, 64, 65, 67, 112, 122, 156, 169
- attacks 24
- causes of 65
- stepwise management of 66

Arrhythmias 14, 21, 22, 56
Asthma 27, 32
- attack 28
  - severe 25
- symptoms 27

Atrial fibrillation 22
Automated external defibrillator 49, 173
Auxiliary nurse midwife 144
Avulsion 165

B

Basic life support 49
Bleeding 14, 51-53, 140, 141, 143, 164
- disorders, history of 52
- emergencies 72
- gums 165
- mouth 165
- nose 156
- severe 73, 173

Blood 68, 161
- clot blocking brain artery 38
- loss
  - external 14, 73
  - internal 14, 48
- pressure 10, 12, 21, 57, 64, 113
  - high 7, 9, 66, 122, 142, 148, 149
  - low 12, 13, 16, 122
  - very low 66
- sugar
  - high 68, 70, 71
  - low 14, 43, 48, 68, 70
- tests 67
- thinners 52

Body limpness 169
Bones
- broken 81
- weak 83

Brain 38
- attack 36, 173
- computed tomography scan of 37
- infections of 43
- injury 43, 48
- misfires 41
- swelling 51

Breathing
- abnormal 47
- difficulty 17, 103, 108, 113, 122, 152
- emergency 28
- shortness of 4, 10, 17, 18, 23, 27

Breathlessness 28
- severe 29

Bronchitis, chronic 28, 32
Bruising 51, 82, 169
Bullying 60, 169
Burn 85, 86, 88, 174
- first-degree 86
- second-degree 86
- third-degree 86
- types of 86

Burning sensation 116
Burst blood vessel 38

C

Caffeine 22
Calcium channel blockers 11
Call emergency services 29
Cancer, prostate 161
Carbohydrate intake, excessive 70
Cardiac arrest 173
- sudden 48

Cardiopulmonary resuscitation 6, 15, 53
Cardiovascular system 1
Catheter blockages 161
Central retinal artery occlusion 147
Chest
- compressions 167
- pain 66
  - severe 10, 23
- tightness 27, 122

Choking 33, 35, 103
Chronic obstructive pulmonary disease 25, 28, 32
- severe 27
- symptoms 28

Clammy skin 14, 47, 56, 103
Clutching throat 34
Cold
- exposure 98, 99
- feet 14
- hands 14
- skin 14, 56, 99, 103

Collapse 29, 56, 66
- sudden 46, 47

Confusion 9, 10, 14, 29, 52, 53, 70, 99, 108, 103
Consciousness 51, 56, 99
- loss of 34, 42, 51, 113

Convulsions 51, 136, 137
Cough 30, 34, 103
- chronic 28, 32
- red flag signs of 31

Cushing's syndrome 9
Cyanosis 34, 103

D

Death 73
Decongestants 9
Dehydration 23, 56, 70, 94, 95
  severe 14
  signs of 95
  symptoms of 95
Dental abscess 165
Dental emergencies 164
  causes of 165
  stepwise management of 165
Depression 60, 169
Diabetes 23, 148
  medications 70
Diabetic 48, 70
  emergency 68, 69, 174
  retinopathy 148
Diarrhea 14
Dilated pupils 169
Disability 60
Discomfort 152
Disorientation 99
Dizziness 9, 14, 23, 55, 56, 70, 113
  sudden 14
Drooling 108
Drowning 102, 103, 106, 174
Drowsiness 14, 29, 51-53, 70, 103, 108, 122
Drug 22, 43, 169
  overdose 48, 60
  use 52
    excessive 9
Dry cough 27
Dry mouth 70
Dyspnea 18

E

Electrolyte imbalance 22, 43
Emergency
  care 10, 11, 23, 24, 66, 165
  hypertensive 10
  medicine 174
Emotional crisis, sudden 169
Emphysema 28
Encephalitis 43
Endocrine disorders 9
Endocrine issues 14
Environmental emergencies 94
Epilepsy 43, 48
Epinephrine 114
Epistaxis 156, 157
Exercise 27
Extreme thirst 70
Eye 147
  foreign body in 151-154
  injury 148
  pain 148
  stroke 147
  swelling of 112

F

Face, swelling of 112, 164
Fainting 14, 23, 55, 56, 70, 113
Fatigue 9, 14, 28, 70, 99, 156
Febrile seizures 137, 139
Fever 23, 136, 137
  high 43
Fits 41
Fizziness 55
Fracture 81, 82, 165
Fruity-smelling breath 70

G

Gasping 27
  abnormal 47, 169
Glaucoma, acute 148
Glucometer, role of 69

H

Hanging 167, 168
Head
  injury 50, 51, 53
  trauma 48, 148
Headache 9, 51
  persistent 53
  severe 10
Heart 19, 57
  attack 1, 3, 14, 17, 22, 32, 64, 66, 173
  disease, history of 23
  failure 17
  problems 14, 56
  rate 122
  valve disorders 22
Heat 14
  stroke 94, 95
    signs of 96
    symptoms of 96
Hematuria 161
Hemorrhage 72, 73
  signs of 73
Hormonal changes 22
Household pesticides 107, 110
Hyperglycemia 70, 71, 174
Hyperplasia, benign prostatic 160
Hypertension 7, 9, 23
  causes of 9
  classification of 9
  essential 9
  primary 9
  red flag signs of 10
  secondary 9
  severe 10
  stepwise management of 11
  symptoms of 9
Hypertensive crisis 10
Hyperthyroidism 9
Hypoglycemia 70, 174
Hypotension 13
Hypothermia 98, 99
  mild 99
  moderate-to-severe 99

I

Illnesses 70
Immunoglobulin 128
Incontinence 169
Infections 70, 141
  severe 14
  signs of 133
Injuries 173
  high-impact 83
  lightning 89, 90, 92
Insect stings 132, 133
Insulin
  missed dose of 70
  overdose of 70
Interstitial lung disease 32
Irritability 70, 103
Itching 112

J

Jaw
  fracture 165
  swelling of 164

K

Kidney diseases 9
Knocked-out tooth 165

L

Light sensitivity 153
Lightheadedness 14, 56, 70
Limb
  abnormal angle of 82
  deformity of 82
Limp body 47, 103
Lips 34
  bluish 28, 103, 169
  swelling of 112
Lung 19
  infections 28

M

Magnesium 22
Major scalds 174
Medical emergencies 172
Meningitis 43
Menopause 22
Mental health 36
  crisis 59, 60
  disorders 169
Mental illnesses 60
Metabolic disorders 68
Metered-dose inhaler 28
Migraine 148
Miscarriage 142
Monitor breathing 42
Mother's kiss technique 153
Muscle twitching 108
Myocardial infarction 1, 173

N

Nails 28
Nasal discharge, one-sided 152
Nasal foreign body, first aid for 153
National Institutes of Health Stroke Scale 37
Nausea 4, 14, 51, 56, 70, 108, 113
Near-drowning 102, 103
Near-hanging 167, 168
Neurological health 36
Nicotine 22
Nonallergic reactions 132
Nonsteroidal anti-inflammatory drugs 9
Nose, foreign body in 151, 152
Nosebleed 9, 152, 156

O

Obstetric emergencies 174
Obstructive sleep apnea 9
Ocular massage 148
Open airway 42
Open fracture 82
Open wound 82
Optic nerve, inflammation of 148
Optic neuritis 148
Oral rehydration solution 96
Organ failure 73
Osteoporosis 83
Oxygen therapy 148

P

Pain 4, 56, 60, 153
  abdominal 108, 113, 122
  chest 66
  crushing 1
  eye 148
  labor 140, 141
  severe 81, 143, 164
Pale skin 14, 47, 99, 103
Palpitations 21, 22, 24, 56
  causes of 22
  stepwise management of 23
Panic attack 22, 64, 65, 67
  causes of 65
  stepwise management of 66
Paralysis 36
Pesticide poisoning 108
Phlegm 28
Pinpoint pupils 108
Poisoning 48, 107, 174
Post-COVID lung damage 32
Post-exposure prophylaxis 125
Potassium, low 22
Pre-eclampsia 142
Pregnancy 22
  ectopic 142
  emergencies 140, 141
  multiple 142
Preterm labor 141
Prostate, enlarged 161
Psychotherapy 65
Pulse
  absent 169
  weak 99, 113, 169

R

Rabies
  immunoglobulin injections around wound 125
  vaccine 125, 128
Rapid heartbeat 56, 70, 113
Respiratory system 25
Restlessness 122
Retinal artery occlusion 148
Retinal detachment 148
Retinopathy, hypertensive 148
Road traffic accident 52, 76, 77, 173

S

Salivation, excessive 108, 122
Scalds 85, 86
Scalp swelling 51
Schizophrenia 169
Scorpion bite 121, 122, 124
Seizure 41, 42, 45, 47, 48, 51, 53, 103, 108, 122, 169, 174
  absence 42
  focal 42
  types of 42
Self-harm, history of 60
Sepsis 14
Shakiness 70
Shallow breathing 14, 99
Shock 12, 13, 41, 73, 108, 173
  electric 89, 90, 92, 174
  position 14
Sight, dimming of 56
Skin 34, 70
  bluish 47
  flushing 112
  intact 82
Skull fracture 51
Sleep deprivation 43
Slurred speech 52, 99
Snake envenomation, effects of 117

Snakebite 115-117, 119, 120, 174
  prehospital management of 117
Sneezing 152
Social isolation 60, 169
Speech difficulties 10
Sports injuries 52
Stimulants 22
Sting 122
Stress 27, 43, 70
  emotional 56
  fractures 83
Stroke 36, 38, 40, 43, 48, 148, 172, 173
  emergency 172
  eye 147
  hemorrhagic 38
  ischemic 38
  kinds of 38
  recovery 36
  signs 39
  types of 38
  warning 57
Substance use disorders 60
Suicide 63
  attempt 60, 169
  prevention 62
  risk 59, 60
Swallowing 165
Sweating 56, 70, 108
  excessive 4, 14, 122
  severe 23
Swelling 10, 81, 82, 112, 113, 152, 164, 169
Syncope 56

T

Tenderness 82
Throat
  swelling of 113
  tightness 113
Thyroid dysfunction 22
Tongue
  bite 47
  swelling of 113
Tooth
  broken 165
  injury 164
Toothache, severe 165
Transient ischemic attack 148
Trauma 60, 76, 142, 169, 173
Tremors 70
Tuberculosis 30, 31

U

Unconsciousness 70, 103, 108, 169
Universal choking sign 34
Unresponsiveness 47, 169
Urinary catheter 160
Urinary retention
  acute 160
  sudden 161
Urinary tract
  infections, severe 161
  issues 141
Urological emergencies 160, 161

V

Valve disease 56
Venomous snakes, types of 117
Ventricular tachycardia 22
Vision
  blurred 52, 56, 70, 147, 148, 153
  distortion 148
  double 148
  loss 148
    sudden 147, 148
Visual disturbances 10
Visual field 148
Visual loss, transient 148
Vomiting 4, 14, 51, 53, 70, 108, 113, 122

W

Weakness 10, 14, 52
Weight gain, sudden 10
Wheezing 27, 28, 108, 113
Wound
  closure 127
  preparation 126